Lost

Lost

Ruth Troughton

Print information available on the last page.

Rev. date: 11/17/2016

To order additional copies of this book, contact:
Xlibris
1-888-795-4274
www.Xlibris.com
Orders@Xlibris.com
745262

Over the past hour, Dan Walsh had let his mind lose itself in the patterns conjured up by swirling snow, that narrowed his view of the world to the few meters in front of his windshield. The bus lumbered along, held to the road by its power and weight. Random thoughts drifted in and out of his mind--would tomorrow night be it--the night he'd imagined for months? His love for Sue had grown like underground roots, winding tendrils around his heart until now. He'd decided to act. He would ask her tonight. The ring he'd bought lay safe in his pocket; he must have checked a hundred times . . .

The logging truck lunged out of the storm; a monstrous beast from a nightmare. "LOOK OUT!" Dan shouted, more to himself than to the bus load of passengers.

Adrenaline coursed through his body, while his mind flared with terror. All his steering wheel twisting, brake pumping, prayers and curses were useless as the two vehicles followed their relentless paths toward the moment of collision. Time seemed to stand still, and he, Dan, a mere observer.

The logging truck, its running lights clotted with wind-driven snow, had swerved to avoid Dan's bus, but it was too late. It jack-knifed and flipped onto its side. Chains snapped, writhing like snakes, loosing tons of logs to spill across the icy highway. The wave of logs came crowding, tumbling toward the spot where Dan sat, clutching the wheel, knowing a target was painted on his chest. Passengers' screams, as they watched death come for them were the last sounds he heard, before the lead log smashed through the windshield.

Chapter 1

Sarah

It seems ironic that our idyllic family, my husband Dave, our little girl Angela, and me; pregnant and glad of it, should have had our lives shredded at Christmas, of all seasons.

From the time I was born, I had a wonderful life. All I had to do was wish for something and it was mine, whatever it was—well, I didn't get the pony-- but generally speaking . . .

Every time I ask myself, 'When did this bad patch start?' It's like opening Pandora's Box. Where does anything start?--good, bad or simply boring? The rest of our lives start with each breath, but I'm going to pick a moment, and begin.'

Just after leaving Kingston, on our way home to Ottawa, our little girl, Angela settled for a nap. I squirmed around trying to find a half comfortable position. The baby was due in two weeks and restful positions were hard to find. I tucked my left foot up under my right leg and leaned my head against the window; the baby supported against my thigh.

1

With my wool hat a warm cushion against the cold glass, I shut my eyes and let my mind drift. The big soft flakes of snow hitting the window were soothing-- like feathers gently brushing the glass. We'd been to the hobby farm where Dave's parents live; a few miles west of Kingston, for a pre-Christmas visit. With my due date so close, Dave wanted us to be home, sooner rather the later.

Angela had such a wonderful time. She loves her Grandmother Lila's dog, cats, and horses, especially the tiny miniatures with their shaggy coats and small warm bodies. The two of them went for long walks, Angela wrapped in enough clothes for the North Pole, sitting on the pony called Bingo, with Lila trudging along beside, the two of them talking about who knows what.

I enjoy the country in winter, especially the nights when your mind goes from the land to the sky, and the stars seem to sing as the constellations wheel across the sky. For me in this climate, it is best enjoyed from a bedroom window, tucked up safe with Dave's warm arms around me.

I felt so well, that when my friend Jill called begging me to stop off a few days with her, I decided it would be safe enough. Dave had to get back to his medical practice. After bit of arguing, we decided he would drop Angela and me off at Jill's, and go on home to Ottawa. That's why we were on the bus.

I let my mind wander back and forward; a time-passing pleasure as there were no dark shadows to contemplate. Well, one minor one that I dismissed. Lila, Dave thought our splitting up was a bad idea. When she heard I was stopping off at Jill's, she took me aside and said, "I have a bad feeling about this."

She was worried about my travelling by bus, pregnant and with Angela, who could be a handful if she got tired or bored. I brushed her advice aside. I would have two young children when the baby was born, and then Jill's place would be an even a more difficult trip from Ottawa.

I really missed Jill. We had roomed together when we were in University. Jill and I have been friends since. She has a little girl, a bit older, but who loves Angela, and they play together happily. The time with them was pure pleasure, but I was uneasy the last few days. The baby had turned the first night I was there, and after several days, I decided waiting any longer was testing fate too far. We left to go home a day early, rather than wait the extra time, as Dave and I had agreed.

'It'll be a great surprise for him,' I remember thinking.

I was aware of the snowstorm, but the warmth inside the bus and the relief of rest time without Angela's incessant chatter, lulled me into a light sleep. The baby was resting too. He had kept me awake half the night; rolling around kicking my bladder.

A swerve of the bus and a loud shout from the driver jerked me awake. I was reaching for Angela when the first logs crashed through the windshield. The rest was chaos. I don't remember the accident beyond that second. I think I was semiconscious for a few moments because I remember the terrible pain in my head, and trying to get my voice to work to call out for Angela, and screams and breaking glass.

That was the last I remembered for a long time. Vague thoughts registered when the blackness lifted a little. It seemed I was a child again, hiding in a dark safe place. Sounds sometimes reached me, even voices calling my name, but they were like children's shouts drifting across a lake; nothing to do with me.

Chapter 2

Jenna

My name is Jenna Ross. I've decided to write about taking the bus to Ottawa and what happened afterward. I've never tried to write anything but a letter once in a while but now I want to tell my story. If you want to read it you will just have to put up with my bad writing.

Months have passed since the day I took Angela from the bus crash and split my life to before and after. Nothing was ever the same again. I never thought of the people I hurt or if I had I wouldn't have cared.

What I did came out of months of black days and a phone call from my cousin Jean. Come for Christmas she begged me–Ron will be here.

Like always she was planning to drag me to share her misery. Just what I needed more misery. Her husband Jack and his buddy Ron would drink beer hog the TV and ignore us unless we were cooking—the pigs.

I said No at the time but changed my mind when she sent me the bus fare. Besides I hate Christmas now and dreaded being alone this year.

When I saw that wall of logs coming at us I thought we were dead for sure—and for a second I wanted that. The pain of losing Julie the only good thing I ever had in this life followed me like a rain cloud through every day and left me awake half of most nights.

I had been watching them ever since they got on the bus- the little girl Angela– I heard her mother call her– and her pretty mother across the aisle from me.

Why had God punished me with a miserable life and gave that woman so much I asked myself. Her clothes cost a lot while I wore a ratty second hand jacket slacks a size too big and crappy boots from the thrift store. They both were blondes with long hair–and you guessed it–no frizz.

After the God-awful crash of the logs coming end first through the bus window and it flipped over on its side I waited before trying to move– hardly daring to hope I wasn't hurt bad. I had been thrown into the air and landed all sprawled on the windows of the side nearest me. I remember thanking God I hadn't been flung from the other side.

In the mess of bodies I saw the child sit up right next to a man who looked dead. I pulled her to me and pressed her head to my shoulder. She was so scared she hung on like a little monkey. I saw the mother with her legs drawn up lying against the side of the bus above the window, where she had been thrown from the other side when the bus went over. Her body was twisted and blood ran from her head.

My brain leaped to life as if a switch had been clicked on. Before the others got over the shock I was in moving. I grabbed the kid's bag. Then saw the purse that the mother had worn over her shoulder when she boarded the bus. It didn't look like she'd need it– so I snatched it to me.

Then it came to me. God had answered my prayers. Here almost thrown into my arms was a girl to take the place of my Julie.

I'd learned quite a bit about them by watching and listening. They had been at a farm west of Kingston for a Christmas visit. The hats they wore were from the little girl's grandmother. Her name was Lila and the grandfather was Don.

It was hard to think with the screams groans and people yelling to one another– among passengers still alive. There were quite a few moving around but they looked shaken up as they crawled to strangers for help or cried out for God's mercy. Some had cuts from broken glass but others lay crumpled like dolls flung down by bored kids.

I moved my legs and thought– they're able to carry me without much pain– thank God or the devil – whoever looks after me. I struggled to my feet. Under my boots was a mess of broken glass and hand baggage. I held Angela to my shoulder. My brain was working like clockwork. I took time to check if I might get out. But the exit door was now on the ceiling. The storm made that a crazy idea anyway. We wouldn't have lasted fifteen minutes out there. I stepped over a body and made my way toward the back–watching careful for glass that might be stuck in something above and fall on us.

I carried Angela to a spot out of the way under the side wall of the toilet cabinet hanging overhead. It was hard to keep things straight in that half upside-down place.

A heavy long coat had been flung down on the broken window. I pushed it onto the glass to make a seat nearly hidden from the others but gave me a space to see what was going on. Angela was crying loud now but no one noticed in the commotion around the centre of the bus. I rocked and crooned to her until she quieted and fell asleep.

I have to own up—I never spared one thought for the mother who I saw lying maybe dead or soon to be. Well, maybe one. And I'm not proud of myself for it. A worry niggled and bothered me. She might come round and ask for her kid. As time passed I forgot that worry as I watched the passengers try to cope. Is that the word—cope—figure out what to do anyway.

Well isn't this one for the Devil's copybook I thought as I spied on them. They say he looks after his own and ain't that the truth? What a mess—they're all so surprised like they was owed a safe life where death can grab any minute.

I know disaster that's why I was thinking straight— a bit scratched and shaken but I had the kid safe. The little girl was even prettier than my Julie. Her mother didn't look like she was going to make it. I knew she was due any day. Why in the world would she be here? These thoughts slid in and out of my mind—forgot as soon as another thing caught my eye.

Still I kept quiet and watched. They were beginning to get sorted now. Two young men— just boys really were trying to take charge. The one with the yellow hair, Alan, I heard his friend Jerry call him, was heavy built but not fat. He looked strong. I had to smile—such a little rooster. He's not the one who's going to be the boss though he thinks so I figured. Jerry was weedy and thin but I thought he might the one who would do the most good.

After they had gone to the emergency door for some reason— he just got to the job of tearing his shirt for bandages and didn't bother giving orders.

It was awkward to get at the door because it opened upward. Alan was too short to reach even standing on the seat arms and the angle was wrong. Jerry tried but he wasn't strong enough. It was probably frozen shut anyway. I wondered what they thought they would do out there. It was about twenty below and we were in the middle of nowhere. Fear of being trapped I suppose.

They gave up and went back to where a group crouched around the mother. I couldn't see much except her blond hair matted with blood. She looked like a broken Barbie doll except for the swell of the baby in her belly.

Alan claimed he had taken first-aid courses, and pushed through the gawkers. They'd been too scared to touch her, but he wasn't. He and his friend lifted her from the narrow place between the seats. You have to wonder— was he brave or an idiot— it depended on whether he really knew what he was doing. He got a folded jacket under her head and someone else found a coat who's owner was dead and didn't need it– and spread it to cover her.

A man had crawled up to the front but now was back looking sick and shaking his head. The logs had only reached about the fourth row and there were no cries for help from under them.

We have to get help. Has anyone tried to see if cell phones work from here? Kingston has a good hospital and an air ambulance-- Alan yelled above the moaning and cries for help.

They scrambled around trying to find a phone that worked and it looked like the man with the blood on his forehead had one but he couldn't see well enough to hit the right numbers. Alan did it for him.

Everyone seemed to be holding their breath except for the dead at the front. It was like watching a play. Alan's face broke into a grin and he pumped the phone and his fist at the side windows above his head.

He jabbered into it a few more seconds and then yelled. They said it may take awhile but the ploughs are out and the forecast is good so we might get lucky.

I didn't care if the ploughs flew here. I already had my luck. The God that sent me Angela would see to me getting out of here with her. She was mine now. Everyone was thinking of themselves and they should have. It was good for me that quite a few seemed to be able to walk. I planned to hide myself among them. I was good at that—no one ever looked at me.

Then another argument broke out. Wasn't that just men for you? Alan didnt have as tight a hold on the boss mans job as he thought. A big guy in a lumberman's shirt and the size thirteen boots wanted to break open the door and get some wood to start a fire. What a crazy idea. It was cold in there alright but there was enough gas spilt around to blow us all to hell. I could smell it clear back to where I was sitting.

Alan and Jerry argued that someone should get outside and see if the driver of the logging truck was still alive and needed help. The lumberjack showed himself to be smarter than he looked. With a little looking around he found a pair of skis and the poles. He was much stronger than either of the boys and taller too. With some pushing and jabbing he got the door open. That was a smart move. A bunch of snow fell in and the wind out there blew fit to tear your face off.

Jerry was the only one slim enough to wiggle through the opening.

Everyone waited for what seemed a long time but was likely only minutes. His teeth were knocking so bad he could hardly speak when he slid in. He said that he couldn't really see anything. The logs had piled up alongside the bus so he went down to the ground. But the wind was blowing and when the logging truck had jackknifed, the cab was crushed. There was no way to get to the driver. Besides it was just too dangerous to crawl onto the pile of logs.

The big guy, I think they called him Jim, eased the door back down again. By now any warmth that the people inside the bus had generated went outside with Jerry and didn't come back in.

They stood around a few seconds looking at each other and then Alan said with smirk that you'd love to wipe from his face– Have you ever delivered a baby Jerry?

I- I- couldn't no way! Jerry replied throwing a terrified look over his shoulder to where the mother laid on the side just above the row of seats. But when Alan gave him a slap on the back and moved toward her he followed.

Someone probably one of the women had turned her on her side and tucked the coat tight around her. I saw Alan lean close and I could tell by his face that she was still alive.

Alan pointed to a dark stain that was running out from under her body and said something I couldn't make out. But whatever it was I heard Jerry say– No bloody way man- and back away.

Anybody here able to deliver a baby? Alan called out. None of the few women came forward. They huddled together crying and saying they were scared to touch her.

I thought– this is better than a movie.

Now-- another actor stepped-up. He was dressed in heavy pants and a plaid shirt. His hands were big and even from my place I could see they were rough and worn from hard work. He said something to the two young men. They shook their heads.

Then I heard him say No no. I not doctor. My name be Janos Warhol. In Old Country work on farms— help many births. He held out his hands as if they could tell his story.

We shouldn't touch her Jerry said. What if we make her worse?

Nothing's going to be worse than if she has that baby here Alan told him. You could see he considered himself far smarter than poor dumb Jerry. For all Alan's bullying, Jerry was not going to help. He kept shaking his head and trying to move away. Alan saw it too and turned to Janos.

He knelt beside her and slid one hand under her belly and pressed around her sides as gentle as any woman.

He said She bad sick from head but her heartbeat good. I feel baby move. Good strong kick. We keep her warm and wait. I sit with her. Jah. You see if others need help."

Jerry and Alan started to move among the other people. I was afraid they would come to where I was but with the storm it was quite dark back in my corner and they didn't seem to see me. They found the first-aid kit and did what they could.

What if nobody comes? Jerry asked. They had moved down closer to where I was and I could hear every word.

Don't be stupid, it's 2016. Those big ploughs will get through Alan said. Alan didn't answer-- then he said, are you crazy man? This thing goes up in flames we'll be hot all right.

Chapter 3

The snow was piling over the upper windows as the day drew toward evening. It seemed much later than it actually was as time dragged on. The temperature was falling. Most of the passengers huddled in a half stupor, nursing their pain and trying not to think about how long it would be before they froze to death.

The weeping passengers, and the howling wind, drove one passenger beyond the bounds of common sense. Maybe the bottle he'd had in his hand luggage, and was careful to not share, had something to do with it. First, it was muttering and throwing things about. "Give me that god damned phone, I'll get someone. I'll call the Mounties!" he yelled at the top of his voice.

Others yelled for him to shut up, because by now his wife added to the confusion, crying hysterically and berating him for making a scene.

Close to two hours after the accident, help arrived. Sirens wailed, lights flashed, and hope flared among the stranded passengers. Before anyone outside could possibly hear, people began to shout, "We're here! We're here!"

They laughed, hugged each other, or cried in relief. Soon voices and boots stomping on the outside of the bus turned hope into reality. Everyone, except Jenna, held their breath imaging warmth, food or medical care. She waited hoping to take advantage of any opportunity that might come her way.

Jenna knew these next few minutes would make the difference between hard questioning and getting away free. Alive or dead, that woman can do without this child– she felt this inside her brain without articulating a real thought. The mother was young, and if she survived, she could bear other children. Jenna reasoned that Sarah's wealth wiped away any need to feel sorry for her, but this was her last chance to have a child for herself, now that Julie was gone.

God had chosen her as this little one's guardian, as clearly as if he had shouted it in her ear. Angela had slept on her lap since they retreated to the dark corner. Now she stirred and Jenna quickly found a box of cookies shoved into the top of her bag, and slid one into her hand. Jenna tucked her bright hair under the hood and pulled the string tight. The snowsuit was blue and white so no one was likely to remember whether the child was a girl or a boy, blonde or dark haired.

Soon the emergency door was wrenched open and a big man in uniform dropped through. A babble of voices greeted him; everything from, 'thank God you're here' to, 'what in hell kept you so long?'

He gave them a minute to settle, and for his partner, a tall blonde woman, to join him. He said a word or two to her, and then worked his way up to inspect the caved in and smashed front, and its broken bodies.

Meantime, his partner was beginning to get the mobile passengers organized. Everything was made difficult by the position of the bus and the cramped quarters, but when they were counted and checked that medical help wasn't needed, she told them there was a bus waiting to take them to Kingston, where another bus would take them on to Ottawa.

Chapter 4

'Carson' her badge read. Her cool voice was laced with authority. She said "You can pick up your baggage at the bus depot at your convenience. We will have it delivered after the bus is righted and the accident investigation completed. It may take several days."

A few dared object. They muttered about Christmas gifts and other reasons why it had to be now, but Carson's sharp blue stare, and the return of her partner, halted any revolt before it was born.

Meanwhile, a ladder had been inserted through the open door and the emergency crew was waiting up top to help people get down and into the rescue vehicle waiting outside. The rescue crew wanted to hurry this first group off so they could get in to give medical assistance to the badly injured.

Confusion was everywhere in spite of the directions. One of a couple might be hurt and the other refuse to leave him or her. The officers made instant decisions, telling people their loved ones would be looked after and reunited with them. All this confusion was in Jenna's favour.

While both officers were busy shepherding the traumatized, complaining passengers, Jenna watched for her chance to escape. Gradually she moved closer to the ladder. She had Angela in her arms, and was carefully keeping her attention away from where Sarah lay. Second from the end of the line, she stepped forward, and sure enough, the man ahead let her in and asked if he could help with the bag. She'd been worried about getting up the ladder with Angela and the carryall.

She mumbled, 'Thank you', and kept her face half hidden behind Angela's puffy snowsuit.

More nimble than anyone watching might expect, going by her bulky jacket, woolen pants and her cap pulled down nearly to her eyes, she climbed the ladder. Outside the wind and blowing snow turned everyone into an anonymous shape. Angela gasped once in the cold air and buried her face in Jenna's jacket. It was a matter of minutes until they reached the ground.

A man with a clipboard asked for names. Jenna gave a false name, Margarita Landry, an address in Montreal, and she was waived on.

The kind man, who she now realized was Janos, returned the bag, and without a word made his way toward the bus. Jenna followed him as if they were together, but when he sat down she continued to the back.

Most of the people were watching the emergency crews and police doing their work. The Jaws of Life finished a new hole into the bus, and now stretchers were coming out and being slid into the ambulances. There was a flurry of excitement as the air ambulance set down.

Jenna watched as they hurried three stretchers to it, but she couldn't recognize the little girl's mother. She wondered whether she was there, or among the dead. She felt glee and relief at having escaped, but then she wasn't too surprised, since in her mind this was ordained from the beginning.

Soon the bus pulled out onto the newly plowed road. Jenna bowed her head and sent thanks for the help God had given her. She knew that yesterday her body could never

have managed those two ladders--one up and one down--
carrying Angela, but she had felt strong and clear headed.

Now wide awake from her long sleep, Angela asked,
"Are you my new baby sitter? Where's Mummy?"

Jenna had been so preoccupied with her thoughts, she
hadn't given much attention to this living child, who had
questions, and now looked at her with tear filled eyes and
quivering lips. It surprised Jenna that she spoke so well.

"Mommy's going to be busy for a while with the new
baby she's gone away to look for. Did you know you were
going to have a new brother or sister?" At Angela's nod she
continued, "She asked me to look after you for a little while.
I'm your Aunty Jenna. How about a story? I bet you have
books in this bag."

"You have daycare?" Angela asked.

"Now that's a funny question." Jenna produced a
passable chuckle. "Do you like daycare?"

"No, I hates it," was the matter of fact answer. By now
she had a book out and had moved closer to Jenna, but not
touching.

Jenna wanted to grab her for a hug but knew she must
not frighten her. Obviously Angela was used to being left
with strangers. The trick now was to keep her happy, and
not call attention to them until they could get out of this
area and back to Ottawa.

All the cunning she had learned– to avoid beatings
from her drunken father, and the hard years after, would be
needed again. The lethargy dulling her mind since Julie's
death was replaced with a brain that might invent a rocket
ship-- it was so sharp and clear. While reading the book
with Angela, one part of her brain, was already laying out
a plot.

At the bus terminal, Jenna hung back pretending a
problem with Angela's bag until all the other passengers

went ahead of her. The girl at the bus door, Jackie, had spent the last hour answering calls from people who were hysterical, or began swearing at her when she couldn't tell them anything. She hardly looked at the people straggling off the bus as she shivered in her short skirt and clasped her skimpy jacket around her body.

Jenna let Angela walk, holding her hand as they followed the complaining group into the terminal. As she had imagined, just inside the door, a painted hand on the wall pointed the way to the washrooms. A quick look told her that no one was paying attention to them. Everyone had their own problems. They had never expected to be stranded here, 'in the middle of nowhere', as she heard more than one say.

Jenna picked Angela up and whispered in her ear, "Let's have that pee-pee now." She made it sound like an adventure.

Angela whispered, "Yes," which came out more like, "Yeth".

Done with the washroom, Jenna took a quick peek out the door. The hallway was empty. Angela took her hand and they walked together out the front door. Jenna walked as quickly as Angela's short legs could move, away from the bright lights, and out onto the street that ran along the front of the terminal.

The terminal was at the edge of town, but on this cold night no one was on the street. She had to get herself and Angela out of sight quickly. There was a coffee shop in the strip mall that had several cars, including a police cruiser, parked in front. Jenna had a moment's thought of the warm steamy atmosphere, and the taste of good coffee, but the temptation wasn't as strong as her fear.

'Don't ask for the moon,' Jenna warned herself.

Further on she saw a motel; its red 'Vacancy' sign flashing its pitiful hope for all to see. She knew that in winter the motel would be nearly empty. People would be with family, not here to see the sights of the town.

Having a small child out in such a night might draw curious eyes. That was the last thing she needed, some Nosey Parker remarking on her childcare skills, and remembering her to the police. Beside this snowsuit of Angela's was too easy to remember. It looked too expensive to belong to Jenna's grandchild. She thought, 'I will tell people that my daughter married a rich man, if anyone asks questions.'

Thinking of the few dollars in her wallet, she didn't have much choice. The motel it would have to be. Then she thought of the mother's purse. Surely it would contain some money. She didn't want to take it out on the street, so decided to take a chance and hurried Angela off in the direction of the motel.

Chapter 5

Jenna

You can't imagine how glad I was when I pushed open the door of the Rest Easy Motel and found the reception area empty except for a young thing with bright red hair tied in a top-knot and not enough clothes on to flag down a donkey cart. She greeted us with a smile though as if any guest was a good guest on a night like that one. I snuggled Angela down beside a chair and unzipped her bag. I knew she had a stuffed kitten in the there.

I whispered to her. Ask Kitty if he was scared in the bus crash. Maybe he needs some hugs.

Angela dug in the toy bag and pulled out the black-and-white cat and told me his name was Beau. She started to walk him up and down the chair arm and around the seat.

My granddaughter and I need a room for the night. My ride got caught in the snowstorm and isn't coming until morning. I said to the girl.

I tried to disguise my voice by making it higher and more posh than it really was. My woolen cap was still pulled low around my face and I hid it from her by a half turn away as I filled in the form.

19

I used Jane Rogers as a name and gave an address in Montréal. A man I knew lived there and I remembered the postal code for his street. I didn't dare use Jean's. She would be wondering where I was but I figured once she got into the booze she wouldn't bother about finding me. She'd think I changed my mind at the last minute.

I had enough money to pay for the room and I told the girl we would be leaving real early in the morning.

She said OK. Just leave the key on the dresser.

Just as I turned to go to the room, I caught sight of the red light bar on top of a police car as it pulled into the parking spot right in front of the door. That minute near gave me a heart attack. The window was steamed up but I could see the big square shape get out and he came through the door with a stomping of feet loud enough for three men.

For a second I froze with the key in my hand. I sneaked a look, but he wasn't interested in me at all. His grey eyes were having a good look at what was on show behind the desk. My heart had barely slowed to twice normal when another problem near made me scream. The little princess decided she wasn't coming with me. She ran to the back of the chair and peeked around with a giggle. I wasn't having any of that. God's gift be-damned. I took a good hard grip around her waist and picked her up.

"Come along, Sweetie," I whispered-- but she knew I meant it. I gave her arm a little pull.

No she said jerking away. Beau flew out of her hand and landed on the cop's back. He wheeled around with his eyes casing the small room until he saw Angela. A grin flashed in a face full of big teeth.

Ha I didn't expect to be attacked by cats he said with a chuckle. He picked up the toy and gave it back to Angela with the big grin still in place.

I was deathly scared he would hunker down and get a good look at her face but he turned back to the red-haired girl. His eyes had seen an old woman not worth a first glance let alone a second.

I wasn't going to push my luck any further. I threw the strap of the bag over my shoulder and grabbed Angela up. In case the cop was watching I walked with a bit of a limp to the door that led to the rooms.

I could feel Angela winding up for a howl but somehow I thought of a little rhyme to whisper in her ear. It worked and I got through the door and I lugged the bag as fast as I could to #14. I was glad to see it was close to the exit door. I looked back. The door from the reception room was some kind of rough glass and I was fairly sure we were forgot the second we were out of sight. Those two had something going for sure.

The room was the usual cheap motel room, one double bed, a ratty sofa and a tiny bathroom all in drab beige. Even the flower print on the wall looked tired. About one minute after the door was locked I started a warm bath for Angela and while she played in the bubbles I took everything out of her bag. A lot of clothes were in it but not the kind that looked as if she belonged to me. One little jumpsuit looked as if it cost more than my coat.

I hoped there would be something to eat but Angela must have been too old for baby food. I wondered if I dare leave her to go buy something at the machine I saw at the end of the hall. I got her out of the bath and into her pajamas. First she asked if she could watch television and then said she was hungry.

Will you stay right here and watch TV while I go to the machine to get a muffin and some milk? I asked her.

She nodded her head– her eyes already fixed on some cartoon she seemed to know.

The dispensing machine was working a little miracle in that place. It spit out chocolate bars muffins and milk. I hurried back and found Angela right where I left her. I spread a towel across the bedspread and she ate the muffin and drank the milk.

Watching her I knew I had to take some drastic action to disguise us. The police are trained to remember things and that cop would maybe remember us in even that quick look. The stores downtown would still be open but I didn't dare take Angela out again. It was too cold and she was too pretty for people not to remember her and wonder why I had her out on a night like that.

A plan came to me and I acted on it before my nerve failed me. I remembered the sleeping pills in my purse. I got them out and read the label. It said take two before bedtime. I tried to think how much Angela weighed against what I did but couldn't figure out a dose that way. I crushed one and dissolved a small part in a juice pack. I was sure Angela was thirsty enough to drink it as well as the milk. I gave it to her and said she could have a piece of chocolate if she drank it all up.

While I waited for the pill to work, I took out the mothers purse pushed it down the front of my slacks and went to the bathroom. I didn't want Angela to see it.

I found her driver's license. Now I knew that her name was Sarah James. There was no time to practice the signature so the checkbook was out. There was a bank card and under that I saw another credit-card. These all seemed too dangerous to try. Then I had a thought. I knew lots of people kept their PIN number with them in case they forget it. Women usually kept them in their purses. I began to search every compartment and sure enough tucked down in a zipped pocket was a little scrap with 479 on it.

When I checked Angela, she was out for the night.

I left the television on and the night light in the bathroom but I was fairly certain Angela would sleep 'til morning. I asked God to watch over her. At that time, I believed it was His idea anyway that we should get away and some kind of disguise was the best idea. I was lucky with the bus, only a few minutes got me to a big shopping center— a good place to mix in with all kinds of people. I saw The Bay had a sale on and people were going in and out. First I had to find an ATM machine. I walked through the store and just beyond the door into the rest of the center was an ATM set back from where people were passing. I faked the limp again and a hunch just in case there was a camera. I couldn't see any but I pulled my hat down and my scarf up before I joined the line of three others.

I had the card in my pocket and the numbers memorized. I quickly shoved the card into the slot. Seconds later $200 in twenties slid out. I pulled the card and chanced another try. It worked! I knew $400 would barely do but I didn't dare do it again here. Later at the bus station I would try again and throw the card away.

Next I went to the drug store and bought brown hair dye and the cheapest makeup on sale–a lipstick and some foundation. I limped up to the cashier but she hardly looked at me as she took a $20 bill and returned a small amount of change. The cost of that stuff—another good reason I never wear it. I went back to The Bay as good a place as any. I wanted to spend as little time as I had to out in public and I was worrying every minute about Angela there alone.

First I went to the children's department. The snowsuits were on sale for half price and I bought a good one in navy blue. That was followed by leggings and a new dress and some other bits and pieces of underwear, socks and a pair of pants and a pretty top. I looked at the prices and realized that all this would probably cost less than the snowsuit we had to get rid of. I didn't bother with boots. The ones she had would do.

The cashier didn't blink an eye as she toted up the stuff. She wished me Merry Christmas and turned to the next person. I took the escalator to the ladies' clothes department. There I was in luck too. Amongst the fancy coats was a rack of plain long wool ones. I found my size in a dark green. Carrying it, I went to the skirts and sweaters area and found a brown straight skirt and a dark green sweater. Now all I needed were some boots and a pair of leggings. I checked all the prices and this would put me on the way to broke but I wanted to look as different from how I did today as possible and that meant better clothes.

Twenty minutes later, I was on the bus back to the motel. I had been away just over an hour.

I had left the back door wedged just beyond locking. No one had discovered it so I slipped in and got to the room without going by the desk. It had all gone as I planned and I was surer than ever of God's help. When I counted my money I saw I would have $100 left after the bus fare back to Toronto.

I left my hair wild around my head and wearing my old clothes I went to the desk. I wanted the clerk to remember this old hag. The young man on duty was watching TV. Half naked women were screeching and leaping around—kickboxing I think. He hardly looked at me when I asked for the shop.

It was on the other side and had lots of snacks and bottled drinks. I found a large carryall that would be just the thing to hold Angela's bag and my old things. I wouldn't dare to try to throw her things away. She was too smart not to make a fuss. I'd get rid of her bag later somewhere in Toronto well away from where I lived.

Back in the room I went over my plans again. Everything had gone so good that I had to be careful not to get a swelled head and make some fool mistake. I crawled into the bed beside Angela. Tomorrow would be the day. At the end, I would either be in jail or safe in my old neighborhood.

Chapter 6

When the bedside radio alarm woke Jenna the next morning the first thing she did was rush to the window to check the weather. Normally, she dragged out of bed feeling half dead, dreading the hours until she could find oblivion in sleep again. Now, standing by the window seeing the heaps of snow not yet dirtied by the day, her mind fizzed with possibilities, and an absolute confidence that things would fall out as she planned. The day was fine and clear; a postcard winter day. Angela was the wild card. She'd have to handle her carefully. With her high bell-like voice, and that pretty face, she was bound to draw attention.

Early as it was, she had a lot to do. The bus she'd planned to take was a daily run. Jenna had always had a good memory and now called to mind the picture of the bus schedule. Leaving at 9:00 AM, it should arrive back in Toronto around noon. The timing was good. She didn't want to hang around the motel any longer than necessary, but she needed some time to get their disguises organized.

While Angela still slept, Jenna showered and applied the brown dye to her hair. The instructions on the box said to wrap the wet hair for half an hour before blow drying. Tying the towel tightly, she pulled on her old clothes because she didn't want to put on her new ones until she had coped with Angela's hair.

Jenna had to pick Angela up, and shake her gently, before she opened her eyes.

"Aunty Jenna, where's Mummy?" Angela asked, her eyes seeking the corners of the room. "I want my Mummy." Tears welled and her bottom lip trembled.

Jenna had prepared a story. "Mommy's fine. But remember– I told you she was going to be away for a while. Today we are going to have a big adventure. I bet you're a girl who loves adventure. Are you?"

At Angela's nod, Jenna launched into a story about a little princess and a big bad wolf who was hunting her. He had a picture of Angela, who he thought was the princess, but they were going to fool him.

"He's looking for a little girl with gold hair. I have some stuff to make your hair brown, and look, a new snowsuit. He'll never find you with brown hair. What do you think?" she asked.

Angela stiffened. She put her arms around Jenna's neck and hid her face against her shoulder. Jenna's heart faltered for a beat in pity, but the plan was launched. There was no going back.

She hugged Angela against her body and said, "Don't be scared. I won't let a thing happen to you. I'll whack that old wolf if he comes sniffing around, but you must be very good and do exactly what Aunty Jenna says."

Angela nodded several times and darted a look around the room, before asking to go to the bathroom.

Jenna turned the TV on as a distraction and ran a warm bath. Last night she'd noticed that one could see the television through the open door of the bathroom. Now she saw that as another aid to her plan. While Angela soaked in the tub and watched cartoons, Jenna laid out the new clothes on the bed. She carefully folded each of the store bags and put them in the bottom of the big carryall.

She knew that cleaning staff always went through the garbage of the rooms looking for anything that might have been thrown out but still useful. 'People throw away all kinds of things,' she thought, as she remembered her days cleaning hotel rooms. She'd found everything from jewellry to a wig, and that was the clean stuff. She didn't intend to leave any clues behind that might be remembered under police questioning.

Angela accepted the dying of her hair as part of the game, but stuck out her lip when Jenna started to cut it.

"I likes long hair," she sniffed.

"We have to fool the wolf. Remember?" Jenna put on a serious face and waited. Then she had an inspiration. She took the towel from her head and snipped a piece from her hair. "Come to the mirror. I'll bring the chair for you. I like long hair too, but I'm gonna cut mine. It will make us look really different."

With Angela on the chair in front of her, Jenna cut her own hair first and then Angela's. When she was finished, two totally different people looked back at them. At first Angela just stared, then, she said, "Is that Angie, Aunty Jenna?"

"Yes, inside it really is, but let's make- up new names until we're sure the wolf is gone. What do you think? Is that a good idea?"

"Yeth. Yeth! I want Crystal. Mummy wanted Crystal but Daddy didn't like it. You be Joan. I know a Joan." Her little face was alight with excitement.

"Crystal it is, and I'm Aunty Joan. C'mon, let's get dressed. We better practice our new names starting now. I hope that old wolf doesn't have a hair color change of his own. But then, I bet he isn't as smart as we are."

With a giggle, Angela turned back to the TV. Jenna removed her old clothes and folded them, into the bag along with the snowsuit Angela had been wearing yesterday. After dressing in her new skirt and sweater, she went to the bathroom and began carefully wiping the surfaces. She noticed two towels had dye on them. She placed the dirty towels in the bag after wiping the room's surfaces as well. The bag was going to be heavy but it couldn't be helped.

At 7:30 she turned off the television and told Angela they had to get ready. When Angela said she was hungry, Jenna said they would get some breakfast at the bus station. She was relieved that Angela didn't show any bad effects of the narcotic. As Jenna helped her put on her new clothes, Angela paid no attention to the fact that they were not her old ones.

Jenna slipped on her new coat and boots. She stood with Angela in front of the long mirror on the bathroom door and took a good look. She saw a woman no longer young, but still attractive. Makeup covered her sallow skin, and the hair cut changed the shape of her face. She looked slimmer and taller in the well cut coat. She wished she had a hat. The old wool one would look totally out of place with this coat.

Beside her, the little dark- haired girl looked nothing like the blonde angel of yesterday. Her eyes looked almost blue, instead of her natural green, and the dull blue of the snowsuit somehow muted the eye-catching liveliness Angela had shown before.

Another quick look around the room finished this part of the escape plan. She dropped the key onto the dresser; made sure she had everything in her pockets, and shouldered the heavy bag.

"Are you ready, Crystal?" She put a laugh in her voice and laughed for real when she got her answer, "Yeth, Aunty Joan."

As they slipped out the back door of the motel, Jenna stopped a moment to look around. The parking lot on this side was as well plowed as was the main road that she could see over the snow banks. Halfway to the bus terminal there was a steady stream of cars coming and going from a coffee shop. Maybe that would be a good place to get breakfast, Jenna thought. It would be a good test to see if they were attracting any notice.

She whispered to Angela, "That wolf is sure fooled. He is somewhere else looking for us." She straightened her back and said, "Let's go get some breakfast."

Angela looked around, but the idea of the wolf didn't seem nearly as scary in the bright morning sunlight. She reached for Jenna's hand, and passing around a big hump of snow, they followed the sidewalk and went into the warm steamy coffee shop.

Jenna usually didn't have money to spend for something she could make at home, but this morning she resolved to enjoy a treat. She ordered a bagel with cream cheese and a glass of milk for Angela. Everything looked and smelled so good she hardly knew what to order for herself. First, of course, the coffee; then she saw the oatmeal muffins with cranberries. She decided that's what she would have.

With the first swallow of the coffee, she realized she hadn't had any food since early yesterday. She broke off a chunk of the muffin and stuffed it into her mouth, while helping Angela spread the cream cheese onto her bagel.

Already the bus crash and its consequence were fading into the past. As she savoured the hot coffee and muffin, it seemed the best food she had ever eaten.

Angela must have been hungry too because she ate busily, not stopping for her usual bright chatter. As soon as she was finished, Jenna zipped her snowsuit and made sure the hood was well up around her face. The white mittens and boots, that she hadn't replaced, looked fine with the snowsuit.

Jenna's old gloves that she had stuffed in her pocket would do for on the street. 'Probably no one will notice, but it's wise to be careful,' she thought, with a little spurt of pride at her ability to pay attention to detail.

It was only a few minutes' walk to the bus terminal. After they entered, she could see Angela glancing around into all of the darkened corners. She kept close to Jenna's side. There were quite a few people milling around and others sleeping on benches. Jenna looked, but didn't see anyone she recognized from the bus.

An ATM crouched in a corner with the newspaper dispensing box. Taking her time, Jenna bought a copy of a Toronto newspaper. Then making sure Angela was sheltered by her body, she activated the bank card she'd taken from Sarah's purse. It was the last time she would dare use it. She withdrew another $600. From there, they moved into the ladies washroom, where Jenna carefully wiped the card free of fingerprints and discarded it in the wastebasket.

She would have cut it up and flushed it down the toilet if she had thought to bring scissors, but by leaving it behind there would be nothing to say from which direction the kidnapper had left.

While scheming about the card, she forgot to watch Angela. There was a little stool in front of the wash basins which Angela had used to reach the taps. A gush of water and a high pitched screech jerked Jenna back to the present. She ran over to turn off the water. Angela was screaming at the top of her lungs. It hadn't been hot water, Jenna was relieved to see. The snowsuit material had been made to shed water, and it was only the surprise of the sudden burst in her face, that had frightened Angela.

It took Jenna a minute or two to calm her and reassure her that the snowsuit wasn't very wet, and to remind her that they must be quiet. A few minutes later, tickets in hand they boarded the bus.

The other people in the lineup were for the most part cold and sleepy, and no one so much as glanced at the middle-aged grandmother with her granddaughter, off to the big city to spend Christmas together.

Chapter 7

While Jenna had watched, plotting her strategy for disappearing, the paramedics at the crash site had given Sarah a cursory examination and found that her labor had already started. As Janos had feared, the liquid seeping from under her body was her broken waters. They noted her other injuries, the most serious being the head wound.

As it had stopped bleeding, they decided nothing more could be done at the site. The dead would be cared for by others; the air ambulance was for people needing immediate care like Sarah.

Sarah and four others were carefully carried out of the new hole cut by the Jaws of Life in the side of the bus. Seconds after the last stretcher was secured, the helicopter rose like a great bird taking off into the blowing snow. It was lost from sight in seconds, leaving seven other patients to be brought in the ambulance.

When they arrived at Kingston General, the storm was already easing. The emergency team was waiting to rush the patients from the subzero landing pad to the emergency room, where extra doctors and nurses were waiting.

The trauma team assigned to Sarah quickly cut off her clothing and began to assess her injuries in far more detail than had been possible at the crash site. The team leader,

33

Brian Jackson, knew it was going to be wild in here as soon as the ambulances arrived with of the rest of the injured. There were already beds in the hall waiting for his attention.

He had Dr. Vern Watts, from obstetrics, paged for advice on the pregnancy. Also the orthopedic surgeon, John Green was called from his office.

After a quick examination, Dr. Green knew there were broken bones in Sarah's shoulder, and he thought the head injury was more serious than the surface cut. They would have to wait for the X-rays to better decide on the necessary treatment.

Soon Dr. Watts was at his elbow with a stethoscope on Sarah's bulging abdomen. After listening carefully at several spots, he allowed himself a small smile.

"The baby's alive and kicking," he said to John. They read the charts, discussed blood pressure, and the results of any other observations taken at the site of the accident.

"I'd say this is one lucky lady. What do you think of that head wound?" Dr. Watts asked. "The baby can wait for--I estimate an hour, and if normal delivery doesn't look possible, we will do a Caesarean."

"No depression of the skull that I can see. Let's get her admitted upstairs and into X-ray right away, if you think there is time," John answered.

'What a shame all of that beautiful hair will have to go,' John thought. 'Natural too, that color-- blonde, striped with cream'. Even with the bruising, he could see her natural beauty: the sculptured cheeks and rather high straight nose, which seemed perfect to lead ones eyes to the clean-cut lips.

For a moment he found something familiar in her features, but he was distracted by a nurse sent to tell him about the arrival of more injured from the crash site. He would likely have more casualties in soon.

"I'll be a while with these X-Rays, and Jane Doe here, but get them organized. Grey can handle some of them," he said as he turned back to Sarah.

He and Watts agreed that each one of the several injuries needed care immediately, but after a brief discussion, they concluded: the head wound first, then the shoulder and, next but by no means the least pressing, the baby.

They sent her directly to operating room #4 because there was no time to waste. Usually there would be relatives to inform and consent forms to sign, but there was no identification with her, and no time to look for any, if they were to save her and the baby's life.

By now word was around the hospital--the young woman so seriously hurt was a 'Jane Doe' patient-- one lacking any identifying documentation. The nurse who had cut off her clothing told the others that she was someone with money, and it wouldn't be long before a man came looking for her, a father or husband. Likely it would be a husband, because she was wearing a wedding ring. Then there was the drama of her already being in labor.

Once Sarah's hair was cut and her head shaved, the injury could be seen clearly. They pasted electrodes onto her head. Soon computers were flashing the codes that only experts could read.

All through the EEG, the X-rays, and the plaster room, Sarah slept under the effects of her head wound and drugs. John Green had seen such injuries before, but seldom all at once in the same patient.

Vern Watts stayed with her all through the different procedures, monitoring the progress of her labour. An ultrasound had shown that the baby lay in the right position, appeared unhurt and normal, with a heart beat that made him smile. This baby was near to term and would surely live.

After all the diagnostic test results were returned, they studied them together.

"There is no immediate danger," John said. "Later we may have to operate. The shadows on the X-ray showed a slightly depressed area at the side of her head. This is what is causing the coma, but once we operate, she should recover fully. How is the baby doing?"

"The baby's doing great, but I'm afraid we're going to have to do a caesarean section after all."

"Right, her shoulder isn't as badly injured as I had thought." John stuck two more black sheets into the X-ray light board and flicked it on.

"Look here, the collarbone is broken and that elbow will have to have a cast. If the C –section can wait, we can get this taken care of quite quickly, and then she can go over to maternity."

Vern said, "Fine, but don't waste any time. Do you think there's any chance Dr. Bailey is available? He's the senior obstetrician, and I'd like to have him do this. Her body has taken a lot of abuse today. She's going to need close monitoring."

"They were paging him a few minutes ago. I know we had a delivery earlier, and he is probably still in maternity. Let's get the shoulder set and get over there," John said as he clapped Vern on the shoulder, remembering what it was like to be a young man just finding your feet in the medical world.

"Fine with me, Bones," Vern grinned.

John Green was popular with colleagues and staff alike. He'd come from England, and staff in a small town didn't often meet an Englishman. He seemed odd-- in the way he spoke-- but his good nature and care for his patients, had won them over in a few weeks. They affectionately called him Bones. He wasn't fond of his nickname. He didn't know whether it referred to his tall lean body or his profession.

He handled the setting of Sarah's arm and shoulder. The resulting cast was unwieldy but in a few weeks the breaks would be healed.

The next operation in Maternity proceeded normally, except that the staff was the only ones there to welcome the baby girl, taken from her mother's unconscious body. A muted cheer went up as the baby popped her eyes open, and began to scream at the indignity of the rough landing into this world. They gently laid her on Sarah's chest, but Sarah was too deep under the anesthetic to respond.

"What a surprise this lady is going have when she comes around," Dr. Bailey chuckled to Vern, as he stood over the baby unit, running his expert eyes over the nine pound baby girl.

Now that Sarah's broken bones had been taken care of, and the baby safe in the nursery, there was only the matter of the depressed area of her skull and the coma.

It was up to John to take the next step. He immediately went to administration to check when the operating theater could be booked. He would've liked to of had Garth Williams, a specialist in head injuries to assist him, but Garth was not available this week. Then he remembered that there was an excellent man, Jacobs, in Ottawa. He called, and much to everyone's surprise, Dr. Jacobs had a cancellation. He could be with them early the next morning.

John returned to Sarah's room, where he found Vern sitting in the visitor's chair.

"What, you haven't got enough to do?" John asked.

"Yes, I have plenty to do," he answered. "But, I hated to leave her here alone. It seems such a shame that there is no one from her family here. There must be someone looking for her by now. It's too bad her purse was lost in the crash, or maybe someone stole it, for all we know."

"I would say that in the morning, when the dayshift at the station gets the reports from the accident, the bulletin will go out. Some good news--you know that guy Jacobs; neurosurgeon in Ottawa? By a stroke of luck he will be on his way first thing tomorrow to do the procedure. If all goes well, shortly after he operates our sleeping beauty should be awake and tell us all."

Vern nodded his head and smiled, but he didn't get up from the chair to leave.

John studied the chart and stood a moment watching Sarah breathe. The elusive feeling that he should know her was back again, but he couldn't bring it to his mind. Then he jerked his thoughts back to his other patients, and reminded himself, that a doctor could not get wrapped up in one patient's problems, and neglect the others.

He had an urge to tell that to Vern. Then he thought, 'Vern will learn that for himself.'

Chapter 8

Dr. Dave James drove home from his clinic, dead tired. He thought briefly of listening to the news on the radio, but he was too worn out to hear any more bad news; with a storm like this, there was sure to be bad news. He'd had four admissions this evening; heart attacks from shoveling snow. Then a lot of old people got sick around Christmas, but they would hang on until they saw their loved ones again, or some would.

The house he and Sarah owned was out on a small lake a few miles south of Ottawa. Dave sometimes thought of how much more convenient it would be to live in town where winter snowstorms were looked after by the city, but he loved this place. The deep winter silence satisfied some craving inside him.

His four wheel drive vehicle churned through the deep snow on the driveway which wound through the pine trees and up to the house. Stepping out of his warm vehicle into the sharp cold air, he took several deep breaths, although they burned his lungs. He imagined the white birches along the lake shore, and how they looked in moonlight.

He let himself into the dark house; his body hardly able to obey in his mind's instructions. He turned up the thermostat and rummaged around in the refrigerator for something to eat. He hadn't restocked it since he got home. Peeling back the lids on two plastic containers, he thought 'Past edible'; and emptied them into the garbage. A frozen pizza popped into the microwave would have to do, and then sleep.

Sarah and Angela would be home tomorrow. They lit his life with joy and laughter --a perfect antidote to his medical practice. 'It will be great to have them back,' he thought. But even imagining their presence couldn't seem to shift the black cloud of depression that sometimes seized him after a long day.

Once in a while, he wished he had specialized in dermatology. He thought of the quiet waiting rooms, the hopes of patients that he could ease some long term skin condition--ones that would make him a mint of money from Botox injections and skin peels. Instead he had the chaos of crying children, sick and broken adults, old and young and everything in between.

Dave put aside these thoughts and found his way to bed. Hours later he woke with a jerk. When was the bus due to arrive? He should have called yesterday, but they had been run off their feet at the clinic, and there was no answer when he called Jill's house.

He threw back the covers and reached for his bathrobe.

As he filled the coffee pot, he wished he'd been able to talk Sarah out of that visit to Jill. He knew how much she missed her college friends, but that highway was treacherous in winter. Storms blowing across open fields caused drifting and whiteouts. He had seen the results a dozen times, but she had been determined to go, saying it was the last time she would see Jill for a long while.

He'd been hoping she would listen to his mother. Lila's strong premonitions were the subject of family jokes, but she was right enough times to make a person think; in the darkness of the night. He had seen her face when the, 'going to see Jill' idea was first proposed by Sarah.

"What if there was an accident?" Lila had murmured, but only Dave had heard her. She said it louder later, but Sarah pretended not to hear.

For a moment, Dave was there in that fragrant kitchen, the smell of garlic and basil and roasting turkey filling the air. Something in his mother's body language had tugged at a part of his mind, but in the chaos of a large dinner ready to put on the table, it slipped away before he could capture it.

Here in his kitchen, a second of foreboding held him; but he ignored it and turned his mind to the immediate agenda: a shower, breakfast and a call to the bus station. Maybe with the storm coming on Sarah would wait for another day.

But before anything else, he would try Jill's number again. No answer. He set the receiver down gently. A moment of rage made him want to slam it off the counter.

It was frustrating but he had things to do before meeting the bus. He knew the time the bus would be at the station; about 5:00 P.M. He would have time to get in groceries, clean up the house, and lay in plenty of dry wood from the shed out back. Sarah would be exhausted, and a fire always made a pleasant welcome home.

Outside the cold was enough to take your breath away, but the sky was clear, and the new snow lay clean on the ground. It bent the smaller bushes with the clots caught in the needles. Taking a deep breath, Dave looked around the property as he felt for the keys with his gloved hand.

'The ice will be safe to skate and ski on,' he thought. It was covered with snow but he'd clear a small rink. Angela loved a sled ride on the lake and through the forest. He had the rest of the week off, after tomorrow.

The reason he had brought his family to this area, rather than setting up a practice in Toronto or Kingston, was the beauty of its landscapes with its lakes and forests. Before Angela was born, he and Sarah had hiked and canoed whenever they could get a spare moment. He suspected she wasn't quite as enamored with the area as he was. She missed her family; but he loved it.

Two hours later, he returned from the store with a small Christmas tree. He stood it in a corner of the living room before putting the groceries away. Angela would be really surprised to see another Christmas tree. At the farm, they'd had a Christmas dinner and opened gifts just four days ago. Of course, at her age, she might think a second Christmas was normal. Tomorrow he didn't start work until afternoon. They could decorate the tree before he had to leave. At 4:00 P.M. he got out the directory and dialed Greyhound.

"Bus 416 from Kingston -- 4:50 P.M," the bored female voice replied after he asked when Sarah's bus was expected.

'That's fine,' Dave thought as he hung up the phone. 'If I go in right away I can be there when it gets in.' He took a quick look around the house, put on his heavy winter clothing again and jogged out to the van. His worried fantasies-- he knew he was prone to worry too much where his family was concerned-- slipped away.

In spite of the storm yesterday, today's bus must have made it through with no trouble. He imagined Angela throwing her solid little body into his arms, and the heavily pregnant Sarah waddling behind with a smile on her face and a light in her eye that was only for him.

At the station a few minutes early, Dave got a coffee and sat down to wait. A group of men at the next table was talking about yesterday's bus accident.

"There were a lot killed in that there crash," one man, dressed in a half a wardrobe of heavy wool clothes, said to his friends.

"Yeah, I hear there've been three they don't know who they are," he said with the relish of someone baring bad news about strangers.

Dave only half listened. Five killed, three seriously hurt, and many minor injuries-- but too far south to be admitted to the hospital where his patients were sent. It was lucky that Sarah was coming today, or she might have been in that crash. He let his mind drift off to thinking of how he and Sarah would enjoy watching Angela open the toys they'd bought weeks ago.

Just then the bus lumbered into the bay. Dave followed along after the others who were pushing out to greet family or friends. They crowded around the door at the side where passengers picked up their luggage.

Dave was taller than most, and by standing against the wall he could see everything going on. He didn't liked being in crowds. Once, as a child, he'd gotten separated from the rest of his family at a hockey game, and was so terrified that he never got over it.

The driver stepped off first then turned to warn the passengers about the spot where another bus had dripped, and left a slippery patch. Slowly, the passengers began to disembark. An old man was helped down the steps by his wife, and had to endure her scolding him to "Hang onto the rail!" Then a young mother came with two children. She was trying to control them without yelling, and not having much success. The one called Jimmy was the big problem. He leaped the steps two at a time and ran toward the station with her shouting, "Jimmy, you come back here right this minute! You hear me?"

Dave watched with a smile tugging at his lips. Soon they would have two racing around their house. He wondered idly whether Angela would enjoy a brother or sister, or be jealous of either one.

Suddenly the flow of people descending the steps dried up. The driver had the baggage compartment doors open and was beginning to drag out suitcases and bags. Dave looked at the bus windows expecting to see Sarah maneuvering herself and Angela to the front. The tinted windows shadowed the inside. He couldn't see any movement.

He pushed forward; an awful premonition twisting his gut. Stepping up the stairs, he looked down the bus but it was empty. He jumped back out and shouldered aside the other passengers. As he plowed toward the driver, he left a wave of grumbling and angry shouts in his wake.

The driver had his back turned, and didn't answer Dave immediately. Dave grabbed him by the arm and jerked him round.

"Hey, leave off! What's the matter with you?" the driver snarled, as he tried to pull away.

Dave fired a barrage of questions. By now, he was so upset that he was almost shouting; and he was a man who rarely raised his voice. In fact he prided himself on always being cool and collected. Suddenly, he realized what he was doing, and apologized for his behavior.

The driver was slightly mollified at this more reasonable tone, but he was tired and wanted to get finished. "You're mistaken, Man," he growled when Dave had described Sarah and Angela. "No one like that with a little girl was on my bus today--just that woman over there with that brat of a kid."

For a moment Dave stood unable to think of the next step. The words that would accuse the driver of lying to him, gathered at the back of his tongue. But before they escaped, he accepted the facts, and began to rationalize them. Maybe they had got off at another stop and had taken a taxi home. They might have passed on the road without either realizing it. He raced for the van and gunned it onto the road out of town.

Chasing his headlights up the drive, he realized the house was dark. The early winter darkness had swallowed the world except for the tunnel before his headlights. 'They must have decided to stay with Jill,' he reasoned. But why hadn't Sarah called? She knew he would be at his clinic. She'd promised they would come today. He counted back the days. Yes, today was the day they'd agreed upon.

Slamming the van into a skidding stop, Dave fumbled out his cell phone and dialed Jill's number. His bulky glove dialed an angry man who yelled, "This had better be good. I'm dripping all over the carpet. Is that you Jack?"

With a mumbled apology, Dave forced his shaking hands to obey him, as he closed that call and dialed over again, this time without his glove.

When Jill's quick pick-up and perky, "Hello," came through, Dave asked to speak to Sarah without waiting to say the usual niceties.

"Is that you, Dave? Sarah isn't here. She left yesterday morning. Isn't she home? She decided to go a day early to surprise you. I tried to get her to wait, but she wouldn't. The storm warning was all over the news, but you know Sarah when her mind is made up."

"No, she didn't come yesterday," Dave croaked-- his voice stiff with fear.

"Could she have stopped in Toronto? Maybe she decided not to go on after all." Jill's conciliatory voice might have made her little boy feel better, but it didn't work for Dave. He hung up with an abrupt snap.

Jill never worried about anything. He was wasting precious time talking to her. He was sure Sarah's parents had gone on the trip they were planning, but maybe she had been tired, and decided to stay at their place. He tried their home number, but the phone rang and rang in the empty house. Shaking with anger and fear, he left a message anyway.

He pocketed his cell phone. He would start on other friends she might have contacted from the land line in the Toronto house.

As he was turning the key in the lock, the conversation he had overheard in the bus terminal came back to him. He walked straight to the phone and dialed the RCMP.

Chapter 9

A man frantically looking for is wife was nothing unusual to the desk sergeant. He only began to listen when Dave mentioned the bus crash near Kingston yesterday.

"Yes! Yes!, the one due at 4:50 yesterday. I met the one today, but she wasn't on it!" Dave wanted to scream, but contained himself. This was living a nightmare! No one seemed to appreciate how he felt. Fear and frustration clogged his throat, but he took a deep breath, and got control of his voice.

"How long has she been missing?" the country voice drawled out.

Dave explained again. She was supposed to have come today, but she came yesterday, and she wasn't on the bus she should have taken today.

"And she was pregnant, you say. Just a minute, I'm bringing up yesterday's accident reports. Yes, the bus traveling east from Toronto was in collision with a logging truck. All passengers on that bus have been accounted for," he said. "Five dead, but none of them fit the description of your wife. Air ambulance lifted three patients, one woman and two men, to Kingston General Hospital. Ten others came in by ambulance. Mobile passengers were sent to the bus station. Try the hospital there."

Dave dropped the phone onto its cradle with a clatter. His head a swirl of fear, hope, and a possible agenda, he shifted from foot to foot. What first? Call his office? Secure the house? Then he realized he had to stop and really think.

'First secure the house,' he thought. He turned down the thermostat, and checked the locks on the windows. He listed off several other things including notifying his clinic, and did them. Satisfied that he could safely leave, he quickly packed a bag, making sure he had bottled water with him. Within twenty minutes he was back in his van and headed out.

The road he needed to reach the main highway was slippery. He forced himself to drive carefully when every instinct was clamoring for him to hurry. He'd tramp down hard on the gas and then have to ease off, gritting his teeth at every skid. He'd seen many results of driving too fast at night on winter roads to risk his own neck.

Two hours later, he strode through the doors of Kingston General. One glance at the clean floors, and the faint hum of people going about their business, assured him that all was as it should in a good hospital. He banished thoughts of flashing lights, police sirens, twisted metal and broken bodies; and what it was like to face families to tell them that their loved ones were dead. He had never prayed in this life, but now he prayed that he wouldn't have to be one of those people.

He was approaching the reception desk when he heard his name called. "Hey. Dave. What are you doing here? Don't you have enough work in Ottawa?"

Dave turned and saw his old friend John Green. He was delighted to see him, but still couldn't bring a smile to his face. Before he could say anything, John's face changed from delight to shock.

He burst out, "Oh my God! I knew that Jane Doe looked familiar. You know, I only met Sarah once, and I never connected her with the patient, brought in from the crash yesterday. Sorry, Old Boy. With all her injuries, we had to rush and decide which to treat first. I am happy to tell you it all came out right. The baby is fine. Mind you, Sarah is still in the coma from her head trauma, but that's normal, and we expect her to wake-up in the next day or two. Your Doctor Jacobs came in and did the op on her head. I set her broken collarbone myself."

Dave could feel his mouth opening and closing like a fish out of water. With every bit of information, which John obviously thought he had already heard, he tried to process it, and catch the next piece as it flew by. He stood with his arms hanging straight down at his sides. He didn't seem to have the strength to lift them. As a doctor, he should be delighted that Sarah was alive; but as a husband, he could hardly bear the thought of her lovely body broken and in pain.

He found himself looking at the snow melting off his boots, making puddles on the floor, and noticing that John was in regular clothes, not green scrubs.

The moment of denial brushed aside, he took a deep breath and said, "And where's my--- my little girl? Where's Angela?"

"The baby's right in Sarah's room. They had her in the baby care unit for the first few hours while we operated on Sara's head, but Vern-- do you know him? He's our resident here in obstetrics-- felt the baby's cries might reach Sarah and make her struggle toward consciousness."

"Cries," Dave stumbled over the word. "Was she hurt?" He turned as if he might rush off and do something.

John reached out a hand to gently turn him back. "No, not more than in any other Cesarean-- I just meant the usual cries of a newborn."

Finally, Dave realized the misunderstanding; John was talking about the new baby that he himself had completely forgotten, in his worry for Sarah and Angela.

"Where's Angela?" Dave finally got his frozen lips to say.

"Who's Angela?" John asked in confusion." Sarah was alone when she was brought in. Air ambulance flew her from the crash site. Hang on. I'll get a list of all the others brought in and you can see the names on it. We have identified everyone, now that you're here for Sarah."

"Angela is our other child. She's only two and a half. Where is she? She's got to be-- the bus, the bus--she was with Sarah on the bus!" Why couldn't John seem to understand? Dave felt he would go mad, if he didn't get an answer without dragging every sentence from his friend, one word at a time.

John looked shaken and puzzled. Dave was tempted to launch into an explanation for the misunderstanding about the times, and how he'd found out about the crash. But he caught himself up short. It was action he needed.

He was about to say so when John said, "Here, you go to Sarah's room. I'll get on the blower and make some calls." He put his hand on Dave's shoulder. "We'll find her, and she'll be safe until you can pick her up. I'll contact the police and Child Services right away. Write a description." John turned to leave.

In the middle of considering the description he would give of Angela, Dave was trying to remember what she was most likely to be wearing. An awful sinking feeling, come to him in the middle of these possible scenarios. 'What if someone, hearing the description, claimed to have her-- when it wasn't true?' As a doctor he was well known in his area. Many would rush to help, but the criminal underbelly there wouldn't hesitate to take advantage, and try to extort money from his disaster.

He stopped and called after John, who turned and came back. "John, let's keep this only with the local police and RCMP for a while--no outside information." He explained his fear of scams.

John argued, "The papers can reach thousands." He went on to explain his thinking, and the reasons for going public, but finally he agreed to wait until Dave got advice from the police.

Chapter 10

Sarah lay as still as death, her pale complexion a greenish white in the partially darkened room. Now that he was here, Dave felt something shift in his brain that brought the doctor forward, and set aside the worried husband.

He removed his heavy coat while standing beside the bed, his eyes absorbing and analyzing all the signals he could see. He touched her wrist and was reassured by her regular pulse, and her normal breathing on her own.

A cry from the corner jerked him around. There was the new baby they had planned and waited for. Her crinkled newborn face called up memories of Angela's birth. His nose strung from the tears pressing behind his eyes. She was so tiny, for all of her nine pounds. And then, with a sound somewhere between a laugh and a sob, Dave gathered her up into his arms.

She let out a little snort and opened her milky blue eyes. She seemed to study his face, and then after a wide yawn, she sighed and fell back to sleep.

"Another old soul in the family, I see," he murmured.

This was one of his mother's favorite saying about babies born into her family. He never knew whether it was said to make the new parents feel that their baby was special, or if she believed the old Irish myths, that he had, as he grew up, put aside as nonsense.

He dropped a kiss onto her cheek and held her close, inhaling her unique baby smell. He thought of the fragility of life, and momentarily in the joy of this new child, he forgot his anxiety over Angela.

Laying the sleeping baby against his shoulder, Dave sat down near Sarah and began to talk to her. He tried to project his love through levels of her unconsciousness, to where she might hear him.

He thought about what he knew about coma. It wasn't understood even by doctors like him. The patient could wake-up in hours, or months, or years. The current thought was to keep talking to them in hopes that they might hear at some level.

He tried to speak as they used to lying in bed at night, talking after being apart throughout the day. That time of soft murmurings had become a ritual with them. Here though, it was difficult without any response.

Hearing a noise that could only be called a squawk, Dave turned to see the duty nurse standing in the open door. She was a stranger to him, and therefore he would be a stranger to her. He could just imagine her shocked response at finding him holding a baby beside an unconscious mother.

He turned to her and said, I'm Doctor Dave James. Sorry to startle you. Sarah is my wife.

"We're so glad to see you!" she exclaimed once she recovered from her surprise. She walked to the bedside. After a quick look at Sarah, she turned back. "You understand that after the bus crash, no one had time to sort the luggage for identification. Not that they could tell which bags belonged to which passenger. She had nothing in her pockets to help identify her and no purse."

Dave carried the sleeping baby back to her climate controlled unit. He loved holding her but he knew she was safest there.

When he inquired how they were feeding the baby, she said, "We've put the baby on formula. Sarah had to have so many drugs to prevent infection, that her milk is unfit for the baby, even if she does wake up."

Seconds after the nurse Simone left, Sergeant Baker, from the local police force, rapped gently on the doorframe. He beckoned Dave to come out into the hall. His square head sat on a square body, but the sharp blue eyes, set close to the bulbous nose, belied a first impression that he wasn't the sharpest knife in the drawer. After a handshake and introduction, he got down to business.

"Are you sure the missing child, Angela James, was with your wife on the bus from Toronto to Ottawa on December 22rd?"

"I know Angela was with Sarah. Sarah's friend Jill Duncan told me so." In spite of his resolution to stay calm, Dave heard his voice rising in anger. Surely the police were not going to suspect him of lying to them. He had great respect for the police and their difficult job-- handling death and injury-- even before it reached the hospital. He was going to suggest he could do without this kind of help, when Baker explained.

"Hold on. I wasn't accusing you of anything. There was a child of that description on the bus before the injured passengers were removed. One group left by bus just before the air ambulance arrived. A witness saw a woman, and a child fitting your description, board the bus headed for the Kingston. The witness is injured, and has no memory of seeing any child after the accident. She saw three men move your wife and lay her on the floor. We checked with the paramedics but they didn't see a child either."

"Someone has taken her! God knows what for!" Dave caught himself before he swore and hit something. His stomach twisted so violently he nearly threw up, and only practiced willpower held back the bile burning his throat.

Baker said, "Let's not jump to that conclusion yet. Someone might have taken her home and will bring her in. People do all kinds of stupid things in the midst of an accident."

Somehow Dave didn't think Baker had much belief in that theory; he didn't. Not for one minute. Then again, anything was possible. People did make extremely stupid decisions under pressure. After an accident, he'd seen one man sitting in the mud, who had cut off his toes with an axe, because they were caught under the truck wheel and he panicked.

The RCMP would have bulletins out on radio and on television. And had sent a team back to search around the crash site. If Angela had been thrown from the bus, she might have been buried by a snowplow. Baker didn't tell Dave this. He'd thought of it himself.

Baker said the site was still being investigated, and that he knew Dave didn't want any names released when the RCMP sent the report.

Already the survivors were being questioned. It was a matter of tracking every one of them down. Baker explained how the people who were not injured were sent on ahead, but they had all been accounted for except for one or two. The names were being checked against the lists from the bus station, and if Angela had come in that group, she would be on the list.

"There was one woman, who didn't sign in here but there was no mention of a child with her. Don't worry, we'll find her," Sergeant Baker said, before proceeding like a small tank toward the door.

Dave didn't have his confidence. Whoever took Angela would be far away by now. His mind totally blanked out when he tried to imagine what kind of person had taken her. He was still standing in the corridor staring after Baker, but he was not seeing the policeman's uniformed back. His mind was leaping from one terrible possibility to another, when John startled him by touching his shoulder.

He said, "You should get some rest. When did you eat last?"

"That's not important now. I can't leave Sarah. "Dave rubbed his hands over his face as if he could wipe out the last hours and replace them with new realities.

"We'll fix that," John replied.

Dave watched John speak to the nurse, Simone, who had been standing by Sarah's bed. John had always had an eye for pretty nurses, and Dave bet himself a corned beef sandwich that this one was in John's sights. He shook his head and gave John a hard look.

"Simone, could you bring one of those visitor's chairs in here? If Dave won't leave, we will have to bring food and a bed to him. The cafeteria might still be open. We need some sandwiches and hot soup if possible."

Dave saw that John couldn't help himself, as he followed his demands with a practiced sexy smile.

"Yes, Dr. Green, right away," she said, turning from the bedside and going down the hall to where she knew a reclining guest chair sat in an empty room. Minutes later she rolled it up the hall and slid the unwieldy chair against the wall outside the door.

The two men quickly came through the door to get it, and safely position it between the baby unit and Sarah's bed. Not waiting for thanks, Simone had left for the kitchens.

The cook was just finishing his last inspection before leaving when she arrived, but he'd heard the Jane Doe story and said, "What do you need? Poor guy must be out of his mind with worry."

Simone told him what she needed, and filled him in on the exciting details, while he made chicken salad sandwiches and brewed a pot of tea. All on a tray with a tea towel over it, the cook started to turn out lights. Simone balanced the tray on one hip and rang for the elevator.

Going up in the elevator, Simone idly wondered if Dr. Green intended to stay all night. His work with Sarah was over, but he might stay as a friend. Careful, she thought. That damned English accent-- I can't seem to get past it. Everyone says he has the morals of a tomcat; been there, done that.

Once she had delivered the tray, she stood a moment with empty hands. She knew she should leave the room but she should check Sarah once more. After all she was the night nurse, and responsible for her.

Something Dave said triggered a memory. She had overheard someone talking about a patient who had been on the bus that crashed. He had a broken hip and was still in the hospital. Wally! Wally, something.

Dave saw her hesitating and broke in on what John was saying. "I'll be here now, Nurse, if she needs anything."

"It's not that," Simone said. "It's just that I remembered something. It isn't much, but it might be helpful." Stumbling a little because she was unsure of her facts, she mentioned Wally.

By now John was listening as well. "Good God, I was the one that set his hip. I'll go talk to him. He might well have some pertinent information. No one told me he was one of the bus casualties." Dave rose to go with him but he said, "Let me do the legwork. If it's anything that sounds useful, I'll come back and get you. Eat! That's what you need now."

Sitting close to Sarah, holding her hand, Dave was torn between wanting to do his own legwork and wanting to be near her. Sooner than expected, he heard John's footfalls outside. He rounded the doorjamb and started to talk before he came to a standstill.

"Wally Oxter isn't the brightest soul because he's on morphine. I'm not sure, that at the best of times he's playing with a full deck, but he perked up when he heard why I was asking him about the accident. Here's the gist of it. Yes, he remembered everything. He hadn't passed out-- he'd seen the logs driving straight toward the bus, the impact, and remembered being flung across the bus to the other side when it went over. He said how weird it was trying to figure why everything was up side down. He'd landed facing the back of the bus on the bottom windows which were broken. He had heard the men discussing Sarah, but the only child he'd seen was carried by her grandmother as she climbed the ladder out of the bus with the other ambulatory passengers. 'How did you know it was her grandmother,' I asked. 'He heard the woman tell the policewoman so,' he said.

Dave had listened hard, but still he made John repeat some things and questioned others. He could feel a tiny layer of pessimism peel off the weight pressing on his body and mind.

"This is our first real lead, John. I think we should get Baker in on this. I'll try calling him, but if you see him first, tell him," Dave urged, before he stepped out into the hall to make the call. A second later he stuck is head back in, "Wally's room? 411, right?"

He was in luck. Sergeant Baker was just getting into his car to go off, but when he heard Dave's news, he went back into the hospital to meet him at Wally's bedside.

Chapter 11

On entering the ward, Dave saw three occupied beds but only one patient who could be Wally. His grizzled hair stuck up in spikes; what there was of it. His face was shrunken and gray. Before he saw Dave, he was gazing toward the window, as if longing to be out going about his business, whatever it might be.

When Dave spoke, the old man struggled to pull himself up on his pillow. A weak smile flickered across his face, as if he was glad to have company, but not too sure if he deserved the attention.

"You look like you've trouble, young man," Wally said. "Is this about the little lost girl?"

"Yes," Dave said, "My little girl. I hear you may have seen her?"

"That bus crash was a bitch, wasn't it?" Wally spat out. He made a gesture at his broken hip before he began to tell about what he had seen. There was no information that Dave could see as being helpful.

"Think again about the little girl, Wally. She's about this tall." Dave held his hand at a spot just above his knee. "Did you see her hair? Was she wearing a white and blue snowsuit?" Dave's mind boiled with questions but he held them in, afraid he might put too much pressure on the old man who'd begin to make up answers just to please him.

Wally twisted his face, as if that could make his brain work better. "I never saw the kid standing. The woman was carrying her. Wait, I just remembered this-- she was quite old and short. Her clothes were old and plain-- all dark colours. I only saw the little girl for a minute, but now I think of it, the snowsuit was like you say. Yes!" Wally smiled proudly at having noticed more than he'd realized.

Dave gave him a pat on the shoulder and said, "Good man. That's a great help." His mind leaped ahead to the next step; leaving Wally behind. He turned to go, forgetting even to say 'Thank you'.

"Will you come again?" Wally asked.

"Sure I will." Dave dredged up a half-hearted smile before hurrying out to meet Sergeant Baker. He knew it had been an empty promise, even as the words left his mouth.

Baker was waiting in the hall outside Wally's room. He had talked to the old man earlier.

"It sounds like it might be a starting place," Baker said. "Do you think the old fellow is telling the truth, or just picking up on what we want to hear?"

"I'm sure not. The old boy is sharper than you might think. He seemed pretty sure about the woman and the color of the snowsuit. I think we should go with it. They must have come to the bus station. There was no other place the bus stopped while coming from the accident site."

"That's the trouble. She must have somehow disappeared before she had to register. It was pretty chaotic. I looked over the place and they could easily have gone to the washrooms and hidden there until the coast was clear."

"But she couldn't have had an accomplice. It was all random--the crash, escaping injury, getting away from police scrutiny-- there must be something else." Dave knew he sounded desperate, and he was.

"We're far from finished yet. People are beginning to answer the call that we put out on the radio for information. Unfortunately, most of the passengers, those who walked away, were so taken up with the injured that they have no memory of her. She had to stay somewhere in town overnight. I would put my money on the possibility that they boarded the return bus to Toronto the next morning. She would want to get back to home territory," Baker said.

Dave knew that was idle speculation, and pressing Baker for answers, was wasted time. Still, it gave him the illusion of doing something. After asking if the RCMP were searching outside his jurisdiction, Baker assured him that they were, but hadn't shared much information with local police. The drop of hope Dave had felt with Wally seeped away. He left Baker and returned to sit beside Sarah.

He talked to her late into the night, until he fell into a fitful sleep. In a dream he was arguing with Sarah, who had grown strangely large and ugly. In the dream, he grabbed her trying to hold her with him. She turned into mist and drifted away.

He startled awake and was horrified to find he was bent over the bed shaking Sara's unconscious body.

John heard Dave yelling from where he was at the nurse's station, and ran down the hall. "Dave! For God's sake! Stop! What you're doing?" he shouted. He jerked Dave back and would have struck him, except that Dave was a good four inches taller and ten kilos heavier than he was.

Dave came to himself, and for a moment he thought he was hallucinating at seeing John standing there with his red hair standing on end like an indignant woodpecker.

Sarah lay too near the edge of the bed, with her covers half on the floor. He was trembling, and for seconds he was incapable of getting the jumbled sounds falling from of his mouth to assemble into words. He fought the sour vomit pressing at the back of his throat.

"Where? Where did you? Thank God you're here. I'm just about crazy. There's another thing I didn't mention. I've got to get back. My locum only gave me four days. A good friend of mine in Ottawa will take over Sarah's care-- not that she hasn't had the best here. I want to move her tomorrow.

"Aren't you forgetting someone?" John turned to the baby unit, picked up the baby and laid her in Dave's arms.

"You're right. I have to get a grip, don't I?" Dave said as he lifted her to kiss her face. "Poor little thing hasn't a name yet. 'Little Stranger,' you were supposed to be our boy."

His voice trembled but did not break. He knew strength to bear this would come from some iron core deep inside; he just hadn't been able to tap it yet.

John said, "Well look, you can't do anything tonight. The police will find Angela. Sarah is on the mend physically, and the baby looks great. I'd recommend another day, but they are fit to transport. I'm going get you a mild sedative. If you don't sleep, you won't be any good to anybody."

Reluctantly, Dave agreed. As John's footsteps receded down the hall, Dave sat admiring his new daughter. In two days he would have Sarah and the baby transferred to Ottawa.

It was Christmas Eve.

Chapter 12

Lila

How I wished I could be with Dave when we first got the terrible news of Sarah's accident, and even more tragic; Angela was missing. But he's a grown man and there was nothing we could do from here. He has made his home in Ottawa, and I know he is very happy with Sarah and cares for Angela in a loving, giving way that I haven't seen in him since he was a boy.

When they set out, we'd already celebrated Christmas here on the farm, several days before the day itself.

I inherited the Irish love of horses, and finally when Don retired from his career in the Civil Service, we bought this small farm here in eastern Ontario. I take in old horses if they are in reasonable health, and if not, I arrange a dignified death for them, so they aren't left uncared for to starve in some last ditch hell-hole. A pair of miniatures, saved by the Humane Society, found their way here too.

Angela is crazy about those little horses. There's a mother and her six month old baby-- it's only slightly bigger than a good sized dog.

They seemed to enjoy a human that didn't loom over them, and the foal ran and played with Angela in the snow.

When she screeched in excitement, he ran away and hid behind his mother and had to be coaxed out again with bits of apple.

Dave and Sarah left together, and Sarah and Angela went to visit Sarah's friend Jill and Dave to drive the long trip back to Ottawa. I was stunned at what I considered such a dubious plan. Sarah was so far along in her new pregnancy, I wondered how she could contemplate that long bus trip in winter conditions. On the other hand, she is a wonderful mother, and I know she has missed her friends and wouldn't live near Ottawa except for how much Dave loves their country place.

Not wanting to come on as 'know it all' mother-in-law-- a big lie; I managed to not say the words I was dying to, but that might damage Sarah's feelings for me. I do think she likes me, as I do her. So, handkerchief in hand, I stood at my good old man's side and waved them off.

I remember the house seemed to die a little when the last car door slammed, and Don and I stood in the open door, clutching our sweaters to our throats. Inside again, Don shoved another stick of wood into the stove.

Straightening up, he turned to me and said, "What's that face for?"

"I just felt a chill that had nothing to do with standing in the open door," I told Don, 'Put on a face of your own, you silly old bugger,' I thought. I knew what was coming next.

"Now Lila, don't you start. I won't hear a thing about your premonitions. You know it's all just nonsense. Of course you're right sometimes, you're bound to be. But you can no more tell the future than; oh well, we've gone over this a million times. I wish we could stop."

I've never been able to prove that I can see the future. It's never as straightforward as if someone says to me, 'you're going to fall down and break your arm'. The warning may come in a dream, or sudden, in the middle of doing a household chore. It's hard to explain, and I best not try, as no one ever believes me. But I know what I know.

That cold had settled on my heart, but I had laundry to do and a lot of tidying up. Darling that she is, Angela can make more mess in one day than half a dozen adults in a week. 'Just wait until the little accomplice, coming soon, gets onto his feet,' I thought, as my hands busied themselves.

In a distracted moment, I dropped the brandy decanter with a 'god-awful' crash. That didn't please Don one bit; it had been his mother's. However it was empty, and that was a good thing, I reminded him.

We didn't talk much that afternoon. We were both tired. I got together a light supper of salad and leftover turkey, and after dinner Don went to his books and I to watch television.

The real Christmas was certainly an anticlimax. The tree already looked old and tired. We tried to be cheerful for each other. I spent as much time as I could with my horses. The old ones needed loving care with brush and currycomb, and being with them calmed me. Don had his woodpile to chop and spent some time at a wood carving project of his.

Three days later the telephone ringing in the office brought us both running. Although Don hadn't said much, and refused to discuss the danger Sarah could be in on those winter highways, I knew he was as anxious for news as I was.

"That's them, I bet," Don said as he picked up the phone before I could grab it.

"Hello, is that you, Sarah? He was so sure he was right that he didn't wait to get an answer but continued, "How did the trip go? Figured out the entire world problems at your

friend's, did you?" He was always teasing Sarah about her
interest in New Age philosophies.

Then I saw Don's face fall, and he lifted his right hand
to press against his chest. I leaned over and pushed the
speaker button so we could both hear.

"Dad, Mom, I have terrible news." Dave's voice sent
icicles dripping down my spine.

Writers speak of your heart leaping in your chest. I felt
as if mine had leapt out and crashed back as Dave started to
tell us the story of what happened-- the bus crash, the fact
that he'd lost hours while he looked for Sarah and Angela,
and then his trip to Kingston. He told the story frontward
and backward, mixing in names of people I'd never heard
of. I tried to keep track, but once he got past Angela's
disappearance, I hardly took in anything at all.

Finally, Don hung up the phone and we stared at each
other, speechless and overtaken with the most horrible
feelings of uselessness. We had given Dave what comfort
we could, but that was little enough.

I wanted to say, 'I told you so', but I didn't. Behind my
eyes, a white pain seared; the onset of a migraine.

Don looked as if he had aged ten years in those twenty
minutes.

Dave hadn't wanted us to come to their place yet. He had
moved Sarah and the baby to the hospital in Ottawa. The
search for Angela was in the hands of the local police and
the Mounties. He seemed hopeful that Sarah would recover.

I wondered if the poor girl wasn't better where she was--
in the coma. I could only imagine her terror when she heard
that Angela was missing. But then I remembered the new
baby. That had to be a joy. Sarah's parents also must have
this news. 'Mary will be absolutely devastated. Sarah was
always Ralph's favorite when their family was young, and
they absolutely adore Angela.' The pain in my head became

worse as more anxieties crowded in. Ralph was a lawyer, knew the law and the way police worked. No doubt he would soon be using his 'Old Boy's network to spur them to cover every clue. I prayed through the pain.

Don saw me clutch my head. He took my hand and said, "Come lie down. I'll make you some tea."

His kindness burst the dam holding back my tears. I let him guide me to the couch-- fussed about getting a blanket and making tea. I dared not talk about what might have happened to Angela--I would start screaming and never stop.

Foolish thoughts swirled through my pounding head. 'So much for ultrasound' I thought; 'they were so sure the baby was going to be a boy.'

Left to my own devices I would be on the bus to Ottawa tomorrow morning, but I suppose it's only right that Mary go; but still.

Chapter 13

Don

Writing diaries for women isn't my thing. But Lila asked me to write this part of her story; my story too. We have been together for a long time, the dreamer and the skeptic.

The only part of hers I don't agree with is that, 'silly old bugger' crack. She's called me worse in our years together to be sure. It's a wonder we are still together, we're so different; like chalk and cheese as they say, but love is a knotty rope full of snags, and ours was woven strong to last.

That night, after we talked with Dave, we felt so dislocated (the only word I can think of) we could hardly form a sentence between us. We usually read awhile before going to sleep, but one would pick up a book, and with hardly a word registering, put it down and propose some different scenario than the dozen so we had worked over earlier. Finally, we fell asleep out of pure exhaustion.

Toward morning, I came awake with the feeling that something was wrong. I sat up and fumbled on the bedside lamp. Cursing my near blindness without my glasses, I sat a minute listening to the house. Our old house is very quiet. It was built to last in an earlier century. From outside there was nothing other than the December wind howling around the loose barn board, the one that I didn't fix last Fall. I prayed that Angela was warm and safe-- whoever had her.

By now my mind was clearing and I become aware that the sound I'd heard was in the room. Lila! I was sure she had been quiet only seconds ago, but now I heard her breathing; labored and rasping. She was facing away from me. Rather than pull her toward me, I got out of bed and went around to her side, put her lamp on and leaned over her.

Her skin was gray and beads of sweat stood out on her forehead. I tried to wake her with a little shake, but she flopped onto her back. It was obvious she couldn't hear me, but the worst of it was her half open eyes. A rim of white showed from under the lids. I tried the questions you're supposed to ask someone you think is having a stroke; she didn't seem to hear me.

I got to admit that I completely panicked. I could no more imagine life without Lila than I could imagine it without legs.

'Call 911,' something shrieked in my head. I cursed myself that I didn't give in when Lila had wanted a telephone in our bedroom. For a second or two I couldn't remember where the phone actually was, but I knew it was downstairs.

In my first semi- leap toward the hall, my bad hip nearly collapsed but I hobbled to the top step of the stairs. Then it struck me, I wouldn't be able to dial the telephone without my glasses. With more curses, these beyond the mild 'damns and goddamns' Lila allowed, I had to sidewinder back. A big step with the good leg, drag the other behind, repeat.

Lila looked just as she had when I left, but I couldn't see the glasses. By now I am completely shaken out of my usual calm. My hands shook as I stared at the table, where I know I put them. Then I saw a glint of light inches from my big toe. They had fallen off the night table onto the carpet.

Sticking them onto my face, and moving as fast as I dared, I got down the stairs. There the, phone sat on the hall table, where it had been all the time.

One of the reasons we bought this place is that it is close to the town and a good hospital. I had barely had time to get dressed before the ambulance was at the door. The paramedics and all their equipment thumped up the stairs. I stood back out of the way, trying to recall forgotten prayers. A nerve under my eye kept twitching and all I could think was, 'Goddamn, I don't need this now!'

At the hospital, I was sent to the waiting room. I knew Dr. Homer would do the best he could to save her. It seemed hours before he walked through the door. I worried about Dave, and how I was going to have to tell him about his mother-- and about my blood pressure. It must be off the charts! Where the hell was he?

Does trouble always come in batches?

When Dr. Homer burst through the door of the waiting room, he startled me out of the half doze I'd fallen into. He pulled over one of the chairs and sat down beside me.

In a quiet voice he said, "Lila has had a slight stroke, but is now sleeping under the drugs we gave her. You will notice; one side of her face is pulled slightly down, but she should recover completely with rest and care. Don't be surprised if her voice is slurred at first. Otherwise, she's healthy and strong. Has she had a shock of some kind?"

I told him the events of the evening and the upsetting news. He was sympathetic and said something like, it was not surprising.

I asked, "Can I see her now? 'Bad grammar!' I thought. 'God, the things that go through your head in a crisis!' Then, he led me down the hall to her room.

I took a chair beside her bed and reached for her hand, the one that didn't have the IV needle stuck in the back of it. The doctor asked me something, and I had opened my mouth to answer, when we both were stopped in mid thought.

"When can I go home?" was croaked from the bed. Then her voice steadied. "And don't stand there talking about me as if I were dead." She'd slurred a few words, but it was obvious she still thought she was in charge. I knew my Lila was back.

"Don't try to talk," the doctor said, patting her arm as he gave me a wink.

With an exasperated sigh, Lila grew too tired to fight and muttered something neither of us understood.

And that was probably just as well.

Chapter 14

Jenna

We were lucky on the bus trip. No one paid the least attention to us. Angela was an angel. I told her stories that I remembered from when I was a little kid before my mother died.

I was only six when she died and I thought Mama was the best mother in the world. She made our poor life in a Montreal slum into a fairy tale. She cooked all our meals herself sometimes picking weeds and wild strawberries if she could save a few pennies or get us on a farmer's wagon out to the edge of the city. She told me stories about the early French settlers the Indians and the missionary Sisters who cared for the poor in the early days.

It was to make me proud that I was French. I wish I had listened better.

But Angela was too young for those stories so I asked her what fairy tales she knew. I pretended I'd never heard of them. She giggled at how dumb I was and had a great time telling them to me. Her face would light up like you couldn't believe.

I had to keep Angela's attention because I was afraid she would chatter about her visit to her grandmother's farm and let something slip that someone on the bus might hear and remember. Soon though she fell asleep and I was sorry I had let those memories of my mother come to me because once Mama died my life became more horror story than fairy tale.

Why my mother married my father has always been a mystery to me. I guess there's no knowing. Maybe he was a different man before he lost his job at Redpath Sugar. I suppose he thought he would work there all his life, and I never found out what turned him into a nasty drunk.

Instead of the good working-class men he worked with he turned to criminals for company. This happened soon after Mama took sick. She lost a baby boy and was never right after that. For some reason– he would never tell me why, but I knew he blamed me.

I tried to hide from his drunken friends who liked to pinch and touch me. I learned to keep my mouth shut too. If I tried to say no and squirm away he would laugh and call me his little whore. I didn't know what it meant but I knew by their dirty snickers, that it was something bad.

Then one night when I was ten he fell in front of the tram. What passed for social services at the time sent me to the orphanage kept by those same Sisters that my mother used to tell stories about.

Believe me they were no saints. Not the ones that worked in the orphanage. I was put to work in the laundry. Every day from six to ten in the morning I sweated over the boiling vats, summer and winter.

At ten o'clock, I went to class under hard-bitch teachers with their clappers and rulers. At the end of the day I'd to go back to the laundry until dinner time. Then we had readings and prayers in the chapel.

There was no time to make friends. By the end of day every one of us was so tired we staggered to our beds.

The dormitory was full of crying every night. The girls would try to keep quiet but those night sobs killed all my belief in the church. It was years after that I began to believe again, but I never went back there.

The first year was the worst. The food was plain but better than I had been getting at home from my father. I grew and my heart learned hate. By the end of it the crying of the others didn't keep me awake.

I made two friends Monica and Teresa and we got good at acting nice and being bad. We would pretend to obey the sister's every rule but traded jobs with others so we could work together. Dusting in the chapel we'd mock the statutes by asking them nasty questions and making up even worse answers. We mocked them all but Mother Mary. We didn't quite dare to go that far.

We'd lie flat in the form of the Cross on the stone floor before the altar and confess wicked sins that sent us into screams of laughter.

I let the priest look up my skirt was the worst one I could think of. Monica and Teresa went way further. The nuns would have killed us at some of the dirt we thought up there.

We were caught and strapped but that only made us more careful.

I was sixteen when I was sent from the orphanage. They found a job for me, a job in a good Christian home but I never went there. I wasn't tall but I was quite good-looking and looked older than I was. I found myself a job in a bar on St. Laurent Street.

I was like a caged animal let loose. This time I picked the men that wanted me and I told myself I wasn't the whore my father called me, because I didn't take money but I went to shows and clubs with them and sometimes to their beds.

I hated them the men who slobbered over me. My heart grew hard like a stone.

At the bus terminal it was easy to get a taxi. It took us halfway to my street. We got out there and waited for a bus to take us nearer to where I lived. I didn't want anyone who knew me see me come in a taxi in my good clothes.

Before we got the bus we went into a café to use the washroom. It was down a short hall separated from the main room. I could only be seen by customers there for a few seconds while we passed the double doors. I changed back into the pants and jacket I went north in.

Back in the little alcove by the door I bent close and whispered to Angela. Just in case that old wolf is around we'll watch for the bus from here and get on quick. Can you do that?

'OK. Hold my hand', she said.

Soon the bus pulled up and we lost no time climbing aboard.

My street was a side street not far from the waterfront. All the houses on it were only fit for the wrecker's ball. My little house looked even worse than I remembered. I thought the porch had sagged under the load of snow on it. We had to wade above our knees to get to the door. I knew I would have to get out of this neighborhood. Everyone knew or could find out your business in a minute. Angela would stand out here like a red flag.

The next morning I called an old friend of mine Mabel and asked her over. I told her that my sister's daughter wasn't able to take care of her little girl and had asked me to keep her for a while. Could she look after her until I found a new place?

I said I can't stay in my house. I can't sleep. I thought I saw Julie out in the hall before I left. It scared me bad. That's why I had to leave.

I nearly laughed out loud at her face. We were at my kitchen table and I never saw Mabel leave tea in a cup and biscuits on her plate but she was out of there like a shot.

Next morning after I left Angela with Mabel I walked east to the place near where old factories used to be. There . I found a four apartment building with a sign saying apartment for rent. This was near to where I worked nights and the street didn't look too bad. I took down the number and went to the first call box I saw. The rent agency said they would send someone right away to let me see it.

It was second floor back and was in need of a good scrub but the stove and toilet seemed to work and the radiators were putting out a steady heat. I didn't have time to be choosy. I signed the lease. The man gave me a key and said I could move in any time.

I hurried to the phone again and phoned Jack Slate who had been a friend of my Billy. After he and Julie died together that October afternoon I gave Jack the truck beaten up as it was. I knew he would help me move. Jack wasn't too happy. It was his buddys birthday and they were planning a booze-up but I offered him $20.

I wouldn't have let him turn me down anyway. He only had Bills truck because I couldn't stand to look at it after the accident.

After seeing the signing of the lease and forking out for the first month's rent I found a little store that had a table or two in the back where I could sit down with a cup of tea and think. On a piece of paper I wrote down a list of things I would need. An odd thought came to me that almost made me laugh— when you have to move it's good to be poor. Just think of those rich people trying to move everything they own. I can pitch my stuff into a few boxes and be off. I suppose it was funny in a sick way.

The Sisters always said I couldn't keep my mind on anything for five seconds. I went back to serious thinking. There was most of $250 left. I'd need a bed for Angela. First I thought crib then—no. She wouldn't be sleeping in a crib for long. A little dresser for her things would be nice-- and then bedding. This was adding up faster than I could count.

There was a lot to do if I wanted to move right away. There were stores along the street on my way back to my old neighborhood. My eye was caught by a sale sign. Inside they sold unpainted wood furniture. It was half the price of what I expected and I imagined it painted pink and blue. The headboard had shelves and it was low to the floor so if Angela fell out she wouldn't be hurt.

Cash sure talks. I soon figured out the man on the floor was the owner. I said I'll want the set delivered this afternoon; before 5:00.

He hemmed and hawed but when I started to put the money back in my purse he found he could do it after all. Curtains and other things could wait. My old sewing machine still worked.

I stopped at a phone booth and called Mabel. I told her my news and asked how Angela was doing. Mabel laughed and said she had a nap and is watching cartoons but she asked me when her baby-thitter was coming back.

I breathed a sigh of relief. I've a small cleaning job to do Mabel. I'll be home by suppertime. Thanks.

Stopping at a hardware store I bought cleaning stuff and hurried back to the flat. I couldn't believe I had got this all done in one day. I didn't want to spend one second longer than I had to in my old neighborhood. Losing one child and turning up with another in less than two months would be sure to set the tongues flapping.

I liked the new flat. Everything on one floor made cleaning it easy. I scrubbed the walls and floor of the room Angela would sleep in. There was a sickly tree that had grown between the building wall and the alley to the backyard. Its top grew to above the window. It was only a little bit of green but was better than looking at the brick wall on the other side.

By four o'clock I was getting afraid the stuff wouldn't come but the bed and dresser was humped up the stairs before 5:00. The room still looked sad and empty but I still had $150 left to find a cheap rug and curtain material.

I locked up and hurried back. Angela was starting to like me. She ran over and grabbed my knees when I came in she was so happy to see me. Mabel had made some spaghetti and since I hadn't bought any groceries, we had supper with her. In return I had to lie like a trooper. She asked me questions about Angela's mother and when was she going to come for her.

She's such a little card Mabel chuckled. The things she says; what imagination for such a little thing.

Lord I thought what has she been saying? I made believe I didn't hear her and wondered out loud if I would be able to sleep tonight after what I had seen before I left. That got her mind off Angela's stories you bet!

My poor old body had been running in high gear and I wanted to flop into bed in my old house, but there was still work that wasn't going to do itself--two more days 'til I could move. I put Angela down on my bed. I hadn't even unpacked the carryall. Now I dug out Angela's bag and emptied and put the mother's purse and the fancy snowsuit back in with the clothes I wore on the trip north. Them I'd stuff in a garbage bin.

Right away I would have to get rid of it all. I came up with the idea to make a parcel wrapped in Christmas paper and leave it somewhere on a park bench.

I called Jack again and I made him swear he would move my stuff and be sober. I dragged up a bunch of boxes from the cellar. The first thing next morning I started to pack.

Chapter 15

The many complications of turning up in a neighborhood like hers with a small girl hadn't entered Jenna's head, when she followed her impulse to snatch Angela, but who would think of returning God's gift?

Jack arrived in the early afternoon, sober but barely, with his red eyes and his excuse for a beard a day longer then yesterday's. All the things Jenna wanted moved were marked so she went ahead with Angela.

Although she had never liked her house much, it was where she had lived with Julie and Billy. She had promised herself to set aside all bad memories, but when she was going through it last night, she had wished that she could burn it down with everything inside.

When she started to gather her stuff to move, she noticed how dirty and worn she had let things become. For now, she would have Jack lock the door and she would decide what to do with the rest later.

In the shed behind the house, she'd found an old stroller from when Julie was a toddler. Washing it didn't improve its scraped and missing paint much, but it was in working order.

Angela looked it over with a sour face. "Don't like that. I walk." She set her feet as if daring Jenna to shift her.

"It's a long way and too cold," Jenna said hoping a stern tone would settle the matter.

"I walk!" Angela screamed, stamping her feet.

Jenna knew this was a watershed moment. Who was going to be boss? Julie had been a timid little thing, but this one was used to getting her own way. Before she decided how to handle her, Angela stepped on a piece of ice and her feet shot into the air. Landing on her backside, she made no effort to get up, as big fat tears gathered in her eyes.

"Oh, you poor baby," Jenna whispered as she picked her up. "See, it isn't a good day to walk." When she put Angela in the stroller, she got a sad look from big blue eyes, but no resistance.

When everything was in the flat, Jack offered to stay and help her, but Jenna said, "No."

She paid him his $20. If she hadn't needed him so badly, she would never have let him know where she lived. She didn't want him coming around cadging money when he was drunk. In this new life, she might be as poor as before, but Angela was not going to be exposed to drunks; their fights and bad language.

Angela wanted her toys from the bag. The old things had been hidden away last night, but Jenna went into the closet and got out the toys. Toys were something that anyone might buy for any child, she told herself. Jenna showed her the room with the shelves in the headboard of the little bed. Angela clapped her hands and set to arranging the cat and mouse game, which gave Jenna time to think.

Getting out her checkbook, she looked over her savings; sparse to say the least. Her pension came to the bank and would be in next week. She would get the paint for the bed, and maybe a poster or two to brighten the wall. She still had a job, but to work she needed a babysitter. There was just this week to find one. A wave of fear slid like a snake through her chest and coiled in her stomach. She was not sorry for what she had done, but she had not thought of all these complications.

First things first, she thought as she remembered how perfectly she had planned and carried out Angela's abduction. She would solve this problem too. The answer was already there in her mind; she only had to wait and watch. Invigorated, she hustled off to do more unpacking while Angela was happily playing.

Over the next week, she watched the teenagers coming and going on the street. Most were either rough looking boys, or girls with short skirts and faces caked with makeup. Some of the language coming out of the mouths of both sexes would shock a lumberjack. It was nothing Jenna hadn't heard before, but she didn't want Angela picking up talk like that.

However, there was one girl she watched for when she heard the teens outside. Her name was Jo. Jenna had heard one of the girls, call her from across the street as Jo came up the walk to Jenna's building.

Jo looked about sixteen--a tall girl with long, straight dark hair and a serious look about her. She dressed better than the others; in knee length skirts or pants, and nearly always wore a bright knit hat. She belonged to the large and noisy family that rented the front flat downstairs.

One afternoon before New Year's, Jenna and Angela were coming from the store and met Jo on the front steps.

"You're the lady that moved in upstairs, and this is your little girl. Are you all settled in then?" Not waiting for an answer, Jo hunkered down beside Angela. "Hi, I'm Jo. What's your name?"

"This is my granddaughter, Angela. She's staying with me awhile," Jenna answered.

Angela was smiling at Jo. "Your hair is pretty. Can I touch it?" she asked.

"Sure you can." Jo said and picked up a jet black strand to tickle Angela's nose.

Jenna knew, from the girlish giggles, that Jo was the best she could find.

"I know we just met, but I'm looking for a babysitter. I clean offices." Jenna made a vague gesture toward the high-rise buildings to the north.

Jo's face broke into a smile. "I would love to have some babysitting. I'm in high school, and Dad and Mom hardly ever give me money."

Jenna noticed that she had good skin and didn't wear makeup. She spoke well too. Jenna wondered for caring. 'Lord knows my English isn't great,' crossed her mind. They'd made the girls speak properly in the orphanage, but it had been in French.

A few minutes later, Jo carried Angela up the stairs while Jenna followed with the stroller. Jenna showed Jo around the flat while Angela ran off to see her stuffed animals, while Jenna explained her hours.

Jo said, "This is going to be great. I have the worst time doing my homework with my bratty sisters sharing my room. Here I can have all evening once Angela is in bed. Why don't I come back tomorrow and help you get finished setting up? Maybe I could paint Angela's furniture, and if you have to go buy anything, I'll look after her."

Jenna was a bit taken aback by all this young energy. She wondered where she could get paint that fast. Then she smiled, "Great idea! I can see you're going to be a real godsend." Something tight inside her loosened. This good luck could only come from one source. Heaven had smiled on her today.

"It's a good idea for Angela to get to know you," Jenna continued. I am almost a stranger to her as well. Poor child has been passed around from pillar to post since her mother took sick. Cancer you know. There's no chance of her beating it and I seemed to be the only one able to take her. Well, we all have to play the hand we're dealt, eh?"

After Jo left, Jenna found a scrap of paper to make notes and looked around the apartment. It was pretty straightforward. You entered by a door that opened into a tiny entrance that in turn led to the central hall with the kitchen at the far end. On one side two doors opened off the hall. One was a bedroom that would be Jenna's and the other was the bathroom. On the opposite side was the small bedroom that was Angela's. Next to that an arch opened into the living room.

What Jenna liked best about the layout was that the kitchen spanned the whole width of the flat, giving plenty of room for Angela to play while Jenna cooked, or sewed with her machine on the table. Two big cupboards, one on each side of a good sized window, were still empty. Jenna thought of all the junk she had jettisoned back at the old house.

"I'll burn the lot," she said aloud--a thought generated from the bit of sunset red glowing in the window; but she knew that was nonsense. A house could always be sold.

Midmorning Saturday the ringing doorbell froze Jenna mid–step. While her mind scurried about trying not to imagine a policeman, Angela ran over and grabbed her around the knees.

"Is it the wolf?" she whispered. Jenna damned herself for ever having made up that story.

"No, it couldn't be. He doesn't know where we are. Let's go see."

Jo's eyes sparkled over a big cardboard box. "Hi, Mrs. J. and Angela! Can I come in?"

Jenna felt the blood rushing to her head. Relief washed over her and she scolded herself for not having more faith. Angela had let go of her dress and was smiling shyly at Jo.

"Of course come in. You're sure looking pleased with yourself. Call me Jenna. Come down to the kitchen, you can't swing a cat in here."

In the kitchen, Jo started to open the box and then stopped to explain how she had run down to the corner store for a bottle of milk, and noticed that the secondhand store was having a clearance sale. The woman knew her and said she could bring some things to see if Jenna would buy them.

"I wish I had money of my own. She had some good stuff but I found these," Jo said, as she ripped at the tape holding down the box flaps.

On the top were five simple little books 5¢ each and a roll of plain white paper that would be perfect to scribble on, with a whole box of broken crayons that had been thrown in free.

By now Angela was on the chair beside Jo giggling with excitement. A big piece puzzle came out and a funny little bedside lamp. A brown rabbit held up a carrot under a green leaf shade.

"How much does she want?" Jenna asked. The lamp had an upscale look, one she recognized from her years in Montreal. "It's Hummel or something like that," she said.

"Three dollars," Jo answered.

"Well that's reasonable enough. I'd say this little lamp, let's see if it works first, is easily worth that."

Jo carried it over to the counter and plugged it in. Nothing happened. Jo's face fell. "Maybe it's the bulb," she said.

Once the old bulb was replaced, the light shone down on the rabbit and his carrot. Angela clapped her hands and pulled on Jo's sweater, "Come Jo. Put him on the bed top!" When Jo didn't answer, Angela yelled, "Now! I wants it now!"

Jo stopped and dropped to her knees in front of Angela. "Do I speak to you like that?" Her voice was soft but firm.

Tears trembled on Angela's lashes. She wiggled and looked to Jenna for help. Jenna's heart ached to hug her, but Jo was doing the right thing.

Angela solved the standoff by launching herself into Jo's arms, "I's sorry," she whispered. "We do it now. Please."

What could they do but laugh?

She named the rabbit 'Nibble' and introduced him to her doll Betty, and seemed to forget the bad moment.

When Jo put on her coat, Angela asked, "You mad at me? Stay and play."

Jo gave her a hug, "Course not! I'll be back in just a little while. I have to go pay the lady for Nibble."

Jo was a little bit like having a whirlwind coming through your house, but Jenna smiled at the thought; such a lively girl and great with Angela. It was hard to not enjoy her enthusiasm.

Jenna knew she had felt more real feelings, beyond fear, in this half-hour with Jo, than in the previous three months.

Chapter 16

They started the New Year together. Jo said her father usually got drunk. He would be down at the bar, and her mother had a friend coming in. Jenna invited her to have supper with her and Angela. She made biscuits and roasted a scrawny chicken to serve with carrots and potatoes. She used the last of her flour and shortening to make a butterscotch pie, using a box of powder for the filling. Her one extravagance was a can of spray whipped cream.

After Jo gave Angela her bath, they let her play with the puzzle and crayons. After a while Jo started to draw. Jenna sat watching and could hardly believe her eyes as she saw animals and people flow from under the pencils and crayons in Jo's hands. Angela kept asking for more but Jenna could see Jo was clever, and made sure Angela tried on her own.

Jenna thought it was the best New Years she'd had for years. A flash of guilt dimmed her pleasure for a second-- but God had given her this, hadn't He? Why shouldn't she have some happiness in her life?

Three days later, school started and Jenna had to go back to work. They soon fell into a comfortable routine. Jo brought her homework and Jenna went to work. The first night, Angela cried when she left. Later, Jo said it was only for a few minutes and she was easily distracted. A half hour of play, a story or two and she went to sleep with the bunny lamp on.

Late nights when Jenna dragged herself back home, Jo would be asleep on the couch. But a soft word and she was awake and up. Jenna always waited at the door to hear her go into the apartment downstairs. Then she made herself a cup of tea and a slice off toast before she went to bed.

Although Angela seemed happy, she sometimes cried and cried for no reason the others could fathom. Jo would hold her and rock her in an old rocking chair of Jenna's, until she was exhausted, and finally slept. But Jenna knew only too well-- and make up excuses to Jo. 'She is missing her Daddy,' or any other lie that came to mind.

By now she had told so many lies, she was having trouble keeping them straight.

One afternoon, Jenna had to go shopping, and Jo came up after school. When she got back with the groceries, Angela was watching cartoons. Jo came into the kitchen to help put things away.

Laughing, she said to Jenna, "Angela's got a great imagination. She told me this story about her grandmother and the farm, and all the funny animals that live there. She even told me that Gran Lila was a witch. She said she'd heard her mummy tell her daddy that. Can you imagine-- a witch? Maybe we had better ease up on the fairy tales."

Jenna found herself speechless. She wanted to laugh, but this was dangerous territory. She was afraid to make up a new lie that Angela might blow to hell any day. Angela was learning new words at an amazing rate and was asking questions Jenna found harder and harder to answer. She faked a coughing fit so violent, that by the time Jo had fussed over her and put the kettle on, the conversation moved on to other things.

One night Jenna had cleaned all the offices but the last one, and she took her time with it. It was the drafting studio. One wall had a dozen shelves to tidy, but she set to, thinking the sooner begun the sooner finished.

She enjoyed looking at the drawings although some just were a mess of lines. The concept ones were best--soaring skyscrapers or lovely houses set in trees with maybe a lake or gardens. She thought Angela might have been born to the kind of people who could afford to live in places like that.

While she was empting the wastepaper baskets, she sometimes found barely used sheets of paper and took them home with her. Tonight, behind the garbage can, she found a large corkboard. It would be difficult to manage on the bus, but she could imagine it on Angela's wall covered with her and Jo's pictures. She thought she'd give it a try.

After midnight the bus was practically empty. The driver, whom she only knew as Jimmy, said, "What you got there Jenna? Can I give ya a hand?"

He hopped down and carried the board into the bus and saw her seated. "Why are ya still workin?" he asked from over his shoulder, as he put the bus in gear.

"Oh, it costs to eat you know," she mumbled.

He laughed and said, "Now ain't that the truth?"

The next afternoon when Jo came in, she was delighted with the corkboard. She and Angela fell into excited plans for what they would do with it.

Once it was up, Jo put on a sad face. "It's awful bare isn't it, Angela?" she said as they stood looking at it. "I know—let's do a picture of you so everyone will know it's yours. What do you think?"

"Do it. Do it." With each 'do it!' Angela's voice became louder. "Then I draw Bingo," she shouted.

Jo covered her ears to let Angela know she was getting too loud. "Come on," she said heading for the kitchen. She caught Angela around the waist and set her on a kitchen chair while she dug out a sheet of the heavy paper Jenna had brought from the studio.

"Sit still, now, or you might end up looking like Bugs Bunny." Jo laughed.

Angela gave her a very grown–up look. "Draw me and no Bugs Bunny," she said. She posed as if Jo had a camera, instead of a pencil.

Finally, after Jo had been working ten minutes or so, Angela couldn't stand the suspense any longer, and came around and climbed up onto Jo's knee. She studied the picture, and then said, "Draw Mummy."

"Ok, I'll try. What does she look like?"

"Like me."

Jo studied her baby face, the blue eyes and the wide forehead. She went to the cupboard and got another sheet of paper and set to work. She tried to make a game of it. "Will we give her a big nose?" she asked.

Angela didn't answer. Jo stopped drawing and Jenna heard the breath she drew in when Jo realized Angela didn't think that was funny. She had a face like a thundercloud, and didn't respond to Jo's smile.

"No big nose then. I'll make it the most beautiful nose in the world."

When it was finished, a strange woman, but very much like Angela, stared at them from the sheet of paper. Jo couldn't know how accurate a portrait her pencil had created.

Jenna drew a sharp breath as she looked over Jo's shoulder.

"Oh my God--it's her to a T," someone in her head shouted. Her heart was pumping so hard she had to sit down. She staggered to a chair, her knees so weak she wondered if she could ever get up again, but he girls hadn't noticed anything. After a few deep breaths, she relaxed. She must not have yelled out loud as she thought she had.

Angela studied the drawing with a serious face. Then with a scream, she grabbed the sheet of paper and tore it into bits. Neither of the women knew what to say or do, when Angela threw herself onto the floor, pounding it with her fists, screaming and kicking at the chair legs and Jenna's, when she tried to pick her up.

"Maybe you should leave her," Jo suggested. "I'll sit here beside her and wait."

When Angela wore out her anger, and only hiccups and sobs were left, she allowed Jenna to carry her to the rocking chair. A few minutes of rocking and she drifted off to sleep.

Later Jo said, "I'm sorry. I never thought--I shouldn't have . . ."

"Jo, don't. It wasn't your fault. You're so good for her. I don't know what I would do without your help. Let's take her down to the lake tomorrow. It's cold, but we'll pile on enough clothes to sink a ship."

Jo giggled and agreed. Jenna's colourful language always made her laugh.

Well bundled up, all three made their way through the back alley and over the old unused railway track, through the hole in the fence, and down to the water.

A bitter wind blew across the open water, over and around the huge blocks of ice pushed up onto the shore. The gulls screamed and swooped overhead. It was cold enough to take your breath away. Waves crashed onto the sand, between the jumbled piles of ice, making Angela scream in excitement. She chased gulls, picked bits of driftwood, and seemed totally immune to the cold.

"Come on Jo, I am half frozen. I can't run around like you and Angela," Jenna called, as Jo chased Angela around a big block of ice for the tenth time.

As they walked along the alley on the way back, a small black cat, with white feet and a white tip on its tail, peeked out from a pile of discarded boards. Angela squatted and called, "Kitty, Kitty."

When the kitten ran to her, Jenna warned, "No. No. Don't touch it. It might scratch you. She was too late. Angela already had the kitten clutched to her chest, nose to nose.

"Can I keep it, Aunty Jenna?" Angela begged. "Aunty Jenna. Please!"

Jenna hadn't forgotten that at their first meeting she'd told Jo that Angela was her grandchild.

"You must wonder, Jo, why she calls me Aunty instead of Grammy," Jenna said. "I don't know either. I don't bother to correct her. I guess she hears people calling me Jenna and wants to use that name. What you think about the kitten?"

Jo didn't answer for a moment. "Surely such a little cat wouldn't eat much." She hunkered down so her face was level with Angela's. "Put him down. We'll let him decide whether he would rather stay here or come home with us. I know that you want him, but it would be bad to take him if he didn't want to come with us." She began gently untangling the tiny sharp claws from Angela's snowsuit.

Angela set the kitten down with a sound close to a sob. But instead of running away, the kitten wound itself around her legs. When they walked away, it followed them, its tail held high. Angela was wildly excited, running backwards, in and out between Jo and Jenna, checking every second on the kitten and yelling, "He's coming! See, he likes me!"

"What will we call him?" Jo asked later, as they stood watching the kitten lap up milk. "It will have to be something special, won't it Angie?"

They tried several names but none of them seemed to fit. Angela ran to her room and brought back her stuffed kitten Beau. The toy's black-and-white markings bore an uncanny resemblance to the living cat. As she waved the toy, she said, "He looks like my, Beau. His name is Beau!" So 'Beau' he became.

Beau marked a turning point for Angela; gone were the tantrums and the screaming fits that seemed to come from nowhere. He sat on the toilet seat and washed his face, while Angela had her bath. He slept in a little basket beside her bed, and followed her everywhere.

Chapter 17

Sarah

I would prefer to recount my story of the aftermath of the accident with crisp incisive word pictures, as if I were in a court of law. Unfortunately, my first memories after the bus crash lie in my brain like pieces of glass from a shattered window.

Certainly, there was a moment of blurred vision and confusion. 'My shoulder,' I thought, 'there's someone weighing it down' and when I raised the other arm to push the unwelcome intruder aside, that arm seemed heavy and clumsy.

I thought, if I rub my eyes, I'll see. That didn't help. I still could only see a blank white sheet above me. I ran my free hand over my face and felt some kind of a cloth covering my head. I couldn't feel any hair. That might have freaked me out, but the idea that I was bald under the cloth was too bizarre to follow up on. I lay, trying to assess my body, part by part. It hurt just about everywhere. Fighting panic, I tried bending my knees. Thank God, they seemed all right, but what I planned to do with that piece of information never had a chance to flower.

I heard quick footsteps, and rolled my head the slightest bit to the left. A petite dark haired nurse shot through the door, already giving orders. "Lie still. Don't try to get up--you'll pull your needles."

Well, pulling my needles didn't sound very pleasant, but at least now I knew where I was--nurse, needles-- hospital. She did a bit of fiddling around with the equipment and gave me another order.

"Don't move. I'll only be a second." She dashed out of the room.

My heart had stopped thumping in my chest now, but my head took it up. I wanted to close my eyes but curiosity won over pain. I didn't think the nurse's last order included eyes. That looked like an infant unit in the corner, but there was nothing in it that I could see. I became aware of the intercom paging Dr. James.

'Isn't that funny,' I thought. Something about the name lay on the edge of my memory. At least I knew I was in a hospital, as I drifted back to the comforting dark, where there were no decisions to make, or orders to obey.

When next I awoke-- first thing I felt was the pain in my shoulder and the grandmother of all headaches. Opening my eyes shot red- hot needles deep into my brain. While I tried to make myself believe I could survive another go at looking, I felt someone holding my hand. It was a big warm hand, and the weirdest feeling slid up my back and into my chest. I didn't want to open my eyes; I squeezed them tight, hoping he would go away.

"Come on Sarah, open your eyes. You can't imagine; I've been crazy with worry."

That voice? Dave. In a flash, memory came flooding back–the pre-Christmas time at Don and Lila's farm, and the trip up to visit my friend. Oh God-- the sight of the logs crashing through the windshield. My urge to escape was pushed aside by pure terror.

"Where's the baby?" I screamed, fumbling my one good hand over my flattened belly. "Did I lose the baby?" I tried to get up to do something-- anything-- but Dave grabbed me and forced me back onto the bed.

"Stop! Stop it! The baby's fine. You'll hurt yourself. They have her in the nursery, for her bottle. The nurse is just outside; she will bring her. Here, promise you'll be quite? Yes? I'll help you sit up."

The same nurse, Betty Hein, who had scuttled away to page Dave, came in carrying a tightly wrapped infant and passed it to Dave. He loosened the blankets, and laid my baby in my arms. 'So beautiful,' I thought; translucent skin, long eyelashes and a rosebud mouth.

"So this is our little boy?" I asked. "Angela will love him."

At a strangled sound, half sob, half curse, I looked up. Dave leaped to his feet, and then dropped back into the chair beside the bed. Tears seeped out through his fingers clasped across his face. The nurse swooped over and took the baby to the unit in the corner and quietly left; easing the door shut on her way.

I couldn't think of anything to say. What could you say to man with a broken heart, because with a breath stopping premonition, I knew there was something terribly wrong. My body went cold with fear.

I had been married to Dave for five years, and I had never once seen him cry. His best friend had been shot in a hunting accident near our home, and he had been the one called to help carry him out; but for all his skill, he could not save his friend's life. He had not shed a tear. At that time I thought that the tragedy that scrolled through his working life had dried his tears for always.

What had I said? Something about Angela loving the baby was all I could remember. I knew I looked awful but there was no doubt that I would recover-- was there?

"Dave, Dave! What is it? Isn't the baby all right? Please tell me if he isn't." I kept myself from screaming by clamping my mouth shut. The pounding in my head intensified, as if it would burst any minute.

For a long moment, he didn't move but then he straightened and wiped his face on his sweater sleeve. "The baby wasn't a boy after all, and she's perfectly fine, but that isn't what this is about."

"The baby's a girl? Oh. If it isn't about her, what in God's name is it about?

Girl or boy, I didn't care--I was close to loosing it and screeching. I could see him struggling to find the right words, and if I had been physically able, I would have struck him for keeping me in suspense. Every second that passed my panic grew.

When he began to talk, it was about our trip to see his parents, and my trip to where my friend lives, east of Toronto. If it were something about one of the kids, he'd tell me right away.

My pounding pulse calmed, but the image of those tears pouring down his cheeks wouldn't leave me. The strangeness in his manner warned me--he was leading up to something.

"Tell me," I whispered. "Is it Dad? Has he had a heart attack?"

"No, Mary and Ralph are fine. In fact they will be here tomorrow. They are both back home now and waiting for me to call them. You know you've been unconscious for almost two weeks."

No, I hadn't known, but I couldn't explore that shocking information just yet.

Dave had gotten up to pace around the room, but now he pulled the chair closer to the bed, sat, and reached for my hand. With his face only inches from mine, I wished he would kiss me, and we could go back to the days when we only needed each other. I looked at his haggard face and knew he was suffering, but with his next words, my world shattered.

"It's Angela," he said. She's been missing ever since the accident. She wasn't with you when they brought you in. Every police force in the province is searching but they haven't found her yet." His head dropped to his chest as if he couldn't bear to look at me.

My mouth opened and closed but I was unable to say a word. A bright light flared before my eyes--and pain-- as if my head would burst. I heard a woman screaming, and I had to run– to go–but I was tied in a nightmare. "It's my fault," a voice screamed through the white light. "Lila warned me but I wouldn't listen."

I could feel Dave's hands on my arms, trying to hold me, but I fought to escape that awful voice. I heard the crash of broken glass.

Through his ragged breathing, Dave kept saying, "We'll find her. We'll find her!"

I felt a needle prick and fell into darkness.

Chapter 18

Nurse Betty was standing outside the door when Sarah went into this hysteric episode. She had been at a loss as to what she should do. Her every instinct urged her to push the door open and go in, but this was the doctor's wife, not a regular patient, and she didn't know whether he would want her to interfere.

Just when Betty made up her mind to act, she saw Dr. Carl Wesson hurrying down the hall. He was the doctor that Dave had caring for Sarah.

He bent his head outside the door, listening. "Told her, did he? Get one cc of the sedative we gave her before," he threw over his shoulder as he pushed open the door and entered the room.

Betty hurried to the storage room and got the correct dosage. Back again, she took in the scene-- Dave still struggled with Sarah. Equipment was knocked over and the bed covers half dragged to the floor.

Then with Carl's help, Dave got Sarah straight onto the bed. It took all their strength to hold her. Her heart rending screams could be heard all over that floor.

Carl motioned Betty forward, and she tried getting the needle in without sticking Sarah in the wrong place, or one of the two men trying to hold her.

"For God's sake, come on," Dave said.

Betty found a safe spot and plunged the needle in.

Sarah stopped screaming and thrashing around as the medication kicked in. Although she appeared conscious, she wouldn't respond to questions or look at them. Her rapid breathing and ashen face told them how much the struggle had exhausted her.

"We'll have to keep her sedated." Carl told Dave after he led him to one side of the room. "That shoulder is just starting to knit. We don't want her to have another episode like that. She'll sleep awhile now. I suggest you get some rest yourself. I'll order a nurse to sit with her. You had better have Dr. Willis on standby; she is going to need major counseling."

If Dave hadn't known already, the expression on Carl's face spoke louder than words about the state of Sarah's mind. "Yes, I guess that's best. I knew it was going to be bad, but to tell the truth, this scares the hell out of me."

Dave spoke slowly, as if in shock. His body was still shaking from the struggle with Sarah, and a long scratch from under his ear to his collarbone was beading with blood.

"Dave, you go rest, and not in this chair where you will be startled awake every time she moves. Go to the doctor's locker room at the end of the hall. I don't think anyone is using the sleep room," Carl said, clapping him on the shoulder with a friendly hand. "I'll look after things here. You look like you've done a couple of rounds with a wild cat."

"I guess you're right," Dave was forced to concede. He left Carl to make the arrangements for a night watch. He dragged himself into the shower and fell into a bed; the Doctor's sleep room was just down the hall from Sarah's room.

Two hours later his eyes flew open, and a flood of worries arrived seconds later. His thoughts raced from one problem to the next. He had known that Sarah would take it hard, but this, and the baby! The nurses fed and changed her, but she needed more than that. She needed love and handling-- more than he had time to give. He had been holding her at night while he sat beside Sarah, but he'd had to stop doing it for fear he would fall asleep and drop her. He couldn't seem to make up his mind on a course of action better than 'wait and see.'

Giving up hope of any more sleep, he started down to the cafeteria for coffee. As he walked along the corridors, a buzz of gossip trailed behind him. He had a moment of frightening hallucination-- as if aliens were sucking the life from his body, getting stronger as he became weaker; feeding on his pain.

The girl at the information desk called him over. "Message," she said, passing him a slip of paper. He thanked her, and quickly turned away from her curious stare to unfold the note.

Dave pulled out his cell phone and dialed the number on the paper. He ignored the big red X over a picture of a cell phone painted on a wall two feet from his nose. He knew who would answer. It was his home number. Ralph and Mary must have arrived at his house by now.

His stomach did another version of gut wrenching. Ralph had his own ideas and, as like as not, he would try to grab the reins of this situation and take over. Dave could only imagine the frustration he must feel at the lack of any trace of Angela.

The second he picked up the phone, Ralph began to talk. "Mary and I just got here. What can we do to help? Have you any news of Angela? How's Sarah?"

"No, nothing definite on Angela but some good news-- Sarah came out of her coma today." Dave started to explain but Ralph didn't wait to hear the end of the sentence before he said, "That's great!"

Dave heard the phone drop on the table, and heard Ralph shout, "Great news, Mary! Sarah's out of the coma!" Then, there was Mary's excited voice in the background. Already he had half lost Ralph. Dave began to sweat. 'This is just going great!' he thought. 'I think they have forgotten I am still on the line.' Finally, after several futile 'hellos,' Ralph came back on with a flood of questions.

"Please, Ralph, I can't do this over the phone. I'm in the hospital at Reception. Why don't you come in and stay in town? The Northland, where I'm staying to be close to Sarah; it is good and right near the hospital."

"We'll come right away," Ralph answered.

"Call me when you're settled in the hotel," Dave said.

Although having Sarah's parents to contend with was a distraction to him, he knew they would help with her grief, and the terrible guilt; he could only imagine, because he felt it too. Sarah would have never insisted on going off on her own if he hadn't supported the idea.

Dave remembered he hadn't had his coffee yet. He trotted down the stairs to the cafeteria and forced himself sit and have a muffin, although it and the coffee tasted like nothing any sane person would eat or drink. He wanted to check on Sarah again, before he met Ralph and Mary at the hotel. They would be half an hour or so getting there. He headed up, taking the elevator this time.

Sarah's vitals were good, according to the readings on the monitors. 'Except for the rise and fall of her chest, she might be taken for a corpse.' Dave thought. 'But she's alive,' he whispered, as a wave of love pushed aside his fear.

When Dave walked into the hotel lobby, he was pleased again at the pleasant atmosphere the owners had created with native rocks, shrubs and falling water which echoed the rocky landscape of the park across the street.

He found the Ashley's in one of the alcoves in the coffee shop; hidden by a bank of chrysanthemums and a dwarf birch. It gave a little privacy from the stream of people coming and going.

Before the Ashley's' saw him, he paused a moment to watch them. How old they looked! He had never thought of them as more than middle-aged, but today they looked old. He could have sworn Mary's hair was grayer than the last time he had seen her, and Ralph had more stoop in his long back. Dave hated to put more stress on them after the year they'd had.

He slid into the seat opposite Mary. He got a quick squeeze from Mary's hand, and a handshake from Ralph that conveyed more than just words.

Dave was quite aware of the reservations the Ashley's had had about his marrying Sarah, but over the years of their marriage he'd become fond of them.

"Tell us what is going on with Sarah," Ralph spoke first, which was usually the case whenever a question needed an answer.

"We want to see her right away," Mary spoke up. Tears brimmed in her eyes.

Dave tried to explain what had happened as calmly as he could. They listened in disbelief, as he recounted Sarah's behavior when he told her about Angela's disappearance. Seeing the shock on their faces, he realized that he'd never actually told them everything. Now he tried to fill in the holes; the work the police was doing, the few witness reports, and he tried his best to put an optimistic a spin on the whole situation.

Ralph began a landslide of questions, but Mary laid her hand on his wrist to stop him. She wasn't a person to place blame, and didn't want to hear the whole thing rehashed again with all the 'maybe's and might-have-been's.'

Ralph cleared his throat, as he did when he planned to be confrontational. He spoke to Dave civilly, but the red tide that washed up his face from under his collar, gave away his agitation. "What's the next step? I want to see Sarah right now."

Dave hesitated and then said, "I think it's a good idea if you could be there when she wakes up after this drug induced sleep. It will be a while yet. Maybe seeing you both will prevent another hysterical episode, and we could encourage her to talk about Angela's disappearance, and hear what she remembers. She might have information that would help in the search."

"Whoever took Angela had to have been on the bus. Sarah may have spoken, or had contact, with that person sometime during an earlier part of the trip." Dave said.

He could see their frustration and knew they wanted to go back over the whole thing; how foolish it had been for Sarah and Dave setting out to see Don and Lila in mid-winter, and on from there.

Dave wasn't ready to walk that path now with Sarah's very sanity at stake. He got to his feet leaving his cooling cup of coffee on the table. "I have to get back, and you'll want to get settled in. I don't expect her to wake tonight, but tomorrow morning she'll be woken as part of hospital routine. You can see her then." he said,

Mary clung to his hand a moment before she let him go. Ralph looked dissatisfied, and resentful that they weren't allowed to rush to Sarah's beside, but agreed to check in and meet at the hospital at 7:00 A.M. the next morning.

Chapter 19

Late that evening, Dave stood at Sara's bedside, hoping that in the morning she would wake up naturally. He thought she had withstood the transfer up from Kingston, two weeks ago, really well. He'd been so happy when she came out of her coma. He should never have told her about Angela so soon. 'But she might have injured herself if I hadn't been here when she found out,' he reasoned. Her sleep this morning seemed normal sleep--she'd wake up when the hospital started up for the day.

He had gotten permission to get her on the maternity floor so she could be in the same room as the baby. He didn't know how long the hospital would allow it.

'What about the baby? God, I still haven't thought of a name! Dave had a terrible moment, when he felt as if his well-controlled world was slipping from his hands

Before Sarah was moved to the new floor, Dave sat in the visitor's chair beside her bed. He was too restless for sleep. For a long time he held the baby as she slept on his shoulder,

The next morning, well before the hospital started its morning routine, Dave was showered, shaved and waiting for the Ashley's to come, or Sarah to wake-up.

Before 7:00, they came to the door. Dave held them back a moment, explaining, "Sarah's not awake yet. Come in and speak as normally as you can. She'll be disoriented from the drugs we gave her and need time to sort things out. The baby is in the baby unit. We feel it's important to keep her close to her mother."

Mary started toward Sarah, but seeing her still asleep, she turned to the baby. The tiny girl stirred and yawned. Mary whispered to her as she touched her tiny hand.

"You can hold her," Dave said.

But before Mary got a chance to pick her up, the small crinkled face turned red, and a loud cry brought the nurse's quick footsteps, coming to take her for a diaper change.

"Mom," Sarah whispered, bringing Mary back to her side. She groped for her mother's hand. "Where's Dad?"

At first she seemed half awake, but she managed a weak smile for Ralph as he stumbled up. He'd held back, waiting for Mary to go to Sarah first. He stood silent, his face pale at seeing her bruised face and shaven head. Mary tried to make normal conversation, but Sarah was having trouble focusing on what she was saying.

Dave shifted uneasily from one foot to the other. Sarah was barely listening; her gaze scanned the room, but avoided eye contact with him.

Shirley, the nurse on morning duty, came back with the baby and a bottle of milk, both of which she handed to Dave where he was standing near the door. Bouncing the baby gently in his arms, he slid the nipple between her lips, and turned toward the bed.

Sarah's outburst was so sudden they all staggered back, stunned. The screams tearing from her throat, and her leap from the bed froze even Dave, hardened as he was to medical emergencies. He held baby Grace close to his chest.

Terrified, Mary and Ralph reeled toward each other. The overturned nightstand, and the IV she had ripped from her arm stopped her for a second. Then her eyes rolled back and she crumpled to the floor.

Seconds later the room was full of staff. Nurse Shirley took the baby from Dave, and he gently pushed Mary and Ralph out of the room, and lead them to the lounge. He didn't stop to comfort them but raced back.

Two orderlies had lifted Sarah back into the bed. Thinking back, trying to make some sense of Sarah's behavior, Dave realized that this was a job for Dr. Willis.

'Dr. Willis to room 216 was repeated four times; rather than the usual three. It lent urgency to the call that Dave welcomed, but dreaded too. He felt the call like a sentence of banishment. With Dr. Willis on his way down from is office on the Psychiatric ward-- Sarah's care would now be truly out of Dave's hands.

Remembering Ralph and Mary, he hurried back to the lounge to tell them to wait. He explained about Dr. Willis.

"Sarah's seeing a psychiatrist? Like hell! It was just the shock of seeing all of us!" Ralph was close to shouting.

Mary went to him and took his hand, "Shush, Dear. Dave knows best. We just have to make the best of it."

Dr. Willis, stout and middle-aged with a neatly trimmed beard and warm brown eyes, slid into the room. He moved so quietly in his rubber soled shoes that Dave hadn't heard him coming.

In Austria, Willis' homeland, he had studied the works of Freud and Jung; then, after years in London, he tired of big cities. He could have been a banker, except for his warm brown eyes, but an expression in them made you feel that he had no illusions about this world of mental illness.

His three piece suit was slightly rumpled, but his deep and lightly accented voice was as reassuring as a warm blanket.

Dave knew him well-- as Willis was the only psychiatrist on the hospital staff. He stepped forward to shake his hand and give him a quick update of Sarah's physical condition; the accident, her injuries and now the latest episode.

Dave knew he must step away as he was too emotional about Sarah to trust his own judgment. He offered to leave if she would allow the doctor to talk to her.

"No, son, you can stay unless your presence bothers her. Let's wait and see," he said.

As Dr. Willis stood by the bedside, looking at Sarah, he mused aloud. "Poor girl, it's enough to turn anyone's mind. On top of the pain from the accident, the missing child, for which she blames herself, and the hormonal changes that birth brings on. We have our work cut out for us."

He asked some technical questions and how much medication she'd received. He pinched her arm gently and moving to the bottom of the bed lifted the blankets from her feet, and pricked one with a little silver pin he'd removed from his breast pocket. There was no response, not so much as a flicker of an eyelid, or a catch in her breath.

"This deep sleep doesn't appear normal to me, or consistent with the amount of medication you report. And you say she was perfectly alert when she awoke earlier, before today's episode?" Pinching his lip, he picked up her chart. However, the information had been taken before she had lost consciousness the second time. He studied the monitors for new blood pressure readings. He listened to her lungs and heart.

"What do you think, Dr. Willis? Dave couldn't help himself. He knew if he'd been the usual kind of husband, he would not have been privileged to remain in the room while his wife was examined.

"Her vitals are good. This may be an emotional response-- nature's way of blocking out the guilt she must be suffering," Dr. Willis said-- still watching Sarah's motionless body.

"But no one blames her. It was an accident."

"She blames herself. I've seen this more the once in new mothers whose babies have abnormalities or die. In their emotional state, they believe it's punishment for something they did. It's an escape, but I believe she will recover with time and care."

"But why did she reject the new baby? She seemed to love her the first time she held her. She looked so happy." Dave hung onto his professional façade; all that kept him from bawling on Dr. Willis's shoulder.

"Was that before you told her the child, Angela, was missing?" Dr. Willis asked.

"Yes. Yes, it was. Could fear of losing this baby too, have sent her into a sort of hiding?" Dave was trying to be logical, but his mind kept slipping off into the refrain-- 'What am I going to do? Why did I ever let her take that bus trip?'

"Before we work from this angle, I would like to have X-rays of her injuries to make sure there wasn't further damage from her fall out of bed. Also, I would like to move her up to the psychiatric floor where I can keep an eye on her."

Dave could feel the blood draining from his head as he staggered a step backward. He suddenly felt weak, afraid he was going to pass out. He'd expected this, but never in his life had he felt so helpless.

Dr. Willis touched him on the shoulder. "Come away now. You'll be able to see her as soon as she's settled upstairs."

Outside the door he remembered that he still had to break the news to Mary and Ralph-- news that Sarah wasn't likely to wake up soon, and would be separated from Grace.

Chapter 20

Lila

Having a stroke is no picnic in the park, but I feel better each day. Don is trying so hard, but he's as clumsy as a musk ox among the teacups, and is terrified of sickness. It's beyond me how a grown man, and a smart one at that, can be so useless. I chased him out so I could get some rest from his fussing, but then had to call him back to find out who was on the phone.

As he stood in the doorway, I could tell it was bad news and he was trying to avoid telling me. "Please don't keep things from me, Don. You know I've always faced up to things. I would rather know the truth than lie here worrying." He never could hold back when I spoke to him in that tone of voice.

"Sarah's on the psychiatric floor and Mary and Ralph have taken the baby home with them to care for her," he said, all in one breath. I hadn't fully taken that in when he said, "They asked that you name her. Her hair is dark, like our family."

I can't tell you my feelings at this bit of news: joy, fear for such a little one without her mother-- gratitude to the

Ashley's for their consideration, and to tell the truth, a bit of jealously that I couldn't be the one to look after her.

Mary had been sick last year, and must remember the frustration of lying about useless, when a crisis in your family occurs. But I can take part, and names are important. A good name must be grown into, and that builds character.

In a second, a name came to me. I said to Don, "Grace. We will call her Grace, and her name will remind us to never lose hope of finding Angela; if not for the grace of God, we might have lost all three."

Don smiled a real smile for the first time since I had my stroke. These moments of pleasure only lasted until we remembered that Angela was still missing.

"Yes, perfect, and an old family name from the time when my family were Quakers. May she live up to it in all ways," he said.

A secret private fear of mine had lately added itself to the others. I might never be well enough to take care of my horses again. Don had shipped them to friends of ours who run a rescue centre for old horses. I know they'll find them a good home, if I can't have them back, but I don't see how I can live without them.

Of course, I don't tell Don. He would think it foolish-- after all they are only old useless animals to him. I sometimes feel in that category myself. But I loved how they would come running at my call, pushing forward nosing my pockets for treats. I did get Don to promise that he would keep the two miniature horses until we know for sure how well I recover from this.

The mother, Bingo stands about 39 cm at the shoulder and has a lovely disposition. I so treasure the memories of Angela riding her.

When they were here for Christmas, there had been a night starting with rain and finishing with a cover of snow which bonded to the wet surface, making it great for walking. In the late afternoon of the next day, Dave and I put Angela on Bingo. One of us on each side of her, we walked up the lane behind the house, talking a bit but mostly at peace. The setting sun glazed the snow with pink frosting, and, in that moment, every part of my life seemed perfect.

I have trouble talking, a relief to Don, I'm sure, although I knew he would be the last to admit it. We both avoided speculation about Angela, especially Don. He thought it upset me too much; as if not talking about it took the fear way.

Our daughter, Anna, and her husband, Joel, snatched a few days from their busy lives to come see us. I guess Anna had forgotten how old I am. Her shock at seeing me for the first time since my stroke would've been funny in other circumstances. She hesitated as if I was so fragile I'd break; before she choked out, "Mom," and hugged me.

I quickly steered the talk to her life. Usually it was always about her career, but this time she brought a lovely surprise. She was expecting a baby and she seemed unfazed at the changes it will bring to her life, and their marriage.

When they left, we soon fell back to our old routine, and I began to wonder when we would see Grace. Within the week, Dave called and said they would be bringing her to visit us soon. Mary and Ralph were going to visit their friend Roy, who lives close to here, while Dave and Grace stay with us.

For the first time since her last episode, he was leaving Sarah for more than a few hours-- other than when he was at work, or took time to snatch a few hours of sleep. It seemed Dr. Willis had no idea, if or when, Sarah was likely to come out of her deep coma.

That night I was so frustrated, feeling so useless, that Don read me a stiff lecture about positive attitude, while he puttered around nearly patting me like an old dog.

As he left the room, I retaliated with, "And supper? What gourmet delight shall we have tonight?"

I know he did the best he could. It's just that sometimes even quarreling is preferable to worrying. A terrible thought crossed my mind-- that even knowing the worst-- would be better than knowing nothing. 'But, I will NOT think that way,' I told myself, during a stiff lecture about positive thinking.

After I wrote the above, I felt so low that I only wanted to sleep. In a dream, I gave myself a good talking to; that seems weird, but I could see myself lying on the bed, and the ghost of myself, really irate, face flame- red, finger waving, saying, 'Buck up and have a little faith. Angela is alive and will come back to us.'

I was not going to let this stroke kill me or, worse still, become an invalid. I called Mary and she seemed really happy to hear from me. She talked a lot about Grace and the things Ralph was pursuing in the search for Angela. She said the latest RCMP belief was that Angela had been taken back to Toronto.

With tears in her voice, she told me that Dave was the rock on which they leaned, and it was a blessing that he was spending so much time talking to Sarah, trying to pull her back.

Chapter 21

"My word Ralph, we'll have to buy everything again. Oh, why did I give away all Angela's baby furniture?" Mary was learning all over again that caring for a newborn full time, was a far cry from keeping a baby the odd day or two. And what about the trips they had waited years to take? But still, the baby was so sweet, and of course she wanted to keep her, but in spite of everything against it, a small stone of resentment had to be swallowed occasionally.

Ralph was really pleased, but for all his promises of being able to help, she was the one to get up in the night, and to do the laundry. She was thankful that Grace was a good little thing. She seldom cried and seemed content on the formula.

Her new hair was going to be midnight black, and she looked far more like the James family than Angela had as a baby. Except her eyes; they were Ralph's, the deepest of brown.

The hardest part for Mary was that every sight of Grace reminded her of Angela. It nearly drove her crazy to think that Angela was likely right here in this city--maybe somewhere she passed by every day.

Trips to the grocery store weren't merely chores that had to be done now. Besides the groceries, Mary looked at every child, as if expecting to stumble over Angela. Every blonde girl-child made her heart falter for a second, while each face was never the one she wanted to see.

Her nights were exhausting with terrible nightmares; jumbled images in the morning, when she tried to remember them. Sometimes Grace cried in the night. Mary always came upright with a start-- Angela's name on her lips.

Ralph had hired a private detective, but so far he'd come up with nothing the police didn't already know. The woman that Wally had seen carrying a child off the bus seemed to have disappeared into thin air. The list of passengers arriving in Kingston hadn't contained anyone answering Wally's description.

The police had turned up an account of an older woman and a child in a motel the night of the accident, but they came to the conclusion that it was exactly what the desk clerk reported; a grandmother with her son's child, in town for Christmas shopping.

Chapter 22

Jenna

Thank the good Lord that I found Jo. She's one of those kids you find in a slum once in a while. Every drunken street bum or tired beaten wife makes them more set to work their hardest and get away.

She reminds me of myself that last year in the orphanage. The more the nuns preached meekness at me the more I set myself to do what I wanted. But Jo has more smarts than I had. She works hard at her school work and always watches to better herself. No pimp is going to fool her with stories of easy money. She told me one day that she would never marry any man who drank.

She stayed with us at the time of this bit I want to tell about happened. Jo was real good with Angela and she said she loved her evenings here where it was quiet. She still stayed in to help her mother most often after her father had been on one of his sprees.

The little sisters thought they were going to have free run up here but Jo put a stop to that the first time they came to the door. She said they'd be underfoot every five minutes if we let them in once.

She helps me. Imagine me being taught cooking lessons by a teenager—to make better food for Angela that don't cost more.

That course at school was what set her off. She sat in bookstores reading cookbooks she couldn't afford to buy memorizing the recipes. She and Angela mucked about every Saturday making something new. Some days the girly giggles that come from the kitchen I never knew what would turn up for supper.

The old sewing machine got more work than it had for years. I made over clothes for Jo that she got at secondhand stores and some for Angela too. I never knew what Jo was going to turn up with. She was like a crow with a good eye for stuff. In return for sewing for her she didn't take any pay for babysitting.

I'll tell you what happened to change things.

I had a nasty turn one day. Jo and Angela were down at the beach. It was the first time they ever come in at that time of day and I wasn't making supper. Jo was surprised to find me lying on the couch in the living room.

Are you sick Jo asked when she saw me laying in the half dark.

I opened my mouth to say no but then I knew this wasn't something new—just worse. I'd been feeling tired and laid down to rest but when I woke up I felt like my head was spinning. A nagging pain ate deep in my gut. It wasn't the first time I felt it but then it hadn't been bad enough to worry about.

I'm not feeling very good I answer her. I don't think I'll go to work tonight. We can warm up that stew I made yesterday for supper.

Do you want me to stay? Mom won't care. It's payday. Dad will be drunk as a skunk. I don't want to be there anyway.

Although she almost never said anything but I knew she was afraid of her father. We were standing in the hall one day in front of the door to their apartment when he came in. He was sober just off his shift at the garbage sorting depot. He totally ignored me but I saw him put his hand on Jo's back. It looked like something a kind father might do but I saw her stiffen and her quick look at me to see if I noticed.

I often wonder why God allows men like that to live and takes little souls like my Julie.

Jo was looking at me and I could read the word PLEASE in her eyes. Angela solved the problem by asking for Jo to stay. Naturally I said yes. Most nights I liked giving Angela her bath and reading her bedtime story but tonight I was not sure I could.

You ask your mother and if she doesn't need you I'd be glad for your help I said.

You don't have to pay me Jo threw over her shoulder as she went through the door. I went on the landing to wait for her answer.

Her father had just come in and crowded in after her. I'd hoped he wasn't home because mostly on payday he went to the bar and wouldn't stagger in for hours. I went back into my place to wait for Jo to let me know if she was coming.

As soon as I heard the commotion from downstairs I took Angela down to the kitchen put her in the high chair with a glass of milk and a cookie and told her to stay there. I didn't want her to hear the fight but I was afraid for Jo.

I heard yelling and an almighty crash, and after a minute or two the slam of the door downstairs. I barely made it back to the kitchen when Jo burst in a bunch of clothes in her arms and her face running with tears.

That's it Jo said as she slumped onto a kitchen chair. The things she'd been carrying slid to the floor. He threw me out. I told Mom that if she didn't stop him I was going to run away. He's really a coward but she won't stand up to him. I'd go to the principle of the school and tell him but then he would bring in Child Services and they would take all us kids. If Mom lost her kids she would kill herself. Can I stay here until I can talk to her again?

She looked so miserable I wanted to say yes right away but then it wouldn't be easy with her and him living in the same building. I had Angela to think about and I didn't know how crazy he might be. When I asked her if he would try to break in, she said no that he would pass out.

When he's sober he is real afraid of the police. They know him from before. Jo was madder than scared now.

I asked her how old Gillian was. Jo and her sister were like chalk and cheese. She was only thirteen but she was well on her way to the street.

Does Gillian help your mother? I asked. What about your brother? Even more useless I told her. We'll have to sort this out later but you can stay for now. All this excitement had me nearly on my knees so I left Jo to put Angela to bed and went to mine. Even after Angela's bath and they were both asleep I couldn't settle.

I had to work. There was no way I could apply for welfare and have them snooping around. But I would have to feel a lot better than this to climb all those stairs and push that vacuum. I'd had these turns before. With the weekend to rest I should be good for Monday night I told myself.

But still a knot of fear was stuck somewhere in my chest. What if I do get really sick? That scared me so much I turned the other way and said to myself -- maybe it's just a bug.

I'd heard that lot downstairs hacking and coughing the last two weeks but Jo seemed healthy enough. Then in spite of myself my mind circled back. I had my bits of savings. It was too bad that truck of Billy's hadn't been insured. He'd forgotten to renew it just days before the accident—just like Billy.

I got pregnant when I lived with one of those men in Montreal—JD. I told him on the way to a party for one of his buddies. He was wicked mad. I should have remembered what a jerk he was. Late that evening I went to the bathroom and was reaching for the door knob to come out when I heard voices in the hall. A friend was talking to JD—his great pal and a pig on two legs if I ever saw one.

Aren't you tired of that whore yet he asked JD.

My man laughed. Foolish bitch thinks I'm going to marry her he answered. She's got a baby in her belly—claims its mine.

I think the rotten bastard had been getting a kick out of stringing me along. As soon as they moved away I got my coat and left. I went to JD's apartment where I had been living. I knew where he kept his cashbox. He had a stash of rings and things but only a few hundred dollars. After I cleaned it out I went through the house to see if there was anything else worth stealing. I decided not to—not out of any honest reason but because things are too easy to trace.

I didn't take any of my stuff but went out the back door. I found a good sized rock in the garden and smashed the pane of glass to look as if someone got in. I walked a long ways before I took a cab to the mall near the bus station.

When I boarded that bus no one would've seen a party girl. I'd bought a cheap outfit and stuffed the hair I'd spent so much money on under a baseball cap and slouched in flats instead of high heels.

I knew it had only been the clothes and makeup that had made me almost pretty.

Chapter 23

Sarah

I awoke alone in a landscape where everything was white with gray in the shadows.

At a whisper of sound I closed my eyes, thinking I could dive back into the darkness if it was something terrible. Hands fussed about the bed. Glass clicked on glass, and when I heard the rattle of the IV stand being moved, I knew where I was.

Twice more in the next hour someone entered. One was male, his voice as warm as summer itself. "I'm here when you're ready," I heard; spoken softly, before a little air disturbance told me he was leaving.

I wasn't ready yet, but I felt abandoned. I almost called out, but then I heard another body settle itself into the chair beside my bed. I recognized the smell of soap--probably a nurse I thought. I sneaked a sideways glance to confirm, and was childishly pleased that I was right.

I felt around in my memory for some reason I would be in the hospital, because this was definitely a hospital. I started by wiggling my toes. I carefully contracted the muscles along my spine. I relaxed and the need to hide left me. Then I was flooded with real memory.

Whatever had happened, maybe they would just let me go home.

Where were my parents anyway? Yesterday they were home because it was a long weekend and neither had to go to work. And, oh my God, I have that appointment Tuesday at the law firm. I have to get out of here because another chance at getting into Basswell & Basswell won't come along any time soon, and there will be a lineup at the door the minute word gets out that there is a position available. These thoughts twisted over and around each other like a basket full of snakes.

I tried to speak but was amazed at the sound that came from my mouth, more like a frog might make than a human being. My throat was a little sore. 'That must be it,' I thought. I remembered the time Dave and I were crossing the Nevada desert on a backpacking trip and the feeling of dust in my throat.

My mind skittered around, and I didn't seem to be able to control it. I lapsed into dizziness at the memory of those desert nights; lying under the bright stars, snug in that double sleeping bag we'd bought in Vancouver.

Why was I thinking about Dave? We broke up so long ago.

The next time I woke up, I could tell there was more than one person in the room. I pretended sleep, although my heart felt as if it wanted to leap out of my body and run away.

"Sarah is awake. She is refusing to open her eyes, but she is awake." He had a nice voice, but I didn't like his smug assurance that he knew all about me.

"Remember when we removed the cast? I saw her response was better, but I wanted to wait until I was sure before saying anything. She's healed nicely; she'll have full use of that shoulder."

Another man answered, "That's good news, but her physical condition isn't what worries me the most."

"Of course, but we will not be sure until we get the chance to talk to her. She fakes sleep when I am in the room, but I know she's been moving around in the bed, and took a drink of water when she thought she was alone. Remember. In spite of the passive exercises we've been doing, she'll be weak. However, she is young and healthy, and she should recover quickly. As to her mental state, we'll have to wait and see."

Lying there listening to them talk about me, as if I were so much meat on a block, made me want to spring up, hit them and tear their eyes out. Mostly, I was furious because the soft-spoken man had seen right through my act.

I opened my eyes and tried to sit up. The room whirled around like a merry-go-around. I fell back. This time with my eyes closed, hoping I wouldn't throw up. If I expected a lot of worried attention, I was sorely disappointed. He laughed.

'OK. Enough of this,' I thought. My head was settling, but rather than risk a return of the dizziness, I turned my head on the pillow toward the voices. It came to me that he must be Dr. Willis. I remember a woman's voice saying his name. There was another man standing near the foot of my bed. It was Dave.

All of a sudden, I started to shake, and it felt as if something began to press on my chest. For a moment I panicked, because I thought I couldn't breathe. I couldn't tear my eyes away from his. I had only felt fear like this that time the bear wandered into our camp. I was vaguely aware that my arms were waving in 'go away' motions.

Dr. Willis picked up my fear, because at an abrupt gesture from him, Dave turned and left the room.

Chapter 24

Dave stood outside in the corridor. 'What was that about?' was his first thought, and then, running it back through his mind, he recalled the terrible expression on Sarah's face. He had seen such fear on patients' faces; the doomed ones, the ones he couldn't help.

He had so hoped that when she came out of this coma, he could take her home, get Grace back, and devote more time to the search for Angela.

He could hear Dr. Willis talking to her, and her answers, but he couldn't quite make out what they were saying. At least she hadn't fallen back into a coma at the sight of him.

The nurse came out. When he moved to speak to her, she shook her head, and continued back to the nurse's station.

It was only a few minutes later, when Dr. Willis stuck his head out and said, "Sarah will see you now. Be very careful. Don't contradict anything she says, just play along. She is very fragile just now. I'm going to leave you two alone."

Dave tapped on the door frame and stepped into the room. Sarah was sitting up, and when she turned her head, he could see the effort it took for her to smile. It wasn't much of a smile, but he was encouraged to go nearer.

"I hardly recognized you Dave. You've shaved your beard. And I see you went back to medical school after all." She motioned to his scrubs and the stethoscope around his neck.

Dave kept his face quiet, but a shiver ran up his back and down his arms. He had shaved his beard five years ago, before they were married.

Remembering Dr. Willis' instructions, he didn't respond but picked up her hand. It lay dormant in his, as if he was a stranger, and after a moment or two, she gently slid it away.

"How're you feeling?" he asked. "I have been so worried." He bent to kiss her cheek, and felt her slight withdrawal. It hurt like a physical blow.

"Was I in an accident? I feel fine now. When can I go home? Where are Mom and Dad? They know that I have that appointment on Tuesday. Oh my God! What day is it? Why aren't they here?" She made a move as if to get out of the bed.

"Slow down. Everything's all right. They will come as soon as possible. We had another bad storm last night."

"Don't be ridiculous. I know where they live. Its ten minutes from the hospital. Call them right away."

Dave could hear the hysterical edge. "Sarah, listen. You're in the Ottawa hospital." He was trying to keep his voice steady, but wanted to swear in frustration.

The whole situation had a nightmare quality. They seemed to be talking at cross purposes. He couldn't establish the almost psychic link he had always felt with Sarah. So many times, one of them would be opening their mouth to say something and the other would know exactly what was coming. That connection seemed broken.

He wanted to bring up the subject of the children, but first had to make sure she was stable enough--because they were no nearer to finding Angela than they had been on the first day.

"Ottawa! What in the world am I doing in Ottawa? I've never been there my life." Sarah pulled herself higher in the bed. "What are you trying to pull, Dave? Is this some kind of payback? Where's that other man that was in here? I want him, right now. Get out of my room before I scream, Dave James."

Dave watched her gathering her breath, and turning on his heel, nearly walked into Dr. Willis as he hurried in from where he'd been listening in the hall. Dave stepped around him and didn't stop to talk.

Sarah didn't want him near her. Maybe Dr. Willis could talk some sense into her. He leaned against the wall outside the door. He felt closer to passing out than he had in all the years of his practice; and he'd seen some horrific things.

"Well, look at you, just awake and already fighting!" Doctor Willis chuckled. "I see you're full of questions. I want you to lay back and rest now. We'll have a nice talk when you wake up. Just remember, you're safe here. I'm putting a little sedative in your IV. Maybe your parents will be here when you wake up."

Dave saw the light that called the nurse come on above the door. A minute later the nurse came hurrying down the hall—Barb-- the one who'd sat with Sarah through her coma. She gave Dave a nod in passing, and went in.

Dave wanted to drive his fist into the wall in frustration. Sarah wasn't herself at all. She was acting like an irresponsible college girl. Neither he, nor Dr. Willis, could predict the next twist in this bizarre situation. Logic told him the childish scenario he himself had been building-- of taking up a more- or- less normal life with Sarah, while they searched for Angela, was only smoke and mirrors. In real life, it wasn't going to happen.

I have to ask Dr. Willis if he thinks she is consciously trying to deceive us, or if this is just another means of escape, now that she has lost the coma option. He thought that idea over, but he didn't think so. Surely, she wasn't that devious. All their married life, she had been truthful and trustworthy--or so he had thought.

His mind moved on to ways he might handle his next visit. He was not going to just go away; the love they shared must still exist. He felt it, through the pain of her rejection. He leaned his head back against the wall and stared at the overhead light, and tried to make his mind a blank.

A touch on his shoulder drew him back. Dr. Willis didn't look at all disappointed, in fact he had a definite twinkle in his eye as he said, "She's all right. You get some rest. Have you called her parents?"

Dave entered the room at noon the next day with a CD in his hand. Sara looked normal, but tired. He was relieved to see that she was lying on her back staring at the ceiling, instead of curled up in a ball facing the wall-- a position he'd seen too many time in the last month. He hoped his face could maintain the upbeat expression he was trying for.

He felt it slip a notch, when Sarah turned her hooded eyes in his direction. Those eyes could push you away with nothing but a cold stare, and Dave would feel as if he had walked into a refrigerator.

Using the strategy he had decided upon, he said in a friendly voice, "I found this last night. You always loved to play it when you were putting Angela to bed. I thought you might like to hear it while you're waiting for your parents to arrive. They're at the hotel and will be here soon.

Sarah's expression didn't change but she didn't meet his eyes.

Damned if I'm going to beg, Dave thought. He turned back toward the door with a firm step. Halfway there he heard Sarah whisper, "Wait. Who's Angela?"

He chose not to answer. She wasn't going to have it all her way. At least something he said had caught her attention.

They had broken off their relationship before she went to law school. It had been one of the most painful experiences of his life, because he'd never really been in love before--but he hadn't been ready for commitment. He'd told her he wanted to be free. He knew it had hurt her badly, but he was flailing around trying to decide a way forward. He still hadn't been sure he wanted to be a doctor, although he had two years as a medical student behind him. He'd only known what he didn't want: to be a married man.

For all his resolution, Dave weakened and turned back. "Are you ready to talk now?" he asked.

A small bit of his earlier anger must have registered with Sarah. Her face hardened and she said, "No, I'm not ready. Maybe later, go away. I want Mom and Dad."

"All right, but we are going to have to talk soon. You may know something about the accident that will help us find Angela."

He turned on his heel and walked out the door. He was going to say Angela's name every time Sarah tried to avoid it.

Chapter 25

Mary's tears overflowed the moment her foot passed the entrance to Sarah's room. Although she was trying hard not to cry, she hated to see her strong- willed child so unlike her usual self. But after a long hug, they both spoke at once.

"Mom, I . . ."

"Darling, how . . ."

Mary touched Sarah's face and her short hair, as if she'd never expected to see her daughter again. Sarah clutched at Mary's hand as if it were a lifeline.

Ralph pushed in between them to kiss Sarah, and to talk about how soon everything would be back to normal. "We're here for you, Sweetheart, as well as Dave. How are you feeling?"

Mary could see the indecision in Sarah's face. She might be awake, but there was something still seriously wrong. Every time they mentioned Dave, an expression came to her face, like a teenager trying to avoid the truth.

Sarah's threw herself into her father's arms and cried with great gulping sobs, and a flood of tears. For once he kept quiet, just holding her and patting her back until she swiped at her face and sat back clutching a handful of Kleenex.

"The doctor says I've forgotten five years of my life! Is that true? My last memory is coming home from law school, July 2nd and--he said it's March! She burst into fresh tears.

Mary and Ralph looked at each other and quickly away. They had always hated giving Sarah bad news. She never took it well.

"Are you strong enough to talk? Maybe Dave or Dr. Willis should be here." Mary spoke in that annoying sweet tone that people use when talking to fragile children, or mad people; the ones they didn't want to push over the edge with too much truth.

Sara looked to be teetering on the edge of control. Her eyes stared out of her stark white face, with rough chapped lips clamped in a stiff line.

"No, I don't want them. I want you to tell me. I don't trust them," she said. "Is it true? So start with that July. It's the last thing I remember."

Poor child, Mary thought. She could feel the heaviness of spirit that signaled high stress creep around the edges of her body; seeping into her mind. 'God help me,' she prayed.

Two hours later Sarah was paler, hollow eyed and trembling. "You want to see Dave now?" Ralph asked.

"No," I'm not ready. I can't be his wife. I don't even remember when we got back together, let alone our being married. And the children. How can I be their mother, and not feel it? Didn't I love them?"

She listened without expression to everything her parents told her, but now tears trickled down her face again.

Mary gripped her hands. "Love them? You're the best mother in the world. You even put your career on hold to be home with Angela. Don't you want to see Grace? She's so sweet now, at three months old. She smiles every time you look at her. We left her with the nurses at the maternity ward today, but we can have them bring her; it would only take a few minutes."

"No. No!" Sarah wailed, "I can't. I can't!"

"Please Sarah, calm down. No one is going to force you to do anything. We're looking after her. Ralph has hired a private detective. We'll find Angela. We'll never give up, not Dave, not his parents. Do you remember Lila and Don?"

"Yes, I was at the farm once when Dave and I were dating."

Mary saw that Sarah was making a real effort to stay calm and focused. She was taking deep breaths and smoothing back the sheet that she had been twisting between her hands. She answered a few other questions about what Mary thought of as the 'safe' past.

Dr. Willis breezed into the room. One quick look around at their strained faces convinced him that they'd had enough stress for today. Turning to the Ashleys', he said, "You look all-in. Go get some food and try to rest. We will all meet here tomorrow morning. Dave can be here then."

"You know him?" Sarah seemed surprised, and not very happy about it.

Mary hurried to counteract any idea that they were all talking behind her back, ganging up on her. She said, "Naturally Dr. Willis sees Dave. The doctor has been taking care of you for him."

Sarah said nothing else but closed her eyes, as she had when she was a child, and didn't want to hear something bad.

Mary saw her hand slide under the covers and down to explore her flat belly, as if there might be some evidence of two children there. "I wish I-I-" she said, but kept her eyes closed.

The others stopped talking, fearing that Sarah was slipping away again. After a few moments of silence, her eyes popped open. "I want to go home, Dad. Please."

Dr. Willis got up to leave them alone to talk over the next step.

Ralph looked at Mary, and when she nodded for him to go ahead, he said, "We'll see. Listen to Dave's side first."

Sarah opened her mouth in protest, but then, a look of weary resignation crossed her face, and she lay back into her pillows.

Mary knew that she was at last beginning to accept the truth.

Chapter 26

Sarah

I really hadn't had a chance to say 'no' to the sedative, because the man who claimed he was Dr. Willis, slipped it into the IV line, and within seconds the room dimmed, and I seemed to fall down a spinning tunnel washed in black ink.

When I was pulled back from the dark, Dr. Willis stood beside my bed again. 'Doesn't he ever go home?' I asked the ceiling.

Some part of me was screaming, 'danger', but I was aware enough to know that there was no escape. I wondered if I were in a real hospital or were these people part of some cult that Dave had got mixed up in. Common sense said, 'that cult idea is ridiculous.'

To fake one room might be possible, but I could hear and see people passing my door, carrying on normal hospital routine. The scratchy call system wouldn't be easy to fake either. For now I would have to go along with them.

This time I was able to struggle up on the pillows by myself, and did feel stronger. At the look of approval on the doctor's face, I thought I would begin my questions before he got a chance to push his agenda, whatever it was. "Please tell me what's going on," I said.

Without thinking I reached out and grabbed his arm. "I need to know what I'm doing here in Ottawa, of all places!"

Dr. Willis gently pried my fingers from his wrist, but as he sat beside the bed, he continued to hold my hand. 'This is the 'father figure' act, crossed my mind. I figured that if I went along with it I might pick up some clues to how I ended up here; although every instinct pushed for me to scream my questions all out in one long stream. But then I remembered the needle, sliding into the IV. I was through with escaping. Now I wanted answers.

"It seems that while you were asleep, you forgot some of your past," he said, as if he gave out that particular bit of news any old time he felt like it. Good God. Yes, that's what he had said, 'forgot your past'. My every instinct rejected that idea. But again, I held back my denial and waited.

"Tell me about you," he said next, not trying to reclaim the hand I had jerked away at his bald statement.

I decided to play along-- answer his questions-- not give him any reason to think I was a crazy person. I admitted I'd acted totally out of control that time Mom and Dad were supposed to come.

I started to tell him about our family-- a nice middle-class normal family. He looked so interested and pleased with me that I told him about having finished my law degree, and how I had come home last week, and that I was anxious to get out of here so I could keep my appointment at Basswell & Basswell.

He just looked at me. "What month is it?" he asked.

"Why, July, of course," I answered. He had told me earlier that it was March and I had pretended to believe him. He didn't say a thing now but got up and walked to the window. He threw up the lower sash. A blast of cold air and a swirl of snowflakes blew into the room.

"March 15th to be precise, he said. He waited for me to up him on that one.

"Winter, how can it be winter?" I heard myself whisper. I was struck with sudden vertigo, and clutched at my bedside railing. Then I watched, as he closed the window, but I could still see the snowflakes dancing in the bit of light shining through the glass. I felt the dark beckon with a terrible pull; I willed myself to hang on. I was trained in logic. There had to be an explanation, and I wanted it to be mine.

"You have lost some time from your memory. I'm sure it is still there and it will come back, but you must be patient and trust us to help you," Dr. Willis said gently.

I was wondering who the 'us' was, until he continued. "Trust Dave; he's the one who has the answers. He's just down the hall. I will have him come in." Before I could say another word, he was out the door.

'Oh God, not Dave again,' I remember thinking. I wasn't afraid of him; I couldn't understand his presumption of our closeness. But, if I wanted out of here, I knew I had better see him.

He stood in the door with a tentative smile. I pointed to the chair and said, 'Come in and sit down.' I was ready to listen.

"While I was talking with Dr. Willis, I heard you say that you had to see the lawyers. I'm sorry to say that that was July 2nd five years ago, and you were admitted to the bar the next year." A bald statement; he never was one for chit-chat.

He followed this ridiculous statement by silence. A wave of nausea gripped my stomach. "Five years! It can't be! Yesterday I came home, and it was summer!" I caught myself just on the edge hysteria. "I know it. I know . . ." But then my gaze was drawn back to the window, and I had to admit that I was wrong.

I couldn't help myself. I turned my back, pulled my knees up and shut my eyes. I wasn't trying to escape; I had to think.

Dr. Willis didn't comment, but said "Relax now." Your parents will be here in a few hours. We'll talk to Dave later.

"Oh great," I muttered. Years lost; the very idea spooked me to the soles of my feet.

After Dave returned, going on about Angela again, I had a terrible attack of the shakes after he left. The name Angela; it frightened me because my mind could not conjure up a picture of her, let alone remember her being mine.

Now the baby! I couldn't remember carrying her, but I had to believe she existed-- she was real, like March was real. That was more terrifying than Angela, who I could keep in the realm of fantasy. I couldn't remember carrying her either, or their births, or, for Christ's sake; that so-called marriage to Dave.

Madness swirled up a stream of darkness, but I gritted my teeth and brought my mind to stillness; a yoga trick that came back to me.

Nurse Barb came in and got me out of bed for a few tottery steps. It was more like she carried me, than that I walked.

I was imaging home as we turned toward the window. A beam of sunlight turned the snow, piled against the glass, into a thousand crystals, and I felt my courage flood back. It flowed down my back, straightened my knees, and ran up my arms to lift my shoulders.

Barb, shorter than me by six inches, tipped her head back and gave me an encouraging grin as she felt me take my weight onto to my own feet.

"You're going to beat this, you know," she said. "You're a strong woman. Look at you, after all you've gone through, you're still beautiful. If I were you, I would go along with them. They're the ones who will help you get your memory back."

After I was back in bed and Barb had left, I thought over what she'd said. 'She was right. After actually walking today, I couldn't wait to get up and get mobile again. My body might be flabby and weak, but I had always prided myself in keeping fit and healthy. And I will be again.'

I was feeling the most upbeat since I had woken. Before I started to slip back into worry, I spotted the disc that Dave had left on the nightstand. As I rolled over to put the disc into the player on the other side of the bed, I felt my remembrance of music awake. I slipped the disc into the player.

I expected music, but the room was filled with the sound of water washing a sandy beach, bird calls and wind, rustling leaves. I closed my eyes and let my mind drift. How I had loved those summers along the river.

I jerked awake, sitting up so fast that for a minute, my shoulder hurt; in seconds the pain eased. In my dream, I was in a canoe on the bluest of lakes. I was sitting in the front, facing backwards, and Dave sat paddling at the back. Between us, a little girl with blonde curls sat playing with a toy horse. I noticed she didn't have a life jacket on. Then the canoe tipped over and I saw her sink into the black water and out of my sight. That's when I woke up.

For a minute I thought the dream was reality and the hospital room was the dream. I ran my hands through my hair and over my face until I realized they were both dry; I was in bed, and could hear voices in the hall.

Mom and Dad came in. It seemed to me that I had seen them only yesterday. After Dad had nearly crushed me with his usual hug, Mom gave him a look that said, 'Let me handle this.' She started with the usual question visitors ask. "How are you feeling, Darling?"

'Just swell; I wanted to scream. 'I've lost five years of my life!'

I had a little crying spell. Can you blame me? They looked older than I remembered, and were handling me with kid gloves. I have to laugh now at how far into left field I had slipped, in that last long sleep. Believe me, it was no laughing matter to be told that my mind was five years back in time, while everyone else had moved on. But Mom meant well, so I got a hold on myself and put her off with as few words as would do. When she pressed for a fuller answer, I cut her off and said, "So start at that July. That's the last thing I remember; coming home."

There wasn't anything for it, I had to go along.

"Dave's the one to tell you. It seemed to us, you were barely home before he came for you," Mom said, and I could see a shadow of the hurt she must have felt.

I felt my own heart harden within me— an echo of that earlier decision. Somehow, odd as it sounds, I was afraid I would lose my soul if I wasn't careful— if I let them tell me who I was.

It looked like I was going to have to face Dave, whether I liked it or not. Just him, I could handle, but the idea of having two children, one lost; to put it bluntly, it scared the hell out of me.

Mom got up as if to leave. I reached out and begged her to stay. I asked my father questions about his work. He fumbled for words, and then he said, "I retired four years ago. These last months I've spent looking for Angela."

That awful weakness flooded through me, but I was stronger now, and looked to the light in the window to focus myself. He went on talking, but I barely listened. Gathering myself together, I interrupted, "I can see Dave but I can't be his wife. I'm not ready. I don't even remember when we got back together, let alone, being married to him."

"But, Darling," Mom said.

Panic swept over me. I heard my voice crying out, "No! No! I can't. I can't!"

Mom stood up, and in the voice she used when I had got hysterical as a teenager, she said, "Calm down. Get a grip on yourself. Dave had to put some time in at his practice but he will be in this evening. And I don't want to hear of any nonsense from you. You listen to him. You won't find a better man if you look a lifetime."

I was taken aback. I'd expected sympathy, and maybe a little coddling. I guess Mom had reached the end of her famous patience. Dad knew enough to keep his mouth shut, and as she stalked out, he just gave a wave from the door.

Chapter 27

Listening to her parents' footsteps fade down the corridor, a black loneliness washed over Sarah, and for a moment she wished she'd died. She definitely couldn't remember. They were playing nice, but she still picked up vibes of blame. Whatever she had done--she'd made their lives hell during her teenage years--they'd always taken her back and forgiven her. Now it felt as if they had abandoned her, when she needed them the most.

'Why should Dave make the decisions?' She wondered. 'They say he is my husband, but I have no memory of being married. None!'

She wiped her face dry of the tears she had hardy noticed pouring from her eyes. She straightened her back and swung her legs over the side of the bed.

"Goddamn it. I'm a grown woman," she said aloud. The words seemed to echo around the room, agreeing with her. "I'm not going to lie here like an idiot and let other people make decisions for me. If I can just get out of here, I can handle Mom and Dad".

For a moment, the idea of not having Dr. Willis's support sent a little shiver of fear down her back. But then he was too clever; he'd see through any strategy she conjured up. He'd force her to remember, and she admitted it now, the idea of remembering terrified her. If she couldn't disappear into the darkness of a coma, she would hide in plain sight.

She slid off the bed and shrugged into the hospital housecoat. 'Can't get any uglier than this,' she thought. She took a few tentative steps, keeping close to the bed in case the dizziness returned. She smiled as she felt her legs hold her weight and her mind remain clear. For the first time since she'd woken up, she was ready to take charge of her life.

Dave walked through the door. He stopped at the sight of her walking, and a big smile crossed his face. "You're walking! I'm so glad you're feeling better. Come sit for now. We have to talk. Your parents want you to go back to Toronto with them. Naturally, I'd like you to go home with me, but you should be near Grace. She's only an infant. She needs her mother."

'As if it were up to him to say what, I can, or can't, do!' She fought down a spurt of anger. Why didn't he leave her alone! 'Careful, something inside her whispered before any angry words could leap out. Don't act crazy.' Calmly sitting back down on the bed, she said, "OK, Dave, tell me the truth. We're really married? My parents keep telling me we are, but somehow, it's just gone."

"Sarah, we've been married for five years, and I love you more than I could possibly say. We have two beautiful children. We'll get Angela back, and you will remember. Give it time."

"What happened after you left me?" Sarah asked.

She was looking at Dave now as if she were the one who had suffered an injustice. Seven years ago, that was. It seemed a lifetime but she still wanted to know.

"Oh God, Sarah, you said you'd forgiven me for that. As soon as I tried to live without you, I realized what a mistake I'd made. I was so screwed up, and depressed at the loss of

Patrick; remember I thought I could cure him, but I killed him instead-- that I hardly knew what I was doing. You forgave me, remember? We've been together ever since."

"No, I don't remember. It must've been after I came home from law school. That day is the last thing I remember. How could I forget? If I loved you enough to marry you, surely I'd remember, wouldn't I? And I don't-- truly I don't--it scares me. I just want to go home, with my parents, I mean."

Choosing not to confront her over her last statement, Dave began to talk about the accident and her injuries; and all else that he could piece together.

Sarah sat listening, but he might as well have been talking about a movie he had seen. She remembered the dream of the little girl she'd had earlier. Was that Angela?

They talked for a long time, mostly about when they first met. Sarah wasn't clutching the bed sheets with white knuckles, as she had when he first came in. She was gesturing freely, as she always had done when she talked.

She understood he wasn't going to blame her, or press her to remember something she couldn't.

A lot more than Dave's beard, had changed since they had first met. He was no longer the rebellious boy Sarah had loved. Some of the attraction was still there. She felt as if her body was coming alive, and she even smiled at some of the stories of what they had shared. She could imagine living with him. And, with a lot of care, they might coax friendship and love back.

Dave

This first connection, since the accident, felt as thin as a spider's web. He decided against showing her the pictures of Angela that he had brought along, and instead, worked at happy memories. If he upset her now, she would have time to brood and avoid seeing him again once she was back in Toronto. When she began to yawn, he decided to quit while he was ahead.

"I'll see you tomorrow morning." He smiled, touching her shoulder lightly as he stood up from the chair.

It tore him inside to accept friendship instead of love, but if he didn't get out of the room this minute, he was going to blow it.

Sarah's voice stopped him in the doorway. "Will you drop by later this evening? It's lonely then in this part of the hospital. Mom and Dad can only come for half an hour at six; something about a baby."

Dave's heart jumped in his chest, but he kept the surprise from his face. "Of course I will, if you'd like to see me," he answered with a smile. But he knew he shouldn't make too much of it-- just one friend seeing another.

'A friend could offer a gift though, couldn't he?' Dave thought, as he left the hospital to go to the hotel. A bewildering array of necklaces, earrings and clothing were tumbled in with crystals and other stuff at the shop where he stopped to look in the window. Back in the days before they were married, Sarah had loved signs of the zodiac jewelry.

Raising children was a lot more complicated than the life she remembered, and of course, law school had changed her too.

One piece caught his eye; a large square amethyst, set in a woven frame of cobweb-thin sterling silver wires, dangling on a silver chain. Amethyst was a stone of healing, wasn't it? Sarah needed that. Besides she had slept through her birthday in February, and amethyst was that month's birthstone.

He hadn't even made it to his hotel room before an urgent call came from his office. There went his visit with Sarah this evening.

The next morning Dave hesitated outside Sarah's door. From inside, he heard angry voices. Dave hesitated a moment longer, then walked in. Ralph and Mary were standing with their coats on, and Sarah was sitting in the chair by the bedside, with a rebellious light in her eye. Mary kissed him, and Ralph put a hand on his shoulder.

"Is there a problem?" Dave asked, looking at Sarah. At first he thought she wasn't going to answer. From the corner of his eye, he saw Mary had laid her hand on Ralph's arm, to keep him still.

"If I go home with them, they want me to take care of that baby. I don't know why, but I just can't," she burst out.

Dave turned to Mary and Ralph, and asked them to meet him in the waiting room at the end of the corridor.

When they left, he led Sarah to the chair and knelt beside her. "I think your mother is finding that taking care of the baby is too much for her, as much as she loves Grace. But, if you'll agree on seeing a psychiatrist, I will hire a nanny to care for Grace, and keep her with me. What do you say?"

Sarah studied her hands. Rebellion was written all over her face. He could just imagine her desperate thoughts, as she tried to concoct a plan to get out of promising to see a psychiatrist.

When Dave didn't move or take his eyes from her face, she said, "All right! Goddamn it, I promise!"

As Dave pushed himself up, he felt the jewelry box in his pocket.

"Something to remember me by," he said lightly, as he dropped it onto her lap. "I'll be in Toronto in about two months, but I'll see you before you leave."

He hurried out, with no relief in sight, and misery hovering over his head, like Sisyphus pushing his stone up the mountain, yet it always rolling down again.

Chapter 28

Sarah's hands shook as she waited for her parents. She wished now she'd asked Dave to be here. She had forgotten what a nice guy he was, and how easy he was to talk to. But she felt weak every time she saw him around her parents. They were so close--when had that happened?

Although she was scared to remember, just for a second she wished she could. They hadn't liked Dave very much when they first met him. Her dad said he was too serious for a girl like her.

A flashback of Dave standing at the bottom of stairs, looking up as she stepped down, came and went so quickly that she didn't have time to capture it.

She closed her mind to such thoughts, and picked up the gift Dave left last night. The amethyst shot purple rays onto the ceiling and walls. She closed her hand tight over it, and dropped it straight into the new purse her mother had brought. She put her hands over her face and began to cry.

Sarah had been expecting to leave right away, but as she sat in her room alone, with nothing of her own but the new purse to take with her, she could feel the familiar panic in her shaking hands, and a tight band threatening to crush her chest.

"God help me," she whispered.

Looking ahead, she couldn't see any way to go; the past a blank and a future that she shrank from with her whole being. The last session with her parents had shaken her confidence that she'd be able to manipulate them, and avoid Dave-- and all the claims he had on her.

Hearing familiar voices outside her door, Sarah struggled to get control and quickly wiped her face with tissues. Instead of just her parents, Dr. Willis and Dave followed behind them. Dave was pushing a cart piled with small boxes.

'Oh no,' Sarah thought, 'they're ganging up on me. Dave never mentioned this yesterday. Why can't we just go?' She thought briefly of staging a fainting fit, but then remembered; Dr. Willis wouldn't be fooled. It might make her look bad, unstable, and not fit to be let off the ward.

Dr. Willis came and took her hand. "Dave has brought some pictures and home movies that we thought you might like to see, to help jog your memory."

'What memory?' she wanted to say; but flippant wouldn't do either. For just a moment blackness welled behind her eyes. 'Hold on, hold on, you can do this,' she silently repeated, until she felt the panic ebb. With a wobbly smile, she said, "Well, maybe just one."

Dave set up the DVD player and slipped in a disc.

"We can turn it off any time you say," Dr. Willis assured Sarah in his clinical voice.

Sarah nodded, holding her breath; frightened of what might appear on the screen. But when an image flashed up, it was a wedding party. It looked to be in a park, and there wasn't a child in sight. The bride had her back to the camera, and in the background, a buffet table loaded with food was set out under tall trees.

The camera panned around the guests. Then Sarah's breathe caught, "That's Aunt Greta! Who is that she's standing beside? Is that Aunt Jane? There's Don and Lila!" Then the bride turned, and Sarah saw her own face.

She couldn't have spoken, if one word from her lips could save the world. Her mind was in chaos. This had to be true! They couldn't fake all of these family members. They didn't all know each other, and her aunt would certainly never take part in any film made to trick her. This– this must be true!

The camera moved on past the group of people surrounding the bride. "There's Jim." Sarah said pointing.

Dave pushed the pause button. "Good. That's a true memory. You hadn't met Jim before the wedding," he said.

Sarah had no idea why she had recognized Jim. Of course, she knew about Dave's younger brother, but he lived in Calgary, she had never seen a picture of him.

"Turn it off, turn it off. Please! I can't take any more!" She struggled to keep her voice steady. "Oh, please, can't we just go?"

"All right," Dr. Willis said quietly. "But I want you to take these home, and promise you will look at one every day. I'll go sign the papers, and you will be released early this afternoon."

Sarah would have promised to walk barefoot on hot coals if it could get her away.

Dave and Sarah's parents met in Dr. Willis's office. They waited for him to speak. He talked about buried memory, and how he'd concluded that Sarah was in denial, but he, in good conscience couldn't keep her in the hospital any longer.

"What would you recommend we do about baby Grace? In our talk about coming home, Sarah has never mentioned her. She can't seem to bear hearing her name, but sooner or later she has to face reality, doesn't she?" Mary asked. "She says she doesn't want to look after her."

Dr. Willis thought a moment, but didn't answer her question, then said, "I know an excellent nanny, Amy. I'm sure she would probably be delighted to get a new job. She isn't very happy where she is.

How about you Dave? You offered to keep Grace with you while Sarah goes to Toronto with her parents. I can certainly recommend Amy. A nanny would take some of the pressure off everybody until Sarah gets used to life outside again. You could take Grace for visits so Sara would not be able to forget her."

"Yes, I can do that. Actually the idea is a good one since I want to spend time with Grace. This Amy-- I'm sure she is suitable, if you recommend her. I'll get on to that right away." Turning to Ralph, Dave asked, "Do you think she will watch the DVDs?"

"If I know Sarah," Mary put in, "She'll look at them out of sheer curiosity, but she'll want to do it in private. I'll make sure she has a DVD player in her room. There's one in the basement." Turning to Dr. Willis, she said "In a few days, if she seems to be settling in, do you think we should start mentioning Angela?"

"I think you can chance it, and freely discuss any progress in the search. Talk to her naturally, without insisting that she should remember. I think if we press her about the accident, it could be counter productive. But, she must see Dr. Robinson every week. This is vital. If she creates a new life for herself; one that ignores the forgotten time-- she may never remember. She, herself, must want it."

Chapter 29

Jenna

The days are getting longer thank the Lord. It's April and there's not much snow left-- a few dirty piles against the buildings and I saw some green grass against a sunny wall the other day when I was out with Angela. I can only take short trips with her. I get tired so easy. Jo runs home from school most days and takes her down to the shore to watch for birds if the weather is fit at all.

Jo can't get over Angela and the birds. It seems such a funny thing in so young a kid. She's always asking their names and wants to know where they live. She drives Jo crazy with questions. Jo says she'd never had any interest in birds before looking at them with Angela. They were just things making messes--like pigeons. Angela loves pigeons because they come close for feed. She thinks their pretty colors make them good.

Jo says they are going to make a bird chart. She's cutting pictures out of an old bird book they found in some garbage. Angela thinks every bird from her picture books will turn up. She's real excited about it.

Angela got bigger over the winter. I expect she must be three now. I'll have to be thinking on a birthday party.

People won't believe that she is still 2 for much longer and her talking is real plain.

That evening Jo took out the new puzzle she had found at the second hand shop. Angela put it together so quick Jo and I could bare believe it.

When will Angela be three? She's getting so tall Sally at the park asked me yesterday. She said she looked a lot bigger than two Jo said.

I hadn't had time to think of a date. Jo sometimes drives me near crazy. I have a hard time making up lies in a hurry. I didn't dare forget any of them because Jo has a memory that hardly forgets a word you say.

In answer I said I haven't had a chance to tell you but it is next Thursday. I didn't want -you know who- to get wind of it. I think we could plan a little p-a-r-t-y. We'll talk about it later.

I picked Thursday because that was my night off. Jo said she would do everything because she knew how tired I was. I still went to work four nights a week then. That's why I had to be careful in the daytime and rest a lot so I would be able to do the night cleaning.

I knew I was not doing a good job. I heard the boss at that art studio grumbling about dust. I was scared to climb the ladder for fear I fall so I had just swished a dust rag around on the end of a stick.

Angela knew something was cookin and did everything she could to stay up. We let her play until she fell asleep on the floor.

We went to the kitchen and whispered over plans for the birthday party. The money dried up faster than mist in August. We figured we could spare $10.

I could make a cake and Jo said that the dollar store had balloons and other cheap decorations. Then Jo thought of a puppet theater. I asked her how she was going to get puppets.

I'll sew buttons on for eyes. She said and grabbed up a sock and drove her hand in it. She bunched the toe between her thumb and her fingers to make a mouth and worked it up and down.

I thought Angela would love it.

The two little girls we decided to ask likely never were to a birthday party so they wouldn't mind if everything wasn't store bought.

I asked Jo if she wanted to ask her youngest sister and was glad when she said no. We couldn't have them all and there'd be a fuss if we only asked one.

The party day Jo took her last class off. I took Angela out to give her time to fix everything up for the party. We didn't go far because it was windy and quite cold.

When Angela saw the room all hung with crepe paper and balloons she didn't seem to know what it was for but stood looking until we yelled Happy Birthday Angela!

She began to laugh and run around looking at everything saying for me for me? It made Jo and I nearly cry- Jo because she loved her so much and me because if I hadn't took her that day her life would be easy with anything she wanted. I'd put aside the idea that she was God's gift in place of Julie. But it was done and I couldn't see of any way to undo it without me ending up in jail. Then I'd say to myself--look how happy she is.

At first they were shy. We knew they would probably be hungry so we had the cake first. There was more on the floor and smeared over their faces than you could imagine but a lot got stuffed in.

After cleanup Jo set up her puppet theater. She'd took the side of a box and painted curtains up the side of the open place she'd cut out and with red and blue stripes and big white stars over the rest of it. Jo done a great job with her sock puppets and a stuffed dog. Even Beau came to watch. The little girls screamed and yelled, and one got too excited and wet her pants.

When the few presents were torn open and we put away anything that might break the girls started to grab Angela's toys. Angela wasn't used to sharing and tried to grab them back but she couldn't manage two of them. I was surprised she didn't strike out but she just went into a corner and started to cry.

The other little girls dropped the toys and began to bawl too. We sent them home.

Jo said to me. What do you think?"

I said, "We're lucky it wasn't worse. No real harm done." Because by now Angela had got over her crying fit and seemed no worse for it.

I spoke too soon because a minute later she came to me and said I want Mummy and go to see Gran Lila. I want the ponies and the cats and dog. Why can't we? Tears ran down her cheeks.

What could I say? More lies? I started to shake but Jo came and took my arm and helped me to my room for a lie down. She hurried back to Angela and I could hear her voice and in a few minutes Angela chattering back. If I ever thank the Lord for anything it would be for Jo.

Laying staring at the ceiling so tired I could barely lift a hand my mind wouldn't settle. That nagging pain in my gut got worse today. I'll have to see a doctor. I knew I couldn't put it off much longer. I'd finally let the bad thought in--I been fighting going there.

Maybe I can just get a pill or something. I have to work. I'm putting too much of looking after Angela on to Jo. Angela needs spring clothes too. All this went over and over in my head.

I didn't have a doctor but could go to the walk-in clinic. Then that led me to worry about Angela. I had no idea what shots she might need or what she'd had. She hadn't been sick since she was with me. I decided to leave that for now but go myself first.

The next day I left for work early and stopped in at the clinic. I saw a young woman doctor who looked about twenty. She poked and prodded and said she would make me an appointment for an ultrasound. She wanted my phone number but I lied and said I didn't have one. The address I put on the form wasn't right either but I told her I would stop in and pick up the form later.

When I went to pick up the form, it was left for me at the desk and I was glad I didn't have to see that nosey doctor. It meant I would have to take a bus to the clinic where they did those tests. It was nearly a month away, on a Thursday at 3:30 in the afternoon Jo could come home a little early. I'd been afraid I'd have to hire a babysitter.

I didn't feel any less dragged out but was more settled in my mind. It was getting warmer and I took Angela out as often as I could. When I couldn't go out she spent hours in her room with Beau watching the sparrows squabble and hop in the tree outside the window.

Angela told him every sparrow's name but of course they all look alike.

I don't know what I will do if I got real sick.

Chapter 30

Dave stood watching the car carrying Sarah out of the hospital parking lot, and out of his life. It turned down the main street and swung east on its way out of town. His chest ached and he felt rejected, and alone.

Dr Willis must've read his body language from where he had been standing behind the family group. Now he stepped up beside Dave and touched his shoulder.

"Don't give up on her, Dave," he said. "She's young and healthy, and needs time to work things out. I'd be interested if you keep in touch. I'm available if you need general advice. I'm no longer her doctor, but hers is a fascinating case. By the way, here's Amy Chow's number for you. I understand the hospital expects you to pick up your baby as soon as possible," he reminded Dave.

"Thanks for your help. I have a feeling I'm going to need it. I'll ring Ms. Chow right away. If I can't hire her, I'll try to find a good daycare," Dave said, looking up from the piece of paper and shaking off the premonition that he and Sarah were lost to each other; she to her denial, and he into the world of work, police files and the disappointment of leads that went nowhere.

Amy Chow's voice, when he rang after returning to the hotel, momentarily robbed Dave of the half-rehearsed proposition he had planned to float by her, in hopes of making her favour his offer. He had expected an accented, rather hesitant voice for some reason. Instead she spoke like any young woman might, one who'd been to university in this country.

"Yes, I would love to meet you, Dr. James. When can we arrange a meeting? In the lobby of the Northland hotel? Sure, eight tonight, I'll be there. In fact, I think I will recognize you. I had to take one of the kids I was caring for to the clinic. Someone pointed you out, and told me your name."

Dave sighed in relief. It sounded promising. He was tired of staying in the hotel and wanted to move back to his own house. He wanted to be there to see Grace every day, and to see the river breakup, and wait for the return of the ducks and geese. He hoped the nanny wouldn't mind living in the country.

He let his mind turn back. Only the news of Angela's loss had hurt as badly as seeing Sarah ride away with not a backward glance for him. He would give her a while, but he didn't intend to give up.

By eight, he was waiting in the hotel lobby. He found himself wanting to pace the room and watch the door. He wanted to have a good grip on events and be in charge. Amy Chow had the sound of a wild card. 'She'd better not be late,' he thought, staring again at the door.

"Dr. James? Thought it was you. Hi, I'm Amy Chow."

Dave gave a start and felt his face flush. "Where did you come from? I didn't see you come in."

"Sorry I startled you. I always like to get a look at the people who want to hire me, before we meet."

Dave didn't think she was sorry at all. He was a bit annoyed at being manipulated, but remembered he couldn't afford petty personal feelings that might cause him to lose a good caregiver.

Amy stood barely five feet, and looked at him with a quirky grin on her face. He thought, 'She's hardly more than a kid herself.' But her resemblance to a child stopped, on the second look. She might have been no more than five feet tall, but she was perfectly proportioned. Her lovely elfin face was surrounded by a cascade of straight black hair.

However, there was nothing flirtatious in her manner, as they sat in the corner of the lobby over coffee, discussing what would be expected of her as the nanny for a busy doctor with a three month old baby, and no wife in the house.

She asked him questions about Grace: his views on child rearing, and the location of his home. She didn't seem put- off at the idea of a country place, as long as she had a car for her own use. Dave said that she could use Sarah's almost- new Ford Focus, since Sarah was in Toronto for the foreseeable future.

"Could you start immediately?" Dave asked, after he had explained his circumstances. "The hospital has been allowing me to leave Grace on the maternity ward, but I have to take her out of there this weekend."

Amy hesitated. "I could. You will have to pay the remaining half of my current rent, as well as the full monthly salary we agreed upon."

Dave didn't like being taken for an extra half month's wages, but accepted with outward nonchalance. "That's fine. You get your things together and I will discharge Grace. We should be able to be ready to leave by noon on Saturday. That okay with you?"

"No problem. Nannies travel light. I want to have a formal agreement drawn up but, we can take care of that once we see how things go. That is why I prefer to work for professional people. They don't mind paying a higher salary to get someone who is a good fit."

She rose from the chair, gathered her coat and purse, and stuck out a small-- but surprisingly strong-- hand for him to shake.

Dave watched her walk away. There was something about her he couldn't quite put his finger on. Was 'the bold Canadian girl' an act? He had wanted to bring up her Korean background, but didn't want her to think it would make any difference as to whether or not he hired her. 'I hope I haven't made a mistake,' he thought. 'I wish she wasn't so damned pretty.'

He shook off the last thought with the mental equivalent of a snort. He'd felt as sexless as a monk since the day he first got the news that Angela was missing.

All of a sudden, depression seized him like a weight on his back. He hauled his body out of the chair and took the elevator to his room. He sometimes wished he was a drinking man and could find relief in alcohol. It wasn't that he didn't like the taste; he feared addiction. He had seen so much damage done to street people and families' torn apart by abuse, even murder.

After a restless night, and a bad start the next morning--he cut himself while shaving-- and the paperwork of getting Grace released to him, he'd had all the stress he needed for a month.

He'd had to see the pediatrician, who was convinced that as a doctor, Dave would want to know every little detail of Grace's feeding regime, weight gain chart, and on and on. Then, when he could finally hold her, she took one look at him and cried as if her heart was breaking. He tried all the little tricks that seemed to work with other peoples' babies, but still she screamed.

'Well, let's see if the nanny can work her magic,' he thought, as he carried the screaming baby toward the exit. Nurses waved, smiled, and went about their business. It was only 11:30 in the morning, and already he felt as if he'd run a marathon by the time he struggled Grace into the car seat-- which the Ashley's had left for him.

As he pulled up at the Northland Hotel, Amy was waiting just inside the door, with enough baggage to furnish a house piled on the steps outside.

'I thought she said she travelled light,' occurred to him, as he looked at the bulky bags on legs, and others that looked heavy, wrapped in some kind of rough cloth.

Dave forgot the mountain of luggage as soon as Amy stepped outside and heard Grace begin crying again, now that the car was stopped. She hurried down the steps and jerked open the van door. In seconds, she had Grace in her arms, and was rewrapping the tight undershirt and the outer blanket. She opened her own jacket and put Grace's face against her shoulder, so that the cold air wouldn't shock her baby lungs, that hadn't yet been exposed to it. The screams subsided to sobs, and then to hiccoughs, and to silence.

"Dammit. How did you do that?" Dave flung the question from under a pile of packages that he had staggered with to the back of the van.

Amy laughed. "They wrapped her too tight. Why hasn't she got real clothes?"

Before he answered, he slammed the back hatch shut and slid behind the wheel. "I never thought to ask for them. Mary only brought a few things, because they thought they would be the ones taking Grace back with them. There's a box of Angela's baby clothes, at the house. We'll use those, until we can buy her some winter things. Angela was born in the spring. All her small stuff will be summer clothes. I should've been thinking about cribs and baby bottles, and all that, but I wasn't expecting Grace to come home with me."

Once they were on the road north, neither spoke for awhile. Dave was trying to formulate how they should relate to each other. It would be so easy to get off on the wrong foot. Too friendly and she might take advantage, but too distant might make her lonely and she would leave.

'Start as you mean to go.' He recalled that old piece of wisdom from his mother. He had never employed anyone in his home before. Sure, it was easy at the practice. Everyone knew their job and their place. 'If only Sarah were here,' he thought. She would be taking care of this-- and I wouldn't be feeling so inept.

He glanced in their rearview mirror. Amy was sitting as near to Grace as her seatbelt would allow. Grace was in the baby seat, with Amy gently whispering to her, a trace of a smile on her face. She was unbelievably beautiful.

He quickly shoved that thought aside, and turned his attention back to the road.

Chapter 31

By late April Grace was happy and seemed to be thriving. With extra salary, beyond her hefty nanny's pay, Amy had taken on most of the housekeeping. She shopped for them all, and cooked for herself and Grace when Dave wasn't home. He looked after its own meals when he came in; his schedule was so erratic, it seemed the best arrangement. She bought everything Grace needed and passed Dave the bills. Sometimes he couldn't recall-- did Angela ever have a $200 snowsuit?

Dave had trusted Amy from the first time he had seen her with Grace, but he had adopted a plan of keeping as little contact with her as he could manage outside of their employer and employee positions. Whenever he spent time with Grace, Amy walked or ran for exercise.

As the search dragged on, Angela was never far from his thoughts. Sometimes he would get up from his troubled dreams and spend hours on the computer, surfing sites having to do with missing children.

He learned that all too often, the very worst time for parents was when their child was found. Sometimes he wished he was a religious man, so he could pray for Angela's return-- undamaged.

Reports of Sarah's progress weren't good. She still clung to the illusion, that he had concocted some sort of twisted plot to make her his wife and mother of his children.

Dr. Robinson was reluctant to discuss Sarah's case, but did reveal that she often missed appointments. The last time he spoke with Dr. Robinson, she'd said, "Sarah uses all the usual ploys to avoid my questions. It would be amusing, if it weren't so sad. She reveals more in what she doesn't say, than in what she does. However, I am convinced that in time she will recover the lost memory. I think this is a psychic state, rather than one arising from the physical trauma suffered at the time of the accident."

After Dave had talked to Dr. Robinson, he tossed and turned half the night before he fell into a deep sleep. When his alarm jumped him awake the next morning, he'd made the decision to go talk with Sarah face to face. Maybe seeing Grace, who smiled and babbled now, could stir some missing maternal instinct. He remembered how Sarah had been with Angela. She'd delighted in every tiny step forward, and reported to him as if they were minor miracles.

Usually, for breakfast Dave merely grabbed a cup of coffee, and had one of the office staff bring something in for him mid-morning. This morning, he pulled up a chair and played with Grace a few minutes. She'd held up her arms, and he couldn't resist picking her up. Amy was busy cooking and cleaning in the kitchen.

He could feel that she wanted to talk, so he smiled and said, "She looks great. You're doing a tremendous job, and I'm sorry I haven't said that enough. Are you all right? You aren't too lonely out here in the country?"

"No, I'm fine. Grace is such a good baby, and I have my painting."

"Your painting?" Dave said, surprised. "I didn't know you painted. Why did you never tell me?" He wasn't making eye contact, but was enjoying Grace's giggles as he bounced her up and down on his knee.

"You never asked," she said. "You're here now. How about some pancakes? I've been dying for pancakes ever since the new maple syrup came out. I bought a jug yesterday."

"Pancakes, eh? Sure bring them on." Dave forced himself to relax, but was aware of her every movement, although he pretended to give all his attention to Grace.

With Amy moving lightly between the cupboards and the stove, he felt a moment of happiness, sitting there playing with his little girl in the bright warm kitchen, and a pleasant companion cooking for him. Then, he caught himself up, and his stomach clenched; it should be Sarah here with him.

"Don't you have office hours this morning?" Amy asked after she'd finished off four pancakes and stood up from the table to start cleaning up.

"Yes, I do. But, I wanted to tell you to get Grace and yourself ready for a trip to Toronto. I thought we could leave around ten tomorrow morning. Does that give you enough time?"

Dave passed Grace back to her and moved to the hall to get his coat.

She followed him, and said, "Sure, my time is your time. How long will we be away? Has something changed with your wife?"

"We'll be there the rest of this week and the weekend. Sarah seems to be recovering. I've got to be back for Monday though," Dave said as he pulled on his gloves.

'All these questions, you'd think she was my wife'. The fleeting thought made him cringe. He quickly pulled open the door and stepped out into the cool spring air.

When they set out the next morning, the road was bare and dry, and the sun sparkled on the hills, and on the roadside bushes. The mood in the car was upbeat; Dave, because he hoped that seeing Sarah would put to rest the uneasy feelings he'd been having lately. Was he getting too comfortable as things were at home? Was he pursuing the search for Angela as enthusiastically as earlier-- and was he spending extra time with Grace as an excuse to see more of Amy? She'd never overstepped the bounds of her profession but . . .

Any time he arrived at the Ashley's, the greeting on the steps outside were chaotic, and it wasn't any less so now. Mary and Ralph were delighted to see Grace, and couldn't stop exclaiming at how she had grown. There was a tear or two shed for Angela, and a few low spoken questions, which Dave answered with a shake of his head.

Amy was welcomed with courtesy and a quick glance between Mary and Ralph. Dave was sure Amy caught it, and hoped she didn't feel hurt, but she answered their questions about Grace with such obvious affection, anyone could see she was devoted to her.

As they entered the house, Dave realized that Sarah wasn't there to meet them. His heart seemed to lurch in his chest, and for a moment, he was disoriented and checked again from one person to the other. But there was no mistake. She was not in the hall, or in the room off of it.

"Where's Sarah?" he asked Mary, after Ralph volunteered to take Amy to the room that Angela had always used when she stayed with them.

"She wasn't feeling well this morning, and I was afraid she had picked up some bug that she didn't want the baby to get," Mary told him.

At first, the excuse sounded perfectly reasonable. But there was something in Mary's face, and the way she held her hands, gripped in front of her body, told Dave there was more to the story than she was telling. He almost challenged her, but then thought better of it. Whatever it was, it wouldn't be Mary's fault.

To break the tension, he said, "Has Ralph had any feedback from his contact with the Mounties?"

"No, he hasn't, but they've told him that they do have contacts across the border, and a low level search is going on there. I daren't think . . ."

Ralph came back down the stairs, cutting off what Mary was going to say. Before he could wave Dave into the living area, Dave said, "Hang on, Ralph. I'm going to run up to see Sarah."

"I don't know if that's a very good idea," Ralph said. "There has been something new going on with her lately, and now, this sudden--whatever . . . She was going twice a week to see Dr. Robinson, and seemed quite happy in herself, although she couldn't remember any more than when she was in the hospital. Then about two weeks ago, she took to her room, and has only come out for meals. Today, she hasn't been down at all."

Dave ran this through his mind, trying to be as logical and objective as possible; given how helpless he felt. "All the more reason for me to go see her, I'd hoped she would have some interest in seeing Grace." With that, he turned, trotted up the stairs, and strode down the hall toward Sarah's room.

Dave tapped lightly on the bedroom door. "Sarah. It's Dave." He turned the knob and pushed the door, but it was locked. "Sarah, come on. Open the door! I don't care if you're sick. I want to see you anyway."

"Go away. Oh God, I'm going to be sick again." He heard running footsteps and her bathroom door, slamming shut.

He couldn't force her to see or talk to him. 'Is this sickness real, or is she faking it?' he asked himself, pressing his forehead against the panel in front of his face. Then he straightened, listened to the silence within the room one more time, turned and went back downstairs.

When Mary and Ralph met him at the foot of the stairs, he shook his head saying, "I can't discuss Sarah right now. Can you give me a few minutes?"

Mary went up to check on the baby, and came back shortly carrying her in her arms. "Amy has a bad headache," she told Dave, when she found him sitting alone in the living room. "Did you know she was subject to migraines?"

"No. She never mentioned it to me," he replied.

"Well," she said, she had some medications, and all she needed was a few hours rest, and she would be fine. Gives me a chance to look after Grace--what do you say, Sweetheart?"

Two more mornings came and went. Amy had recovered, and Mary and Ralph warmed to her quickly as they saw how good she was with Grace. She talked easily with Ralph and was quick to offer her help in the kitchen.

Sarah never appeared, and would only speak to Mary.

On the third morning, Ralph worried out loud, "She'll starve herself if she keeps this up." Silence fell around the breakfast table. They were sitting finishing their coffee. Amy had taken Grace up to be dressed.

Mary turned to Ralph and said, "You can stop worrying about her starving, Ralph. Somebody has raided the fridge every night, and it wasn't any of us or Amy-- it must have been Sarah."

Dave's face flushed red and he threw down his napkin. "I'm sorry, but I can't stand anymore of this. I'll have another talk with Dr. Willis, and let him consult with Dr. Robinson. I can't get anywhere with her. If you're going upstairs anyway, Mary, please tell Amy we're leaving as soon as she can get ready."

Mary and Ralph tried to talk him into staying another day at least, but he had to separate himself from this latest betrayal as quickly as possible.

With Amy and Grace in the van, and thanks said to Mary and Ralph, Dave hesitated at the van door and looked up at the window of Sarah's room.

'Was that a twitch of the curtain, or just a trick of light? Sarah! Maybe I should try again,' he thought--but decided against it. She was probably checking to see that he was really leaving. He lifted his hand in a half wave, just in case she was watching. In that moment, he felt his anger drain away and sadness take its place. What misery and pain Sarah must be feeling to go to such an extent to avoid him?

There was silence in the car for the first while. Grace was asleep beside Amy in the backseat. Dave was busy with the heavy traffic, and Amy was thinking her own thoughts. Then she reached up and touched Dave's shoulder.

She spoke softly, "She was watching, Dave. I saw her clearly in the window when you were putting the suitcases in the back. She must care. Maybe she really is sick?"

"It's--I don't know how I can go on. I see peoples' lives wrecked every day, but have never had to live through anything like this. Sarah and I didn't know we had a happy life. Do people, who worry about disaster lurking around every corner, accept this pain better than people like me, who never expect it?"

"I can't answer your question, Dave. All I can do is to help you get through each day by taking care of Grace." She took her hand away and sat back in her seat.

Dave didn't answer except to say, "Thank you, Amy," but his mood shifted again, and the thought crossed his mind that there might be something hopeful about Angela in his inbox at home.

The hours back were boring and gray. They stopped once in some small town to change and feed Grace, have a quick meal and then drive on.

The farther north they travelled the more they fell back into winter. In Toronto tulips had been pushing up beside the blooming hyacinths, but there was no sign of that along the roads as they neared home. The rocky hills with scant scrub clinging to their sides lay all around. Still, it wasn't hard for Dave to find beauty here. But for some, Amy being one, it was a challenge.

In the house, lights on and a fire in the fireplace, drove off the gloom. He rocked Grace while Amy made coffee. She had been quiet the last miles, but being back in the house seemed to energize her. She quickly changed Grace, tucked her into her bed, and delivered a plate of cookies to the end-table in the living room. Then she sat on the floor with her legs curled under her. Dave looked up in surprise from where he sat, half asleep, watching the fire. She hardly ever came to the living room in the evenings. Dave thought she looked like a contented cat as she stared into the flames. The firelight striking her face accentuated her high cheekbones, and painted highlights within the shadows of her hair. He caught the smell of the subtle perfume she was wearing, but quickly turned his mind away.

In one easy movement Amy stood up and came to stand before him. "Come. It's time for bed," she whispered.

Like a man bewitched, he got up and followed.

Chapter 32

Jenna

I've just been reading over that part of my story when I wrote about that birthday party for Angela. I was so down right then I couldn't go on writing. Summer so far has been pretty good to us.

That prissy little doctor gave me some pills that helped me get some of my strength back. I never took Angela to the clinic. I know I'm a coward but it would kill me to lose her now.

Jo got a summer job in a daycare and was able to take Angela with her in the mornings so I could get a good sleep after working the night before. Jo went back to the daycare until half past three. It has worked out real good.

Jo had some bad luck at the end of June. I want to write it here in my story and I'm going to use some of Jos words because I wasn't there for all of it.

That day she was happy. She washed her hair that morning and it spread like a black river over her shoulders. She fairly fizzed inside-- her feet wanted to dance she said. She knew she'd done real good on them exams.

Old Mr. Mahon's eyes were going to pop when he read her essay on them French poets. And in art, if her picture didn't take first place she'd sign up at the Toronto Zoo to be the monkey's uncle--or aunt! She can be a real card.

I can still see her face when she told me that. She was only here a couple of minutes to tell Angela she would be back to take her out. She wanted to show her report card to her mum. I wished I could have stopped her because I heard a terrible row going on down in their apartment earlier. He acts as bad as a mad dog.

I wanted to call the police but never catch their eye is a rule of mine. The same ones who handled Billy's accident might show up and wonder where I got a little girl with Julie dead.

The door to Jo's apartment was never locked in daytime although they was the first door into the building and the outside one was never locked neither.

She shoved the apartment door open as always and almost turned back when the sight that met her eyes was so bad.

She told me how she stood there frozen to the spot looking around the room. She tried to make sense of the upset tables and torn down drapes as if a terrible wind had ripped through the room. Their only decent lamp was in splinters on the floor next to broken dishes and smashed furniture. The drapes from the window were torn from the rods and were on the couch all bunched.

She heard the loud howls before she saw her two sisters huddled in a corner screaming at the top of their lungs. Jo screamed too when she saw her mother's foot sticking out from under the pile of lace that had lined the drapes but now was a heap of dirty white rags on the floor under the window.

Jo said she dropped her books and ran to her mother. As she flung away the drapes she cried Oh no Oh no!

One look at her mother's swollen red and black bruised face told the story. Her mouth was bleeding. A tooth stuck out through her lower lip. Blood from the cut ran down her chin and neck. Her breath came in groans. Jo hugged her for a minute and then ran to the phone. It wasn't on the table.

From Jo's first scream I knew it was bad. I dialed 911 and gave the address and said. Send the police. I sure had never done that before.

Joe scrambled around looking for the telephone but after pawing through the mess she decided to run up to me for help.

The little girls screams had stopped when they saw their mother uncovered and Jo said she wasn't dead. She told them she'd be right back but by the time she got to the door she heard heavy feet pounding on the sidewalk and three uniformed police officers two men and a woman banged through the outer door.

Jo told me all this.

The poor girl stood in the middle of the room making jabbing motions like an idiot towards her mother. She couldn't stop crying. The woman officer, Bertha Graham gathered up Jo and her sisters and herded them into one of the bedrooms out of sight and sound of the police doing their work.

Bertha waited while Jo got a hold on herself. From her bag she pulled a handful of tissues to mop up the little girls who clung to Jo like monkeys. When they were all sitting on the bed she pulled over the rickety chair that was the only other piece of furniture in the room.

Jo told how she found her mother when she came from the daycare. Tammy the youngest one was staring at the police woman like something from Mars.

She said, 'She's dead– We saw him kill her. He punched her face and she fell down.

Then they started to howl again.

No, she is not dead. Bertha tried to be heard over the noise. Jo shushed them so sharp it shut them up.

When Bertha asked if they had anyone to go to Jo said, Jenna. But there are more of us. I have another sister and a brother. She won't be able to take us all.

That's when I got mixed up with the police. They came to my door and my old heart thumped like a jackhammer but there was no help for it I had to let them in. I can't have those snotty brat sisters here with Angela was the only solid thought that stuck in my mind.

The policewoman was kind and not a bit put out when I asked to speak to Jo in another room. I told Jo I wanted her to stay but I couldn't keep her sisters more than a few hours. My place was not big enough and they were too rough around Angela.

When we told her that, she got out her cell phone and walked down the hall away from us. When she came back she said Children's Aid had a temporary foster home who would accept them tonight. The woman from there was on her way.

I was sure proud of Jo the way she stepped up to speak for her family. She asked the aid worker- You won't put them where we can never see each other will you? I work for Jenna as a babysitter so I'm all right here with her. She asked me to stay.

There were questions that Jo did her best to answer. She wanted to show her family in the best light but she tried to tell the truth too. Jo hugged the little girls and told them she would come and see them soon. At last Bertha and the care woman--I forget her name--left taking Jos sisters.

Angela had been hanging on to my dress but now she ran to Jo. Jo carried her to the door as her sisters left and I saw tears running down her face.

When Angela was asleep Jo and I sat in the kitchen. We were too upset to make a meal. We toasted bread and spread it with Cheese Whiz and made a big pot of tea. Jo asked me why I wasn't getting ready to go to work. She looked at me harder and said Oh this is your night off isn't it? You do look terrible.

I've had my hands full trying to get Angela to eat and have her bath. All this excitement-- Don't be surprised if there are nightmares and tantrums. She wanted to do that puzzle, but don't think for a minute, she didn't take in every word we said.

Chapter 33

Sarah

Finally, I made it out of that hospital. Now, I know my mind was in such chaos that I hardly knew what was true or false. That great gaping hole of time, that I had no remembrance of, colored my every thought. I was angry at Dave, my parents, and just life in general for putting me through what seemed like a pack of lies.

I couldn't sit still. I looked out the window; no joy there. God knows what they were telling Dr. Willis, or he was telling them! I had been a rebellious teen, but isn't everybody? Maybe the doctor would advise my folks to keep me at home, and I wouldn't be free to go out and see my friends.

I wondered if Dave would keep his promise about getting a nanny so I wouldn't have to take care of that baby. I had taken a good look at my belly that morning and saw the scar from what they claimed was a caesarean section. To say I was horrified is putting it mildly. Right then I felt violated, not in charge of my life.

It seemed like an eternity, but was probably only a half hour later, when my mother came in with her arms full of clothes. She put them on the bed and came to hug me.

"You look beautiful. Those short curls really suit you. Come, see the clothes I brought." She smiled bravely, no doubt expecting that I would hate them.

She was trying so hard, for a moment I remembered how much I had loved her. Now she was like a stranger with a map of wrinkles furrowed into her face.

The coat was a plain black pea jacket and the size was right. Not stylish, but it would do until, I could get out shopping. But the others--I couldn't help myself-- "Where did you get these awful rags? You expect me to wear these? Look at this! If this is the way I dressed, before the accident everyone keeps going on about, forgetting might not be such a bad idea!"

Mom's face was a study of disappointment and hurt, but she took the kinder gentler road. "Why, they are yours, Dear. It took a month until we got your suitcase back, but all your things in it were maternity clothes. You bought this outfit in that little boutique at the Eaton Center, just before you got pregnant with Grace."

The fear that had been my constant companion flickered and anger flared in its place. Anger, I could handle. 'They were just not going to give up! Grace, Angela, Grace, very sentence! I'll go mad if they don't stop.'

However, I caught myself in time, and didn't say anything else about the clothes. I went into the bathroom and dressed. A stranger peered back at me from the mirror. I would never have bought this color; it was totally out of style, Eaton's or not. Right then I felt strong and decisive. The best strategy going forward would be to pretend to be this other person, and take charge of my own life.

After I endured more of Mom's chatter, I said, "Have you made any decisions about that baby? I am not going to take care of her. If you haven't, I can get an apartment and live on my own. I am still a lawyer and can find work. Or, I can go live with Jean for a while. I can't live with Dave.

I turned my back to her shocked face. This was an old tactic from my childhood. You proposed something so preposterous, that the thing you really wanted seemed a good compromise. It had worked when I wanted to live with Dave, and my parents thought it was a terrible idea. I threatened to run away with him to the United States, and they would never see me again. I didn't have any intention of doing such a thing, but it brought them around in a hurry.

I guess my mother had learned something from those days too. She didn't respond until I turned back to face her. "Grace is staying with Dave. Dr. Willis recommended a responsible woman to be her nanny. And, as for staying with Jean; Jean has two small children, remember? They'd make far more work and bother than Grace."

Mom actually laughed at catching me in the act.

"Jean has two? The last time I saw Jean she was talking about getting married in spite of being such a career woman. I can't imagine her taking time out to have children."

Quick as I was in this game with Mom, I knew that if she said so, it must be true. But, it was another piece of that puzzle I wasn't anxious to explore.

At first I couldn't see my parents' car but the cold air tasted wonderful after the hospital. I was a little shaky, but with my dad's arm under mine, I chafed at the time Dave took to say good-bye to him. I wanted to get out of there, and I was angry he'd left me for last. I hung close Dad so as it would be difficult for Dave to hug me.

I saw the pain in his face, but my wild need to escape, blotted out any pity I might have had for him.

The car had been right in front of us. I hadn't recognized it because it wasn't the one I expected. I didn't say anything, except "I'm cold," and not even a goodbye as I climbed in and slammed the door. I was glad the windows were tinted so Dave couldn't see my face clearly, but still, I felt a twinge of guilt as I glanced up at his, for sadness was written into all of its lines.

The trip to Toronto was one long marathon of my parents trying to cheer me up. The parting from Dave was harder than I had thought it would be.

In the year after we had broken-up, I had tried my best to forget him by working to keep up my grades. The law department was full of smart good-looking men, with not enough women to go around, so there was no need to be lonely. But today, seeing him standing there on the curb as we pulled away, it was like a black cloud clamped over my head, and just for a second, I felt a terrible need to yell for the car to stop. But the idea of being with him frightened me, and I turned and looked forward, willing the car to hurry away.

After an eternity, we pulled up to our family's familiar suburban house. If, in fact, I had been away living near Ottawa with Dave, nothing seemed to have changed on the outside here. Entering into the great room, I stopped a moment, but the leather sofa, the carpet, and all of the pictures on the wall were as if I'd been here yesterday. Still, I had a niggling feeling that I didn't belong here anymore; something was missing.

Mom, bustling around getting dinner, was so familiar that I began to relax. Later in the evening, after my parents had gone to bed, I thought of Dave's baby. I was so glad we didn't have her with us. I didn't know much about babies, except that they were messy, and took a lot of attention.

First of all, I would have to contact a few law firms to see if I could get a junior position– any position. My feet itched to get out into the city. If I hung around the house, I would have to listen to incessant talk of Angela.

They had talked of nothing else the whole trip. They even planned to hire a private detective, and what Dad had done and what he was going to do; the newspaper ads, and on and on. Listening made my head ache and my stomach hurt.

The second week I managed to get away on short errands, but I always returned when I said I would. There were fewer questions each time. I had plans, and they didn't include seeing that psychiatrist, Dr. Robinson; any more than I could avoid.

But within a week, Mom got an appointment, and I reluctantly agreed she could come with me.

'The Duck,' I called her--because I knew a quack when I saw one. She'd put on a sympathetic face, and did so want to fix me. I wouldn't buy one word of her theories on memory loss. She, of course, never spoke about them out loud, but I thought I could practically read her mind.

She suggested we use hypnosis but I refused. I was terrified of giving over control of my mind to someone else. And what good would it do if I did remember? It wouldn't make me run back to Dave, love that baby, or bring that kid, Angela, back.

Maybe I would remember that I hadn't loved any of them. Of course it was all a delusion to think that, but it made sense to me at the time.

I was moping around in my housecoat, looking out the window at the buds swelling on the trees and the tips of tulips pushing out of the cold spring ground, when a wave of claustrophobia almost made me scream. When I was grounded as a teenager, I had felt like that. Actually, I had smashed the window in my room, which led to real trouble; threats of psychiatrists then too.

Mom, who seemed to feel I needed conversation every second, saw me standing staring out the window, and asked, "Aren't you going to go downtown? You have an appointment with Dr. Robinson this afternoon. Have you forgotten?"

It was like the cage door flew open. "Yes, I remember. I was just going to shower and change," I answered. 'Thank God for lies,' I thought, as I ran up the stairs.

Chapter 34

As I pulled into the parking lot at the shopping center, I felt my depression lift. Dave had set me up with a bank account and a Visa card. Somehow I knew there would be several thousand dollars in that account. I cringed a moment in guilt at using his money, and having no intention of acting like his wife.

'I won't think of that right now,' was the way I handled those foolish pangs. Instead, I was determined to have myself a little treat; scratch that. It would be a big treat.

I couldn't remember the last time I'd bought clothes. The ones in my closet were student stuff. After I'd tried them on, I saw that my body must have changed while I was in the hospital. I didn't like the way they fit now. My butt and waist were a good two inches larger than before.

Mom laughed and said they were so out of style she couldn't imagine why she'd kept them.

The parking area was so big, with its hundreds of cars, that a tremor ran down my back and made my hands shake as I drove around to find a space. Once I got the car parked, I didn't jump out right away. A strange reluctance tugged at the edges of my mind. I wanted to plunge in there but still--. I pulled down the mirror and studied my face. Seen in the bright daylight there were tiny, almost- invisible lines, sketched in around my eyes where wrinkles would one day lie, deep and ugly.

My first step would be a professional facial, and a whole new line of cosmetics. And then with quickening heartbeat, I thought--'a new face deserves a new outfit.' I grabbed my purse, and orienting myself to where my car was parked, I entered the shopping center.

Color and movement swirled around me. But I had been here many times, and even if some of the store fronts had changed, I knew the layout. I set out to see if the Roma Spa was still where I remembered.

Two hours later, with my face still faintly tingling, I strolled down the mall. The above the knee short dresses, like the one I had on, were something new for me. Maybe I'd got carried away a bit, but these deliciously scanty dresses were in every window of all the best shops. They were the nearest one could get to being naked in public; and still be considered dressed.

I'd always hated my long gangly legs, but now, looking down at them flashing under the lavender skirt, I thought they weren't that bad after all. In fact, I was attracting smiles and admiring glances; granted mostly from men.

Once I had slipped into this handful of jersey, and slid it over my silk underwear, I'd felt like another person. Although necessary to carry it off, I heartily wished the high heels didn't pinch.

I hadn't had lunch and felt hungry. I stopped at the pub to look at the menu posted outside the door. After all that hospital food, the very words steak, French fries, and lobster, flooded my mouth in anticipation.

'Yes!' I thought as stepped back. I'd been so immersed in thoughts of a juicy steak, that I hadn't noticed there was someone behind me. I bumped into a big solid man and lurched sideways; my new shoes no help to catch my balance.

I felt the soft squish of stiletto heel on sandaled foot and heard a suppressed curse. It took a bit of prancing around for me to get balanced, and think of an apology. I began to babble something about how sorry I was-- when I couldn't help it, I burst into laughter; even hopping around on one leg, with a grimace on his face and holding his mashed toe, I knew Denton Greenberg.

He recognized me at the same second and quickly straightened up. His face split into a dazzling smile. "Sarah Ashley! As I live and breathe!"

I saw his lightning quick glance around to see if I was alone. I was quick to say, "Denton Greenberg! Oh my God. What are you doing here in Toronto?"

He didn't answer that but said, "Remember doing research at the law library that summer you were dogsbody to Carter and Finch? C'mon girl, we got things to talk about. Going in for lunch? I'll buy."

"That's a switch," I said with a smirk.

We had been great friends. He was one of the few men that made me feel petite. I'm tall, but he's really tall.

As Denton gestured me before him into the pub's dimly lit interior, I remembered what a nice guy he'd always been. Although I'd found him attractive in those days, he'd been engaged to a girl of his own faith. And I was seeing Dave. We were comfortable friends, and by mutual agreement, we avoided sexual bantering between us, although we teased each other all the time.

Seated at a booth well to the back of the room, we spent a moment searching each other's faces, trying to assess the person the other had become. Gangly and gauche then, he had reminded me of a big friendly puppy, but now he was filled out and grown into his 6 ft. 4 bones. The high cheekbones and prominent nose were still there, but the amber brown eyes framed with black lashes-- which many a girl would kill for-- bore an expression which said that he was all grown up. I started to babble something about being so glad to have someone to do lunch with; didn't he feel the same?

He quickly agreed and added, "I sure do, especially when I've got the choice between a boring client and a beautiful woman. Hold on a second." He pulled out his iPhone, turned slightly away muttering something about a last minute emergency.

Snapping it closed, he turned back and continued, "I always thought that under that college girl facade you would--well let's not go into that now, but you always did remind me of a kettle ready to boil."

"You wretch! That's a poor image. Kettles are squat and boring." I couldn't believe it. Here I was flirting with him, fishing for compliments.

"Oh, you were never that, even if some of your ideas were so far off the wall that I despaired of your sanity. Remember that crazy case when you were so convinced that woman was innocent?"

We both laughed, remembering how I nearly got myself put in jail trying to prove my point, when it turned out she'd been playing me like a 'cheap fiddle' all along. My father warned me, using those exact words, but naturally I didn't listen. Of course, I had to cap that with something he had done, so in the next hour we ordered, bantered, and ate something. Later I couldn't remember what.

Denton was now a full partner in this father's law firm, so he told me. Even without the fine suit, I could imagine him standing before the bar. I could see success had come for him, quickly, if not easily. If there was something a little sad in his silences, it was so elusive I hardly noticed.

During a lull in the conversation, I leaned back in my seat and crossed my legs. I caught a tiny whiff of body odor.

I realized, that for the first time in months, I was sexually aroused. I squeezed my legs together, but that only made it worse. 'What if he can smell me,' I thought. 'Oh my God; I have to get out of here.'

I sneaked a quick look at my watch. My parents would be wondering where I was. I snagged my cell, and with a quick, 'Sorry' to Denton I called home.

"Are you still living with your parents? You're pretty grown-up for having to check-in." He had a teasing, knowing look that made me go hot all over.

"No, but you know what parents are like-- a predator around every corner, and their little lamb out in the dark." I made myself look him right in the eye.

"But I'm your old pal, not the big bad wolf." Denton smiled a definitely wolfish smile.

"Speaking of leashes, if I remember, you're pretty tightly bound yourself. You've been married now, what two years?"

All pleasure fled from his face. "She died three years ago; breast cancer. And, we were married six years."

Talk about wanting to kick yourself! While grasping his hands and doing the, 'I'm sincerely sorry,' bit, another part of my mind, and a lot of my libido, wanted more of the warmth of his hands wrapped around mine.

Again, I remembered the lies and the need to leave. A little too sudden for good manners, I scrambled out of the booth. He half stood, but I could see he was going to let me go without further protest.

Two steps forward, I hesitated, "Will I see you again?" I asked; turning back, with no idea where the words had sprung from. I desperately wanted that. He didn't answer. He was already digging in his pocket for his iPhone.

I didn't wait. I bolted for the door.

Chapter 35

Lila

When I woke on the first of April, the black depression I had been suffering was gone --gone away, some time in the night. I felt energy flowing along my arms and legs, making me want to get up and do something; not lie in bed feeling over my troubles.

I threw back the covers and went to the window. The temperature had warmed. There were patches of bare ground where there had been nothing but white yesterday.

I always thought I loved spring but, I've come to conclude it isn't spring I love so much, with its mud and fickle weather, but it's the promise of new life everywhere you look.

I washed up and dressed-- which I had been able to do for myself for about two weeks, and waited for Don to come help me downstairs. He came in grinning. 'The little black mare just had her foal" he said. "She's had a tiny filly. It's going to be a roan, and is already nursing and hopping around the stall. Are you sure her dad isn't a rabbit? She sure acts like one."

I thought he had become quite attached to them in the time he has been taking care of Bingo and her pal Ruby.

It's such a shame Angela couldn't be told, even if over the phone.

That morning, along with my return to life-- as I think of it-- had come the firm belief that Angela was somewhere safe and eventually she would be found.

I hoped that soon I would be almost my old self. My speech had improved to where I only stumbled over the odd word, and I was able to get around with a cane. I wanted to try to go out to see the foal, but Don wouldn't let me.

He said there were patches of ice, and likely we would both find ourselves lying on the ground yelling for help. Besides, the foal would keep for a few days, and he promised to lead Bingo out for me to see her when the foal was strong enough, and if the weather got warmer.

He kept his promise and I was so glad that I'd talked him into keeping the miniatures. They ran loose in the barn and took little care. They wore long shaggy coats, with bright eyes peering out from under heavy forelocks, and they didn't need pampering. The foal was so sweet I got teary thinking how Angela would love it. I named her Angel.

The month of May was hard for me to bear. I knew I had to downsize my gardens and I spent hours drawing up plans. We would forget the vegetable garden. We could buy carrots, but my flowers were my first love.

Don hired Sean Griffin, a young man who hadn't a job right then. I wasn't best pleased because I didn't think the lad knew anything about gardening. And I was right. At first, I was unsure whether he was shy or resentful, because I could hardly get one word out of his mouth. The first week was spent with my wanting to fire him every five minutes, but by the end of the second week, he was catching on. He didn't talk a great deal but he was a natural gardener.

He later said, "You fired orders like a shotgun scatters shot. I couldn't follow because I didn't know even the names of the tools and stuff." One morning, instead of acting as if he were coming to his execution, I heard him roar his scooter as he came up the driveway. He was happy to come to work, and that's what makes a good gardener.

"What's on for today, Missus?" he always asked as soon as I came out.

We dug a trench from the old well and built a pond and waterfall, with water pumped in by a small submersible pump. With plenty of rock available, we built and planted small terraces. Sometimes, when Sean didn't know I was watching, I'd see a small smile playing across his face as he looked over the day's work.

During that time I had another visit from Anna. She always carried a healthy look about her, but now she glowed. I swore later, that the minute I saw her, I knew she was pregnant, but as usual I am poo-hooed. She had expected to see an invalid and fussed a bit to see me busily setting out flowers.

I sent Sean home and we sat down to catch up. Don went to the kitchen to make tea. Anna raised an eyebrow at seeing that. In her lifetime, she'd never seen her father do more than draw a glass of water, and only then, if he was literally dying for a drink

"He's become quite the cook," I said for his benefit. But the effect was slightly spoiled by her answer-- "That'll be the day!"

Don pretended to be angry and banged the pots about, but I knew he was leaving us to talk about the subjects that lay just below the surface of our every thought; Sarah, Dave, and Angela's disappearance.

Because she now carried her own child, Anna let her fears colour her opinions. She said, "I'm afraid they'll never find Angela. She'll be three soon, and probably looks different from all the pictures we have of her--if she's even alive."

I would have none of that. "I had a premonition the other night, not quite a dream. I saw her walking on a street with the CN tower in the background. She was holding someone's hand, but I couldn't see who," I said.

Anna didn't even grace that with an answer. "You know I don't believe in hunches, premonitions, or any other such nonsense, Mum. You're only setting yourself up for disappointment," she stated categorically. There was no one with her feet more firmly on the ground than our daughter.

Not wanting to quarrel, I dropped the subject. Satisfied she'd gotten her point across; Anna told me that she'd stopped in Toronto to visit Sarah.

"I hardly know how to explain what Sarah's like now," she said. "It's hard to put your finger on. She acted like I was there to see her parents, not her. You wouldn't believe that, with her hair short, she doesn't even look the same. And you know how she never used makeup-- well now she looks more like a model than the outdoorsy girl we knew."

Anna stopped a moment to think. "Remember how close we became when she was expecting Grace? She used to call me every week. Now she's like a zombie. Know what she said when I told her about my baby? "Oh that's too bad. You'll have to quit work. I never want to have a baby." Now is that strange or what?"

She didn't wait for me to answer but plowed on. "Dave should never have agreed to let Sarah live with her parents. They treat her like a precious vase; Mary waits on her hand and foot. She needs either to be working at something, or to go home and take care of Grace. I'm afraid she's sliding further into forgetting."

If I hadn't been convinced that this whole terrible episode would pass in time, I would have fallen back into depression. Don was going to be very worried about what Anna said, and I asked her to let me tell him.

She could only stay overnight, and by mutual consent, we talked of happier times and the life changes Anna would make next year. I was surprised to hear she was going to take two years off from teaching to be with her baby.

I talked long and hard with Don. I had an idea that could help Sarah. He said, "You should mind your own business. It's never a good idea for a mother-in-law to stick her nose into a marriage."

"Well, nothing can be much worse than what we have going on now," I insisted. "I may fail but at least I'll have tried."

He grouched a bit but finally said, "Alright, go ahead. I'm not going to hold my breath for this to turn out good."

Early the next morning I phoned Sarah. Mary answered. After I assured her that I was recovering, I asked to speak to Sarah.

Mary said, "Wait, I'll get her. There was a long pause filled with muffled voices, angry I thought. Obviously Sarah wasn't leaping for the phone.

When she came on the line, she sounded distant, as if she was speaking to a stranger– a telemarketer maybe. But I was determined to ignore anything negative. "Could you possibly come and help me out. Don tries but he is a man, and I need some woman company."

She tried to wriggle out of it by saying, "I have to see my psychiatrist next week."

In the background, I heard Mary say, "No, Dear. It's tomorrow you see her."

I pulled out all the stops. Letting my voice quiver, I said, "I need your help Sarah. If you could possibly come, please do. Dave said you don't remember us very well, but I'd appreciate it so much. I can't drive, you know, and I want to do some shopping. Don hates standing around waiting. I need help trying things on, and I don't like strangers– salespeople and the like– touching me."

I'd hoped that last bit might appeal to her better nature, but you can't always get what you want first time around. She said, "I don't have a car and the bus--well you know . . . ?"

In the background, I heard Mary say, "We'll drive you up on the weekend." A bit more muttering and Sarah came back on the line to say that she would come.

It was a railroad job, but other than an outright, 'No', she had to agree. She might not feel she was Dave's wife, but she had admitted to that possibility as a ploy to stop her mother's kindly badgering.

I said to Don, "We have some thinking to do. You know Sarah will help anyone who needs her. She's likely to be more open with me if I act a little worse off than I am."

Don didn't like this idea one little bit. We argued on and off all afternoon and half the evening. Finally, when he saw I wasn't going to drop it, he gave in; I could see he was far from happy. He felt it was a sneaky way to gain her confidence, and if she saw through my plot, we'd be through for good. It might spoil what had been a happy relationship.

Just past noon on Sunday, my old hound Beller-- short for 'bellow'-- let us know the Ashleys had arrived. Don pushed me out in the wheelchair that I had stopped using two weeks ago. It made a great prop for the act I was going to put on.

Sarah hung back, letting Mary and Ralph come forward first. We weren't on hugging terms but we were glad to see them. Don stepped in right on cue to invite them in, while I turned to Sarah.

I locked the chair and struggled to my feet. "Here's the one I want to see," I said, holding out my arms. At the same time, I took a tottery step forward. Sarah quickly reached to support me and I saw something in her face soften. She eased me back into the wheelchair.

Back in the house I explained that I didn't need the chair except to get down the ramp. I didn't want to use it more than necessary. "I am afraid I'll get dependent on it," I told her.

The Ashleys only stayed an hour. They wanted to get back to Toronto before Sunday's rush hour when everyone sped home after having been to their cottages up north over the weekend. The highway leading into Toronto would be packed.

I'd planned a simple meal for that evening; shrimp stir-fry. I used to make these things from scratch. But now Don bought packaged stuff from the store. I threw everything into my wok, spiced it up, and that made supper.

Sarah insisted on setting the table, just as I had hoped. Sure enough, she knew exactly where I kept the knives and forks, plates, napkins and everything else. I didn't say anything, but I saw something pass over her face as she turned to get out the wok. I think she realized she had done this before.

As Sarah steadied me on route from my chair to the table, Don took a pale yellow Chardonnay from the fridge. As he reached to fill her glass, Sarah put her hand across the top. "I haven't had wine since I woke up from the coma," she said.

Don stared at her for a moment. "Why not? You aren't pregnant now, or even nursing, and I know you like wine. Try this lovely white. Forget your troubles-- I'm going to," he said, followed by a loud laugh. "My family says I laugh too loud, but it's too late to change now."

I took a good swallow; not some prissy sip. "Lila, take it easy," Don said, but I waved away his 'go easy' tactics and turned back to Sarah. She'd picked up her glass, and was smiling slightly, as if there was something familiar in Don and me wrangling over nothing.

"We'll have Jill up for a day. What would she like to do?" I asked.

"Jill? You know Jill?" Sarah looked puzzled, and slightly annoyed.

"Of course I do! You haven't seen her since you and Angela were there at Christmas, have you? I would have thought she'd have been to see you. But then, I always thought she was a bit of a fair- weather friend."

I had deliberately said that about Jill. I wanted Sarah to jump to her defence. Oddly, she didn't.

"I don't remember," she said looking away and hunching her shoulders. "I never call her. We got out of touch while I was at law school."

Trying to get back to a more comfortable place, I said, "I guess you have forgotten. It was her you were visiting before the accident at Christmas. Don't worry. It will all come back in its own time. One thing this stroke taught me-- live now, tomorrow you may be dead."

I chuckled, to let her know I wasn't really worried about another stroke---or that she had a hole as big as a truck in her memory.

Don opened his mouth to stop me saying too much, but I thrust my empty glass toward him and said, "Pour me another, and hold your tongue."

Sarah actually giggled. But when I turned to share her laughter, tears were pouring down her cheeks.

Forgetting my invalid role, I got up and put my arms around her. "Come up your room, Dear. It's all been a strain hasn't it? Have a good cry; there's nothing like it. Howl out loud if you feel like it. This stiff upper lip is all very well, but carried too far it can shrivel your soul, and you wind up feeling nothing. A good laugh won't make Angela any less lost."

Chapter 36

After Sarah's breakdown the first night at the farm, Lila had to rethink her strategy. Stubborn rejection was one thing, but last night she had seen the turmoil Sarah was carrying within herself. She hoped it was some kind of a breakthrough, but Don warned her not to get her hopes up, or push too hard. He said Sarah was a strong girl and would want to have time to sort out things for herself.

Lila's instinct told her to pound on Sarah's door and put her through the third degree, but the wiser path of watching and waiting won out.

Sarah's door stayed stubbornly closed all morning. Just when Lila thought she couldn't wait one second longer, she heard Sarah's footsteps go down the upstairs hall, and moments later the shower running.

Lila didn't know whether Sarah would want lunch, or breakfast, but she couldn't sit still. Sarah's place at the table was still set from breakfast, so Lila made some sandwiches and put out fruit, along with a selection of cereals.

She heard Sarah scuff back to her bedroom. Lila thought the suspense would kill her; her heart was thumping much harder than it should.

She had to wonder. 'Who will come down the stairs? Would it be the cold aloof beauty, or the friendly daughter-in-law; or someone in between?'

Lila stayed sitting at the table as Sarah came into the kitchen. Her face was clean of makeup and her blue eyes shone, yet the dark shadows around her eyes accented the pallor of the rest of her face. A tentative smile lifted her pale lips as she came forward and slid into the chair across from Lila.

"I'm sorry about last night. I didn't mean to make such a spectacle of myself. It was terrifying to admit that I remembered being here that first time, back when Dave and I were dating. If that part was true, I had to admit that maybe there really is a chunk of my life missing. Until now, I've only been paying lip service to the idea."

Lila hardly knew where to start. 'Careful,' she warned herself, before saying, "I'm only going to remember the good parts of last night. You know, I pray for your memory to return. When you want to talk about it, or ask questions, then we will talk. You see my stroke taught me another lesson. I used to rush at things, not sparing my opinions. But, I'm going to try not to do that so much anymore."

Sarah's skeptical look said, 'I'll bet!'

Lila was desperate to question her as to what else she remembered, but in light of her last statement, she could hardly jump all over her like wind in a dust storm.

"You know, Lila, when I first saw the farm, nothing looked right, but last night I began to recall little bits and pieces of having been here before. As soon as I went into the guestroom, I remembered the smell of old wood warmed by the sun. This morning the shadow of the Maple in the backyard, threw leaf patterns across the floor. I remembered that from having slept there before."

She thought a moment then continued. "Dave showed me a DVD of our wedding when I was in the hospital. I'm sorry; it was awful. I couldn't remember anything except a vague memory of you and Don from when we had met the first time."

"I have some DVDs here. When you feel you're ready, they might help you remember. How are you making out with Dr. Robinson? She's about as much good as tits on an angel-- from what I could gather from Dave." Lila turned away with her characteristic snort.

"It isn't really Dr. Robinson's fault that I haven't made any progress. I've been lying to her ever since she started her 'therapy'. I'm afraid I can't help jerking her around. She'll believe the most bizarre things. I made up long dreams to fill in the hour." Sarah blushed. "Don't tell Mom or Dad; Please."

Lila laughed. "Poor woman; if only they didn't take themselves so seriously. Now, what do you want: breakfast or lunch?"

Sarah gestured for Lila to sit and then poured herself a bowl of cereal. Lila could see that Sarah was relieved to have told one of her secrets, and not made to feel guilty. The conversation moved on to other things, and they went out to see the garden, where Sean was topping up the fishpond.

Now in mid-May, the garden was in full flower, so he only came once a week to weed and take care of the pond. He and Don had built several rustic seats, which gave a different perspective of the garden. Some flower beds held all red flowers, others only yellow or orange. Sarah seemed relaxed as she praised the work, and laughed at Lila's stories of Sean's early mishaps.

The days slid by. One day they went shopping. Lila bought clothes she didn't need, so as to encourage Sarah to buy some things for herself.

Sarah told the story of her first shopping trip post-hospital. "You should have seen the stupid dress-- and the shoes with four inch heels!"

Sarah laughed, but Lila felt there was pain attached to that story, and she wasn't going to hear all of it.

One day after breakfast, Lila found Sarah in the TV room turning over the DVDs. "Are you ready," Lila asked.

"Yes, I think so," Sarah answered, her mind taken up with the hand written titles. "Dave's written here, After the Wedding. Who's wedding?" She put it down as if it might catch fire.

Lila picked it up. "Oh, that's Anna's. She was married, here at the farm two years after you and Dave were married." Lila felt, rather than saw, the involuntary pulling back, even as Sarah said, "Let's watch that one".

The camera had been hand-held and shaky. Obviously the ceremony was over, and the guests were eating and drinking as they moved around the lawn.

Sarah didn't say anything the first few minutes. Then she sat up and pushed the pause button. "There, I remember that."

The ceremony was obviously over. Sarah and her sister were standing under the maple tree.

"That's when she told me that she'd be married by this time next year, and she was, wasn't she?" She turned with a smile to Lila, who was stretched out on her recliner with a cup of tea close at hand.

Without waiting for an answer, Sarah pushed the DVD into its slot. She leaned forward, hands crushed between her knees, scanning all the faces the camera had lingered on. A couple of times, she changed position, as if she was going to say something, but she let it play to its end.

Lila waited for some comment but Sarah seemed lost in thought. Then she said, "Letting the memories come is good. I think your mind is in conflict, fighting your need to know the worst, but scared it will be more than you can stand. I know, I promised I wouldn't push, but don't you think it would be a relief to know? Sometimes the truth isn't as bad as we imagine."

"C'mon, give an old woman a hand. Don has been busy with the projects he let slide while he was taking care of me. Let's make him something better for lunch than meat paste sandwiches." Lila bustled off to the kitchen.

Sarah stood a moment as her mind played back over the tape. She had an inkling of why she'd felt none of the fear and weakness that usually attacked her at any mention of the lost time. The fear must have started after the accident, and this video was taken before it happened. 'If only I could remember!'

Hearing pots banging in the kitchen, she welcomed the diversion and went to help with lunch. As she washed the salad, her mind wandered again to the reason for watching the DVDs. Without warning, tears started to trickle down her face and drip onto the lettuce. She dropped the colander and reached for the box of tissues.

In an instant Lila was at her side. "What's the matter? Have you remembered something upsetting?"

"Everyone must be saying it was my fault that Angela is lost--and--and-- I don't even remember her! It's my fault; it has to be." Sarah mopped at her tears.

"Even if you were at fault, which one of us has never made a mistake? The question is now is whether you are willing to work at remembering, so that you may recall something you have seen or hear; anything that could help in the search. And then, there is the question of Grace-- but we will not go there now. I'll finish this. Why don't you to go to the garden, and then, in a few minutes tell Don its lunchtime?"

Sarah didn't see Don, and after a few minutes of wandering along the paths, she sat down near the fishpond. Watching the constant weaving of their gold and black bodies between the lily pads, she felt the tight coil inside her loosen. She let herself think of Dave, and how kind he had been to her in the hospital.

'And I betrayed him.' She cringed, remembering her affair with Denton. She wondered idly how come she didn't feel more remorse about that. And then she knew; it was a thing of the body, and only her pride had been hurt by the ending.

She gave a start as Don spoke. "Like fish do you? Personally, I prefer them on a plate with a nice lemon butter sauce. Speaking of sauce, what's for lunch?"

"Oh, Don, I was supposed to tell you lunch would be ready whenever you are ready to come in."

"Lead on. More meat paste sandwiches, is it?"

Sarah laughed. "I think it's a surprise. It sure doesn't smell like meat paste sandwiches."

Sarah had to laugh at Don's face when Lila slid a plate of small perfect lamb medallions before him. Peppercorn sauce glistened over them, and onto the bed of couscous that was generously sprinkled with pine nuts and coriander.

Lila claimed it was nothing at all, as everything had been in the freezer. But Sarah and Don would have none of that. They agreed that they would have looked in that freezer for a week, and not have come up with this.

After the dishes were cleared and Don went to lie down for his afternoon rest, Sarah saw Lila stagger, but quickly catch herself and pretend it never happened.

Before Sarah could scold her for overdoing it, Lila said, "Are you ready for more DVDs?"

"Let me help you up your to room, Lila. We can talk there," Sarah said.

For once Lila didn't argue. A small glow of caring seemed to pass from one to the other, as Lila leaned into Sarah's young strength.

Sarah easily took on Lila's weight. It had been a long time since she had willingly done something for someone else. Once Lila was tucked in, Sarah turned to go.

"Stay a bit. You said we could talk," Lila said.

"Oh yes, about the DVDs," Sarah answered. She sat on the side of the bed. She twisted her hands together and felt as if a weight pressed on her chest. It made drawing a breath a hard thing to do.

Lila took Sarah's hands. "Let me tell you something. I was so angry when I had this stroke, that I cursed my lot. Sometimes I wished that I had died-- I hated being sick and useless. Then one morning in March, I saw the bluebird back. There he was, snow all over the ground, and yet he'd flown here from some summer place to pick out a nesting site, and wait for his mate. A message of hope, I thought at the time."

She paused for several breaths, and then said, "Don't miss the miracle of Angela and Grace. They can live without their mother, but do you want that?" Lila rolled away and pulled the covers up around her ears.

Sarah raised her head in shock; anger flared, then after a moment, it passed. She smiled. Lila surely didn't think she wouldn't see through that bit of staged action.

"I'm glad you told me," she said softly. "I do want to look at the other DVDs, but I'm still scared. Would you mind if I looked at them by myself, when I'm ready? I'll leave you now, Lila. I have some serious thinking to do."

Sensing Lila trying to form another strategy, she decided to leave quickly before that balloon went up. She heard Lila sigh and resign herself to a draw.

Sarah couldn't remember when she'd felt so much in control as at that moment. In her room, rather than lying down on the bed, Sarah sat in the rocking chair beside the window. It was going to happen; she could feel the memories on the edge of tumbling out. Some remnant of her Catholic childhood sent up a prayer; 'Please let me be strong enough to weather this storm.'

She rummaged around in her bag for the journal that she'd been keeping and began to write.

Chapter 37

Sarah

Here I am-- another face of Sarah.

I have regretted the impulse it grew out of-- for more than a while now. There have been many changes since that day I bolted out of the pub after my lunch with Denton. There was that question I'd left hanging in the air; about seeing him. I've rued the impulse from which it sprung, more than once.

I cursed those high heels as I hobbled to Mom's car. I knew that Denton wouldn't run after me. He had too much pride, and there would be no need. He had only to look in a phone book to get in touch.

He didn't rush though. He let me dangle for a full week.

For days after, I couldn't seem to put aside how natural it had felt, being with him in that pub; so different from what I remembered. Denton and I had been pals, who hung out together, sharing bags of chips and stupid jokes. We'd lived in the moment. I never remember sharing anything about family, except the odd complaint. I'd told him about bad dates and all kinds of personal things.

Later that night, I was distracted and short tempered with my parents, and I refused to discuss my missed appointment with Dr. Robinson. Later, as I lay twisting and turning in my bed, I couldn't help but imagine Denton there, with his wicked smile and big warm hands.

I think now that I had repressed my sexual side, and when it returned, it was almost compulsive. Now I wish that I'd fixated on Dave. But that I didn't, is understandable. I still considered him one of my enemies.

Denton was not one to ask a lot about my past. In fact, when he'd asked me if I was married or if I had children, I replied, "No, Dave and I broke up before I finished law school. Remember, you were a year ahead of me." I was practically giving him an open invitation, and he knew it. That day pheromones must have been streaming off me like spoors off a mushroom.

One morning, when my parents happened to be out, I was on the point of phoning Denton's law firm. Five days had dragged by and no call. Then the phone rang. I'd expected one of Dave's calls. He always pretended it was to my parents, reporting on Grace's progress, and of course, the search for Angela. However, I suspected it was more interested to check up on me.

He was going to have a few things to say when he found out I wasn't seeing Dr. Robinson regularly. I'd promised to see her last week, but meeting Denton had put that idea right out of my head.

When Denton's warm baritone spilled into my ear, I felt my whole body spring to life--odd when considering I had to grab a nearby table to keep my knees from buckling. Partly it was from relief that it wasn't Dave, and the rest was happiness that I wasn't going to make a fool of myself chasing after him. That is, if he hadn't wanted us to be together.

I needn't have worried. After the shortest of greetings, he asked me if he could see me that evening; from his manner I knew he meant more than 'seeing' me.

I hesitated for a nanosecond. I hadn't been out on my own in the late evening since I'd come to Toronto. But, the temptation was more than I could resist. Somehow, I knew that if I turned him down, that was it. A man like him needn't beg. As he walks by hundreds of beautiful women must practically swoon.

Flinging aside the knowledge that there was going to be the fight of the century with my parents, I agreed when he asked me if I would meet him that evening. There was a wonderful new musical at the Winter Garden Theater. From the way he said it, I knew he had more on his mind than a night at the theater.

I knew I could drive to the nearest subway station, take it downtown and meet him there. 'That's Denton alright,' I thought, as I gleefully accepted.

Desire was already surging through my body. I wasn't signing up for only the play, and neither was he.

After we hung up, the first thing I did was go to my closet. Scanning the mainly T-shirts and pants, my high spirits fell through the floor. There was nothing there even remotely possible for a fancy evening out.

My parents had only taken one of the cars, so within minutes I was on my way to the nearest shopping center. To get there, I had to drive through a street lined with shops. On impulse, I found a parking spot and went into the one called Diva.

Recalling those four inch heels, I decided I would need new shoes, as well as an outfit for a night on the town. In the shop, I just stood and stared. I couldn't imagine how I could choose. I knew how to dress the old Sarah, the college student, but dressing for Denton would be harder.

But help was at hand, eager to grant my heart's desire, and ready to start at the top. When two sales ladies arrived, I chose the one I hoped was chic- Chinese girl, and not into stripper version high fashion.

By now I had got a grip on myself and told her where I was going. She took me through aisles of sequins, and strapless things that hardly qualified as public apparel. Stopping at an alcove at the back, she pulled out a gorgeous silk pant suit. 'Pantsuit, I thought. A little passé, but gorgeous-- that long flowing top and the full legs split to the knee?

"With your height, I see you in something like this, with great lines," she said with such conviction I didn't dare say 'No'.

"With a long coat, you won't look too conspicuous on the subway, but once you are there, you will knock them dead."

I knew the smug look on her face said she had just the coat in mind; the fish was on the hook, and all she had to do was land me. She said, "Look how the bronze perfectly highlights your beautiful skin. You have to try it on.

The deep bronze slid over my body and hung perfectly, emphasizing all the right places. The neckline subtly suggested that it wouldn't take much effort to see what lay below. As I walked, the pants flowed perfectly, showing only a flash of leg as I turned. For shoes, she suggested a matching pair of strappy bronze sandals with a kitten heel.

I said I would take the lot. 'Thank God for credit cards,' I thought.

She took me over to the makeup section and sat me in front of the mirror. As she worked, she talked. "Under your brows, we will put a little gold eye shadow to highlight your lash-line. I'll do the lids smoky gray.

When she was finished, I was stunned. I'd never worn much makeup; a swipe of lipstick and a little powder was dressing up.

I'd hardly gotten past the shock that the woman in the glass was me, when she was back with a shimmering long grey coat, as light as a cloud.

What could I say except, "Let's see the coat on."

My assistant looked thoughtful after seeing the total effect and said, "You might want to change at the theater. Lots of women do carry their good clothes to clubs, so as not to attract unwanted attention. Still, you would look high fashion in that outfit, even soaking wet."

After turning to see all angles and walking out to the floor, I had to agree. The outfit covered me all over and the way it slid across my skin made me think of Denton watching and waiting-- until he could slip open the oversized shell button nestled beneath my chin.

At the counter, I just shoved my credit card across and didn't look at the bill when I signed it.

My parents were still not home when I got back. I hurried my new clothes up to my room, and spread them on the bed. I had never owned anything so beautiful, but then I had never thought I wanted seductive clothes like these--clothes to preen in.

With that thought, I remembered a movie I'd seen about an English girl seduced by a handsome man in India. When it was all over and she was left humiliated and alone--there was something she said. 'He was a peacock—beautiful, but look at its feet; he's only a dressed up turkey after all.'

A wave of guilt swept over me. Was that what I would be? I was using Dave's money to vamp myself up for Denton, but I felt flirtatious, happily so; no matter how expensive the clothes.

Remembering the relentless badgering by Dave and my parents, and Dr. Willis too, I shrugged away that moment of weakness. I had to see Denton, maybe to be disappointed, if he didn't seem as alluring as before. I knew that was an odd word to put on a man but it was the one that came to mind; impossible to resist.

I knew my parents would soon be in, so I carefully cleaned all the makeup off my face and folded up the empty bags; all those silver ones with *DIVA* slashed across the star logo; and hid them in the back of my closet. Then I got a small carrier bag and carefully folded every scrap of fabric into its bottom. For a complete outfit, coat and shoes included, it took very little space. On top, I folded one of my cotton boy-shorts and a tank top. My mind was working like a fine tuned motor. I had already rehearsed my story.

It was after 4:00 by the time my parents got home. I was sitting in the living room, reading, and had to endure over an hour of listening to an update on how Grace was doing so well. Dave had called-- why hadn't I answered?

When he hadn't gotten an answer, he'd called Mom on her cell instead.

I made the excuse that I'd needed stamps, of all things, and had run down to the post office. I must've missed his call.

Dad had gone to his office upstairs, and Mom was in the kitchen starting supper, when the phone rang. I had been getting more and more nervous about my fictitious story to get away for the evening. I rushed to get the phone, afraid that Denton was canceling.

It was a telemarketer. In an instant I'd pressed OFF and began to talk as if one of my high school friends was on the phone. "Cheryl! Sure I can come over. I'd love to get caught up. You're married you say?" I faked listening by saying 'aha', and the other noises one makes to give the impression you're paying attention. "Seven, that's great, see you then,"

I knew Mom had been eavesdropping on my side of the supposed conversation. It'd been awfully quiet in the kitchen until she heard me coming.

"It'll be great to see Cheryl. You don't mind if I stay over? She's got two movies. Maybe she can help me remember some of the things I've forgotten," I confided. How could poor Mom resist that?

"Well then, we better get supper going. You set the table."

I was jumpy as a cat all through the meal. The phone rang and my heart plunged. Maybe Denton was having second thoughts; but no, it was a wrong number.

When we got up from the table and Dad left, Mom said,

"What's wrong, Dear? You seem nervous. Were you expecting a call?"

"No, Mom. Please don't fuss! I turned to stomp out of the room as I had when I was a teenager, but I caught myself and apologized, saying, "Sorry Mom, I didn't mean to snap. Just before I came down I was thinking that I should see Dr. Robinson more than once a week. I decided I would go see her Friday, if I can get an appointment. My mind was miles away. I'm not used to your loud ring tone, and it startled me."

I moved to help her but she told me to go get ready. "A Girls' night out will do you good," she said with a smile. I felt like a real bitch, but nothing was going to stop me from seeing Denton.

As I passed Dad at the foot of the stairs, I saw him eyeing my small bag.

"Pajamas. See you tomorrow, Dad," I said as I scooped up the keys to Mom's car.

I mentally blessed the saleswoman at the store who'd warned me against looking too rich on the subway. Other people were headed downtown to party; some of them I wouldn't want to meet on the way back after they'd been drinking all evening at the clubs and bars.

It took barely minutes in the lobby restroom to transform myself from college girl, in jeans and a hoodie, to sexy lady. Putting on my makeup, I watched out of the corner of my eyes at the other women preening themselves. Some wore too much makeup, or the wrong kind, but I had been advised by an expert.

I jammed the casual clothes I'd taken off into the bag. I had a moment or two of not knowing what I'd do with it. Then it struck me, the theater would have a place in the lobby to check in bags of any shape and size.

Chapter 38

With the bag safely stashed, I walked into the theater itself. The silk pants swirled around my legs like cool water. The deep plunge of the top revealed a discreet swell of breasts, before dropping to a deep hem line that hugged my hips in scrolls of silk stitching.

I nearly fainted when Denton spoke from behind me, and slid his arm around my waist. "You look beautiful. I was watching you come to me," he whispered into the hair at the nape of my neck.

A shock wave hit me like a lightning bolt that I felt down my back, right to my heels. The old Sarah would have said, 'Yes, and it cost me a bloody fortune,' but now I just leaned onto him so that our bodies touched from shoulder to knee. I heard him draw a deep breath before he chuckled, "Just don't step on my toe again."

I had to laugh. That was so pure Denton. As I swatted him with my clutch, I felt the tension leaving my body. I was just pure happy. It was as if I'd checked in my uncertainties along with that bag.

Just once during the evening, I did I feel twinge of guilt at the lies I had told. But then I thought, 'It's only for now.' If there had been a devil on my shoulder, he would have fallen off laughing.

I don't remember much of the play. I'd feel Denton turn his head to look at me, and my stomach would knot. We didn't even wait for the standing ovation. We left by a side door that led to the small street at the back where he'd parked his BMW. I was going to tease him about his cliché car, but he tucked me in and we roared off.

I asked, "Where are we going?"

He gave me a look that could start a brush fire in a rainstorm.

"Guess," he said.

The details of our affair, if you could call it that; more a kind of madness-- are easily imagined. The upscale apartment, the lies and evasions necessary to keep one party from learning too much about the other . . .

I had to account for my absences from home too. It was all standard fare for someone with an addiction. And sex with Denton was an addiction, in every sense of the word. If we met for dinner, I could barely eat as I sat across the table in agony; my body burning for his touch.

Often, I blushed with embarrassment as his eyes scanned my face, and a smile very close to sadistic, tugged at the corners of his lips. He'd suggest dancing, or drinks with his friends at a fancy club, but I knew he was waiting for me to beg him to be taken back to his apartment instead.

I only had a few hours because my parents might suspect I wasn't seeing Dr. Robinson or old school friends. I would tear myself from his bed, and literally stagger home. The first few times the house was dark and I slipped into my room without waking them. I started to stay out later and later. Then one morning they were both in the kitchen when I came in for coffee. The look on their faces told me that they had a good idea that I was lying to them, and it was going to have to stop.

Instead of a tirade about late nights, Mom said, "You're up late up this morning. You missed him when Dave called. He's on his way down from Ottawa with Grace and the nanny. I'd like you to help get the crib set up in the room across from the second bathroom. I can hardly wait to see Grace again. She must've grown so much."

I had to grab the nearest chair, such a wave of dizziness washed over me. My very first reaction was 'how long until I can see Denton?' With Dave here, there was no way I would be able to sneak out and go downtown. I'd told my parents that I was seeing Dr. Robinson yesterday, so I couldn't say I was going to see her again. My racing thoughts were dangerously close to going over the edge into total meltdown.

Mom didn't seem to notice my white knuckle grip on the chair. Dad started to say that he would carry the crib up from the basement for us. He stopped in mid-sentence. "Are you all right, Sarah? You're awfully pale this morning."

I forced myself to straighten up. "Dad, I'm fine. I think the shrimp Cheryl and I had last night might have been a tad off, but then, it might have been the caramel popcorn. We ate a ton of it while watching those movies."

The tranquil evening light shining across the neighbouring oat field calmed Sarah's mind, quieting her jangling thoughts. One toe pushed on the floor and the old rocker carried her back and forth as she thought over what she had written.

Instead of trying to avoid thinking of her affair with Denton-- not just the end, Sarah let her memory play over other things that had happened. Oddly, it seemed to have happened to someone else.

She wondered who was wearing that beautiful bronze silk creation now. She'd given it to a thrift shop. The memory of the owner's reaction made her smile. She had been torn between her knowledge of what the clothing would bring in her shop, Couture Still, or if she should tell Sarah what they were really worth.

Then Sarah's mind came back to the decision she had to make. Being here on the farm, her heart seemed to beat at a slower rate, and her thoughts become more ordered. All of a sudden she reached a compromise decision.

Days on the farm had a way of slipping away. Sarah helped around the house and yard. Lila never questioned her, but from her being able to find things, and a hundred other incidents, Sarah knew that she was remembering more-- without having to think about it.

Chapter 39

One evening Lila said, "Let's get Angela's pony out. We'll let her graze on the lawn. Will you get her, Sarah?"

"Sure, be back in a second," Sarah answered.

She arrived leading the black miniature with the little foal trotting behind. "I see you've got the right one," Lila laughed.

Sarah looked surprised. "This is Bingo, isn't it? Somehow I just knew that she was the one having the foal this year." She ran a hand over the baby's soft fuzzy coat. It shied away and ran to the other side of its mother. Bingo nuzzled the foal, and then turned back to grazing.

"What's wrong Sarah?" Lila asked.

Sarah didn't want to sound sentimental, but it'd struck her that the mother loved her baby, and had reassured it that it was safe. She was a good mother, not like Sarah herself.

Later that evening, she berated herself. 'What in hell am I waiting for?'

Lila had just asked her what she wanted to do for the evening-- and was there something wrong.

"No, nothing's wrong, Lila. I just realized it was time we looked at some more of those discs."

"Sounds like a plan," Lila replied with a big smile. "I thought you would never get around to it."

Lightheaded, Sarah hurriedly began to sort through them. Everything seemed to take on a slightly surreal edge. By the time Lila arrived Sarah had set up the player and the old TV. Don was left outside to watch over the horses.

Sarah threw the whole lot out on the bed before Lila arrived, puffing from the stairs. They began to read the labels.

"What about this? Lake of the Woods Canoe Trip?" Sarah asked.

"That was your honeymoon trip," Lila explained. She'd thought this would be a safe place to start as Angela hadn't been born yet, or even conceived.

They settled down to watch. The camera rarely showed Dave and Sarah together, since one was always recording for the other. Then came a part where someone else at the campsite must have shot them. They were loading the canoe.

Sarah's stomach felt as if she might be sick. She had hazy memories; this must've been where the dream came from. But, there were no children there.

She stopped the video. She said that she wanted to get on to something more important. She didn't want to spend time on less pertinent things.

Ejecting that disc, she sorted through the others.

"Anna's Wedding? That's odd! Why would that make me feel afraid?" Sarah asked. Right now her mind was a total blank. Of course, she must have been there at Dave's sister's wedding.

"Don't watch if it's too hard for you," Lila said, "But there's nothing frightening there. This was a happy time for all of us."

"Okay, I'm going to watch it," Sarah said, as she placed the DVD into the player and picked up the remote. She laid her finger on the off button, just in case.

After a blurry start, there was Dave standing in his best suit in front of a church with a soaring steeple.

"He hated that tie. He moaned all day, until he could get it off," Sarah said as an aside to Lila. She was rewarded with a chuckle.

Dave's sister was beautiful in an antique gown that looked as if had been handed down from generations of loving mothers. Actually, it came from a theater selling off costumes from a play that had closed after the fourth night. Lila added this bit of information.

As the camera moved over the crowd after the ceremony, Sarah looked for herself. Suddenly the screen filled with her face looking down at a baby sitting on her lap.

Sarah screamed, "NO!" and dropped the remote.

Her scream frightened Lila out of her chair, with a sudden movement that couldn't have been good for Lila's heart. Grabbing the remote from where Sarah had dropped it, she punched the OFF button.

Turning to Sarah, who was shaking and crying, she put her arms around her shoulders, and in a soft voice said, "It's all right. It's only a picture. Let's be brave together."

"Oh God, I remember it all. That's Angela at seven months. How could I ever have forgotten her? Remember how good she was that day? Remember the beautiful dress Mom gave her, and she threw up on it just before we went into the church. I had to put her into her old Osh Kosh overalls."

The dam of memory was broken, and the flood of images threatened to overwhelm Sarah. She gasped for breath between sobs and laughter, while Lila hovered around afraid to say anything that might upset her more.

After a while Sarah got control and dashed the tears from her face. She said, "Don't look so worried, Lila. I'm not going out of my mind. It's just the relief. But if you don't mind, I would like to spend some time alone now. Is that alright Lila?"'

Always, when people spoke of being brokenhearted, Sarah had thought it was a figure of speech, but now the pain in her chest felt exactly as if her heart was being torn in two. 'Angela! How could she have forgotten? 'And Dave! What must he have suffered?' She didn't know how she was ever going to be able to face him.

She cringed, remembering how she had acted toward Dave when he'd brought Grace down to Toronto. She had refused to see him and hidden in her room pretending to vomit, and saying she was so sick she couldn't talk to him. She'd made them all so miserable that he'd only stayed two days.

She'd hardly seen the nanny, but now she recalled how lovely Asian women often looked, and Amy fit that description in spades. She'd pictured a nanny as being middle aged and frumpy.

'Oh well,' she'd thought, 'as long as she takes care of that baby, I don't have to . . .'

Now she thought back to that night after Dave left, and the wicked quarrel with her parents. She'd regressed to about sixteen--screaming and swearing, reminding them, **'I am an adult, and I will do whatever I want!'**

Her mother, pale with shock, had stood her ground. "Sarah, if you pull a stunt like this again, there will be consequences! We know you weren't sick, and we know you have been lying to us; doing God knows what, when you are out of the house. Maybe you should be sent to a hospital for mental assessment."

Her father followed that shocking threat by saying a lot of things that he would be sorry for later, "You're totally out of control! You're not even trying to get your life back together. I called Dr. Robinson, and found out that you haven't been in for a month."

'What if they had found out about Denton?' she'd worried? Even if it was over, she'd be ashamed for them to find out. That's what had scared her into agreeing to go to the farm.

Tears wove patterns of regret on her face, as she thought of how she had deceived everyone she loved, and who loved her.

Although Sarah had washed her face and brushed her hair, the signs of her meltdown could still be read by anyone as observant as Lila.

Lila didn't directly refer to Sarah's memory return, but said, "Take your time, Sarah, but if Angela is found, you've got to be ready for whatever comes. We can't let this tear us-- both families I mean, apart. It was just something that happened. Hundreds of people board that bus every year, with never a care. I am convinced, with every bone in my body, that Angela will come home."

"I want to call Dave soon. I was going to call right away, but I thought we should watch some more DVDs to see if it's only a few things I remember-- there are still be gaps yet. I don't remember visiting Jill, or even getting on the bus," Sarah said in a voice devoid of any of the excitement she'd shown earlier.

"Why don't we just leave it then? Don has been hectoring me about not resting enough. I thought I might take tomorrow off and stay in bed. We can watch more then. Don even volunteered to get breakfast. But, if you'd like, watch by yourself. It's up to you. I don't want to put any pressure on you, Dear." Lila went back to stirring the soup.

Sarah sat, staring at her hands, with an odd glance at Lila's back.

"I'll wait for you, Lila. I'm kind of scared of what I'll see. Besides, you're able to fill in the blanks. I'll go out this afternoon and pull some of those weeds in the flower gardens. I think better there than anywhere else."

The next morning, Sarah helped Lila with getting in and out of the bath, and carried up her breakfast tray, then got her settled comfortably in clean sheets.

Sarah went to the other room, where the TV also had a DVD player attached. As she went through the discs again she looked for the ones that seemed the most useful -- ones that contained pictures of Angela leading up to Christmas.

Sarah heard Don climb the stairs, and the clatter of dishes as he carried the tray from Lila's room. He didn't go downstairs again as she expected he would do. He left the tray on the hallway table and knocked on Sarah's door frame.

"I hear you girls are going to watch movies. Need help with the set up?" he asked.

Sarah managed a smile and said, "Yes. Can you move our gadgetry into Lila's room? " She knew he felt left out. He was used to having Lila to himself.

Settled comfortably on the bed beside Lila, Sarah punched the control. There they were in the kitchen, Lila and Don, Dave and Sarah. She remembered Jim, Dave's brother, had been there snapping pictures on his iPhone. When she saw herself stand up on the screen, Sarah was shocked at how pregnant she'd looked.

"Damn! I didn't know I was that huge," she said.

She told Lila that she had remembered, just this morning, that she had been pregnant with Grace when these pictures were taken. The sad thing was that she had no memory of Grace's birth. And now she felt sorry that she had never held Grace, except for those few hours between her first and second coma.

"Do you think that she'll remember, and ever learn to love me?" she asked Lila. She wiped at the tears welling in her eyes.

"You'll be fine my dear. Grace is just a baby. I wouldn't worry. She is completely opposite in temperament to Angela. Where Angela's all movement and chatter, Grace watches the world from the sidelines, and waits for it to come to her."

Chapter 40

That evening Dave got a call from Sarah. He was taken completely by surprise. The moment he heard her tentative, "Hello," a whole series of events ran through his memory-- knocking on her bedroom door-- her refusal to come out to see Grace, or him. That awful pain, and how he'd handled it. There had been a lingering fear that she might ask for a divorce.

After the trip to Toronto, when he was convinced her sudden illness was faked, he had came home in one of the blackest moods he'd endured since she came out of the coma. Since he couldn't help her, he had to let her parents do what they could. It had tipped him over the edge of good sense, with consequences he still hadn't resolved.

Dr. Robinson told him not to give up hope. She was very reluctant to go into details, but said Sarah was resisting therapy: pretending to cooperate, missing appointments and using all the tricks disturbed people use to avoid their pain. She had suggested hypnosis but Sarah absolutely refused to consider it.

But, she also told him not to give up hope, that in cases like this memory might return in a moment; then she qualified that with, 'or maybe never'.

He hadn't accepted the 'never', so now again a tiny flame of hope sprung alive at the sound of her voice. "Is that you Sarah? Where are you? I can hardly hear you."

She was hesitant at first, as if she were unsure of his reaction, but warmed up immediately when he told her how glad he was to hear from her. In the end it was quite simple; she wanted to see him. And would he come and bring Grace? Finally, she wound down and stopped.

He said, "I'll call you back as soon as I've arranged to get away from the clinic". There didn't seem much more to say and after an awkward pause, he rang off.

Dave went straight to Amy, who was on her computer while Grace slept. One look and she came to him. "Is it bad news, my love?" she asked softly.

He could hardly call up coherent thoughts to express his feelings, because they were so jumbled. He had almost given up hope for his marriage, but there were a lot of unanswered questions yet.

Every day he'd set aside time to follow the progress, mostly false leads, in the ongoing search for Angela. Anxiety over what terrors she might be suffering; if she were still alive, ate away at his stomach causing constant pain.

And, there was Amy. How had his organized happy life get to this point? Right this moment he'd like to switch off the world, crawl into a big black hole, and pull the earth in over him.

Four days later, as Dave pulled up at the farm door, it flew open. Lila and Don looked out, then stepped back to make room for Sarah. Don's hand was firmly under Lila's elbow-- maybe to give her support, but more likely to hold her back.

Grace was asleep, and Amy didn't need to be asked to remain in the back seat until the family greeted each other.

Dave's brain felt frozen as his eyes went to Sarah's face. So many feelings churned inside of him-- he didn't know whether to run to her, or to cry.

She looked lovely. Unlike the last time he'd seen her. Her eyes sparkled and her face was alight with pleasure. He felt rooted to the spot, unable to take that first step, dimly aware of his mother and father standing behind her.

Then she lifted her hands, and with a strangled cry, ran into his arms and burst into broken sobs. At the warmth of her body pressed to his, he could only hold her and murmur that he loved her.

Don and Lila both patted their son's back before they went around to the other side of the van to see their new granddaughter, and to welcome Amy.

Over Sarah's shoulder, Dave watched their reaction to Amy. Her plain clothes did not hide her exotic beauty, which wasn't only physical, but held an inner glow, that spoke of caring and wisdom.

He thought his parents handled their surprise well. If a peacock arrived when you expected a dull brown hen, anyone could be thrown off stride for a second or two. They welcomed her warmly and turned to Grace.

When Dave wiped the tears from Sarah's face, he saw her trembling smile. She let go and stepped back so as to turn with him, and walk around the van to the others.

The ice was broken when Don had said, "Come on in. Why are we standing here like a bunch of immigrants just off the boat?"

They all winced, except Amy, while Don still beamed. If looks could kill, the one Lila shot at Don would've struck him dead on the spot.

"What?" he scowled at her. Amy started to giggle and suddenly they all began to laugh.

They were abruptly sobered when Grace woke up with a cry; Sarah instinctively reached for her, and after a glance, so quick only Dave noticed, Amy passed Grace into her mother's arms.

For a moment Grace continued to cry; then, with a hiccough, she stopped. She studied Sarah with big brown eyes. Dave knew she didn't recognize her mother, but she was a baby too young to fear strangers.

Dave watched Sarah hesitate, but Grace herself solved the problem. A toothless grin melted Sarah's heart. She gathered their baby to her shoulder and just looked at Dave as if her heart was broken. She had missed all those first months and she must bitterly regret it.

Leaving Sarah still hugging Grace, Dave gave this mother and father each a hard hug. "It's like a miracle isn't it," he said. "I can't believe she's her old self again. Three weeks ago, when I was in Toronto, her parents were as upset as I've ever seen them. They were at the end of their wits as to how they could help her."

His face sobered, "But we're still no closer to finding Angela."

Lila answered, "Let's take one blessing at a time. We haven't questioned Sarah about the accident. In fact, she doesn't remember getting on the bus-- but I'm sure she will. Since she had the breakthrough, she seems to remember more detail. She told you, didn't she, that she remembered being here with you and Angela at Christmas?"

Don captured Lila as soon as they entered the house and made her sit down. He showed Amy the room that was all set up with a baby bed, and its own bath, down the hall from the rest of the bedrooms

"If you'd like to wash up and rest awhile," Don said to Amy, "we'll take care of Grace until dinner time. Anything you need, you've only to ask. We can't thank you enough for your help to Dave, when we couldn't be there."

"It's no problem. Actually it's fun," she replied. "Grace is easy to love."

Over dinner, the air swirled with good intentions as everyone tried to pretend that this was just a happy family gathering. Grace sat in Angela's high chair.

In spite of the wine and this coming together, Angela was more present at the table than anyone else. It was as if at any second she might dash into the room, full of life and energy, demanding this or that, telling a funny story about the cats, and probably knocking over the milk jug.

After the table was fully cleared and Sarah and Lila had kicked everyone out of the kitchen, Amy took Grace off for her bath. Don took Dave aside and said, "Let's go for a little walk-- get some fresh air."

The sun was just setting as they leaned on the fence of the riding ring. "Are there any new leads?" Don asked. "Christ, she must be somewhere. It can't be easy to dispose of a body in winter and not have it turn up in the spring. There was heavy snow cover in all that area." Don rubbed his face with a rough hand. He suffered every hour from not knowing and not being able to search for Angela himself.

"Last week, Ralph's private detective was following what he thought was a new lead. But it turned out to be a child that the police had found dead on a riverbank. The body was that of a girl, two years older than Angela."

All over again, Dave felt the agony-- mixed with the guilty relief --he'd felt when he'd seen the pictures. Even his frequent contact with death, didn't stop him from being badly shaken, and those feelings were now mirrored in his father's face.

"Don't tell Lila," Don said. He didn't need to explain.

So Dave kept talking about the avenues of search they were pursuing; daycare centers; parks, and anywhere one might see groups of small children. Don shook its head.

"If someone took her, just to have a child, they wouldn't be likely to bring her out in public, not this year anyway. I would try medical clinics; although I know it's hard to get information from them. But surely the police could," Don said, his voice laced with frustration.

"We've thought of that, but no success so far. With every month that passes, identification will become more difficult as she grows and changes." Lila is convinced she's alive," Don said; his face arranging itself into a little smile, as usually happened when he spoke of Lila's premonitions.

"We all want that," Dave said with a frustrated sigh. "The fact that her body hasn't been found is hopeful. We're keeping up the appeals on television. It's very expensive. Ralph has nearly bankrupted himself and I have spent over fifty thousand dollars so far. You know, I finally sold my Ottawa house? The Toronto property will be ready at the end of this month. Luckily, it was fully furnished. Now that Sarah seems better . . ." He choked up and couldn't continue.

"Take it easy, Son, Don said. I think Sarah is ready to move forward, although mind you, there's still lot of gaps in her memory. With patience and some time to think, I'm sure she's going to be all right. Were you aware of the situation in Toronto? I don't know any details, but I've a feeling it's over, whatever she was doing."

"Mary told me that she suspected Sarah was seeing someone," Dave said. "Unhappy people make mistakes all the time. I made that mistake myself after we broke up the first time. It's a sort of insanity; grasping at a new love affair to forget the pain of the old one. Then one day, you wake up and see it for what it is. I almost left medical school over mine."

"I know it won't be easy, but I'm not going to mention it unless she does." Dave rubbed both hands up and down over his face, as if to wash that partial lie away. 'I guess that I didn't learn that first lesson very well,' he thought.

"Your mother really is a witch," Don laughed changing the subject. "You should have seen it. Sarah never stood a chance. Came here determined not to be what we claimed, but Lila pulled out all the stops. We even met her with Lila in the wheelchair looking helpless-- just what would appeal to the Sarah. Once she let herself remember a little bit, the memories came flooding back. We had better go in or the women will come looking for us." He clapped Dave on the shoulder and led the way toward the house.

Later, over dessert and coffee, Lila turned to Dave. "Tell us about your new house."

"Actually, I chose it," Sarah said. When Lila gave her a, 'Really?' face, she laughed, and changed the subject, to tell them about how Mary had dragged her around house hunting. When she had griped about absolutely hating this house, Mary figured it must be the one her daughter liked best. She'd found fault of the fenced backyard, saying it was a house for people with kids, and clinched her rejection with, "Dave might like it, but that has nothing to do with me."

The laughter was ragged and soon over.

Dave could feel tears pushing at the back of his nose. It had been so long since he'd heard Sarah laugh. In a way, it was a mercy that she was spared those first terrifying days, when he had expected to get news of Angela's death every time the phone rang or he saw a police officer.

The dishes were stacked in the dishwasher and they moved to the living room-- except for Amy, who waited as Grace was kissed good night by all, then she took her upstairs.

After the family news was all hashed over the conversation lagged. There was an unspoken agreement not to speculate about Angela's disappearance. Dave and his parents knew Sarah's pain was still raw, while time had dulled theirs, if only a small amount.

Around ten, Don said to Lila, "You're tired, my dear. Let's off to bed."

"I usually like awhile in my garden in the evenings, but I think I will pass tonight. Goodnight," Lila said to Dave and Sarah.

While they were in the living room, Amy had come down stairs, and had gone outside to walk in the garden, and had yet to come in.

Dave and Sarah went upstairs to see Grace. She was sleeping, curled on her side with one tiny hand beneath her cheek.

"Look, she sleeps just like you," Dave said, as he took Sarah's hand. She didn't pull away but laid her head on his shoulder for a moment. They stood watching Grace breathe, but their sweet Angela crawled into their thoughts like a jealous little ghost, blunting their pleasure in Grace.

"Dave's got you to thank for this, Lila," Don said, snuggling up to his wife's back with his arm comfortably over her waist. He chuckled, and it reminded her of the wonderful times they'd spent together when they were Dave and Sarah's age.

"Not really. It was Anna. I was feeling so useless that I jumped at the chance to do something," she said. She'd ignored his first remark and the second.

The next morning, as Sarah and Lila sat on the porch, Sarah said, "I want to go home, to move into the new house and start to help with the search. I can walk streets in different districts, and I'll be less noticeable around parks and playgrounds than a man would be. I know the city, and I'd be doing something useful. To think I've wasted so much time!"

Dave had been standing just inside the screen door, waiting for a moment to interrupt their conversation. He stepped out now and said to Lila, "I'm going to take some time off too, before I join the new clinic. I've had a couple of offers to start work, but now with Sarah's help, we can really scour the city."

Sarah had a hard time making eye contact with Dave. They had agreed to not tell anyone about last night, but this morning, she suspected that Amy knew.

Chapter 41

Jenna

I had to break off my story back when that hullabaloo went on with Jo and her family. It's fierce on the poor girl but I was glad for me. I knew she would come to me.

I never was or tried to be good. Look after number one-- that's me. I don't love easy but when I do it's fierce.

The week before Jo was worried about the paycheck. Her father had been drinking up every penny he could get its hands on and it might be the last paycheck ever if he lost his job. She told me one night if that happened he would make her to quit school so her mother could go to work. Jo swore she wouldn't but in the end she would have to.

I never thought I would see the day I'd say a good word about the police but that woman Bertha was worth a dozen men tramping around giving orders. She sorted the kids and helped find places for them. Gillian– Jo's sister the makings of a real bitch if I ever saw one. And that brother Alex sulking along trying to look innocent— he ran with a gang last year so I'll bet they won't be able to control him for long. Bertha came back and told us every one was settled at least until Jo's mother got better.

I had to make a lot sad faces but now Jo would live with me. I never had a daughter, or knew I wanted one. I dared to think she would be happy too after the shock of finding her mother near dead wore off. Angela was wild with excitement when Jo moved in.

Jo wanted her single bed from the apartment. It was sealed with police tape but Jo had the key to the back door. We took the bed apart and smuggled it up to my place and set it up in Angela's room.

We hardly finished and set Angela to drawing a picture of Beau when Bertha called. She asked me to tell Jo that she could go to the hospital to see her mother.

I tried to keep Jo home. It was getting late. I told her she could go tomorrow but she wouldn't hear of it. She said she had to know.

Before she ran out with never a thought I said you be careful. Have you any money? Hang on my purse is right here—here's enough for a cab. I shoved the money into her pocket. Jo had no idea how pretty she was and today was payday for a lot of the men on this street and they would be staggering in and out of the bars.

After she left I sat down with a cup of tea. In spite of doing as little cleaning as I could get away with I was bone tired all the time. I had to make myself do Angela's bath—not easy because she had a tantrum when she heard Jo was gone and fought me every step.

The doctor at the clinic told me I might be able to work another month. I would have to go on welfare when I quit. I knew I wasn't right but I never thought of cancer.

The day I heard I put my head down on the kitchen table too tired to cry. In my mind the words I knew it-- I knew it ran over and over. I knew my sins would catch me up. From now on I was living on borrowed time. I thought of praying but how stupid. If God had ever loved me he forgot it long ago.

I'd worried about other things like getting caught and going to prison but dying so soon never entered my mind. I had hardly been sick a day in my life. Like a big black shadow trying to swallow me I tried not think about Jo and Angela and how they might get stuck with a life like mine.

Jo came back late and went straight to bed. I slept poor and got up early. She was still sleeping her shiny black hair spread across the pillow. Dark circles like bruises blackened the skin around her eyes. I'd forgot how young she was until I saw her asleep.

I turned and left the room. I couldn't tell her I had cancer not now. I decided I'll sign the papers to foster her and wait-and-see. Maybe I could hang on longer than they think. Someday I will have to tell her about Angela but we can have a bit of time yet. My breakfast tea was gone when Jo staggered into the kitchen. Her eyes were puffy from crying. Before I could get my mind in gear to say what I should she began to talk.

"Mom died before I got to the hospital. It was a heart attack but he had hit her. Her face was all black and blue. He's going to get away with it. He killed her even if he didn't beat her to death! I never want to see him as long as I live!"

Her hands wrung one over the other as she cried. I made hot chocolate and when she drunk it I got her into the shower. I told her she could have my bed to rest. I would close the door so Angela couldn't bother her.

But I have to work today, she said.

I'll talk to them. Don't you worry they will understand and you can go tomorrow. I'm not feeling too bad. I'll take care of Angela this morning and maybe this afternoon you can take her out so I can rest. I said as I tucked her into my bed.

Angela was bored and acting up by the time Jo came out. She gave me a sickly smile and turned her attention to Angela who was grabbing at her clothes asking questions one after the other without waiting for answers. We coaxed her to lunch by saying that Jo couldn't take her out if she hadn't had anything to eat and she wouldn't eat alone. That got Angela to the table like a shot.

A long walk along the lakeshore and Angela was ready for bed by the time it was dark. We settled into the kitchen for a good long talk about Jo living with us. It was going to be a great help to have Angela at the daycare.

Besides it paid Jo a small salary which she could save for her last year of high school.

We heard the outer door downstairs slam and someone clomping up the stairs. We sat still scared. Trouble was on the way. Great bangs shook our door and we could see it jumping on its hinges.

Oh my God, its Dad Jo whispered. Her face turned ash gray and she seemed stuck in place until Angela screamed and Jo ran to pick her up and hold her tight. In my ratty old housecoat, with my rolling pin the only weapon I had went to the door as fast as I could. The chain was on and that was saving us.

He was a sight to scare the devil as he pushed his face into the crack around the chain. He hadn't shaved in days and his crazy face was red and wet with sweat. The garbage that flowed from its mouth was curses and yells that HE had the short end of the stick here.

Where's my girl? She better get home if she knows what's good for her he roared. He backed off to kick the door and I was able to slam it shut and turn the lock.

I stood beside the door holding my rolling pin over my head. Every kick shook the door. He was big and even drunk we'd be no match for him if he broke in.

I'm calling the police. I'm not going back there to wind up like Mom Jo yelled through the door. Wasn't killing Mom enough for you? I'll see you fry in hell before spending another minute near you.

Silence followed Jo's screams. I pulled Angela off Jo. She was too scared to do anything but hide her face and hang on.

Jo turned to me with a look of disgust that I had never seen on her face. Now he'll blubber and say how sorry he is Jo sneered in a voice loud enough to be heard through the door. Maybe he could fool Mom with that garbage but not me never again. I'm calling the police right now.

Angela lifted her face from where it was buried in my neck and asked is that the wolf? Is he found us?

All I could keep saying was no it's not the wolf' but I was as scared as she was. It wasn't only Jo's father— this was bringing the police close to us again. I knew there had to be posters of Angela all over the city and it only took one sharp eye to put the two puzzle pieces together—the missing kid with a woman on the bus. Someone was bound to have seen me climb the police ladder.

I should never have gone on using her real name. What was I thinking? God Damn my careless brain I thought. I only grabbed the moment and had never thought I couldn't keep Angela hidden.

Minutes after Jo phoned a squad car pulled up to the building and a team of police raced up the stairs. We heard Arthur muttering but the fight had gone out of him. I unlocked the door when they knocked. I heard Jo sob when saw her father handcuffed. He wasn't scary any more--he looked a sad old man.

I used the need of seeing to Angela to get her and me
out of sight as a policeman and a woman came in. Jo took
them to the living room to give her statement. I heard her
tell them that I had nothing to do with it but was a friend
who'd taken her in.

Will he be charged with murder? Jo asked. They spent a
few minutes explaining how the law worked. She didn't like
it but she signed the statement they asked for. Then they
told her she as was a minor so I would have to sign as well.

She came in to stay with Angela and I went out. They
asked me a few questions about the family but I told them
I had only moved in a few months ago and employed Jo as
my baby sitter for my grandchild. They had no way to know
how near to fainting I was. Somehow I held on and didn't
let them see my fear.

The next day they were there again. They were less
sharp and told Jo she was to call the minute she saw her
father anywhere near. He was out under a restraining order
after a night in jail. He promised to stay sober and not seek
go near any family member. Their words not mine.

Jo snorted at that piece of garbage. He can't make me
go back to live with him can he Jo asked me. If it hadn't
been a question we both dreaded, we would have burst out
laughing at the idea of him paying attention to a restraining
order about drinking and if he drank he would be back
after Jo.

We knew he would let the younger children go. After all
it would save feeding them but he was going to fight tooth
and nail against me for her.

Jo said I've been scared of him for years. He never hit
me but lately when he was drunk all slobbery with self–
pity he'd ask to help him do something. Somehow he would
work around to rub himself against me. Mum slapped me
when I tried to tell her."

If he got her back the child- care might send the other children home and she would be stuck with them until she was as worn down and as hopeless as her mother.

She said, I'll run away first—the streets would be better—at least I'd be paid there!

I was scared too. With social services snooping around it would only be a matter of time before they found out how sick I was. Or God forbid find out who I really was and what I had done. Even if they didn't know who Angela was, they'd be taking her away and putting her in some foster home. Much better she should go back to her people. The mother might be dead but there would be a father and grandparents.

This was the first time the thought of returning Angela ever entered my head.

After Jo had dragged herself away to bed I sat alone at the kitchen table. I couldn't seem to settle. Half plans-- maybe would work ran over in my head. But sitting there in the dark I gave up the idea of sleep and just let my mind take its own path.

I worried about what this was going to do to Angela. Not just this last but all the dirt this part of town could throw up— what if I got really sick.

I expected the fright she got with Arthur banging on the door to turn up trouble-- tantrums and crying spells. She hadn't asked about her mother since her birthday party but I knew she never forgot her. The pictures of women she coloured– they all had blonde hair.

After scaring myself into a black hole I began to think of the summer if it turned out Jo got to live with me. Maybe I should give up the cleaning and take in sewing. I no sooner thought it than I decided that's what I'd do.

I made over clothes for Jo. She had a good eye at the secondhand stores. She'd tell me how the girls at school always wanted something like she wore. It wouldn't bring in much but it was something I could do while Angela and Jo were at the daycare.

A few days after in the judge's chambers— I had to take Angela— we heard what would happen to Jo's family. Arthur sat behind a Children's Aid worker a sick sight. His dirty clothes smelled rotten. He was sober though. You could see him putting on the poor me act with his black eye brimming wet above his drunks nose. When the judge asked him if he could keep the peace he started to mumble about his rights but she shut him up with a snap about it being his doing and he had no rights other than what she gave him.

In the end the judge sent Tammy and Kathy to a foster home and Gillian and Alex to a youth home. Arthur had to stay away from Jo's place here with me.

Jo grabbed me and we held hands. I'm never going to be able to prove he murdered Mom Jo said. But now all I want is him to stay away.

Chapter 42

Sarah

When Dave and I came to the new house together, it was without furniture. I had seen it earlier with Mom but had deliberately paid little attention to the flow between rooms, the dark wood floors and a layout that makes any house easy to live in. The rooms seemed larger without furniture, but we were both pleased with its solid construction. A small apartment, overlooking the ravine had been added. It was perfect for Amy and Grace; separate but still close, with a tiny kitchen, sitting room and two small bed rooms.

We stayed with Mom and Dad for a week while we installed our new furniture. Dave had sold all our old stuff with the house in Ottawa. I was so anxious to start looking for Angela that we moved to the new house as soon as we could.

I'm afraid I never considered how Dave felt. He'd loved that country place.

We furnished a new room for Angela. It was an act of faith on both our parts. Amy moved into the nanny suite with Grace. She created beautiful Korean style paintings on rice paper. Because Amy's room was small, we gave her space in the loft area in the attic. One whole end wall was a great window. The previous owner had had some kind of studio there.

"I could never afford such a place on my own," she whispered. In return she offered to look after Grace in set hours over specified days and nights.

We spent as much time as we could with Grace. I prayed she wouldn't carry the inner knowledge that, for a time, I had rejected her. Even as I began to love her, the love was tainted by Angela's absence and my guilt. I was still plagued by nightmares. I spent hours awake at night trying to sort memories from dreams.

We decided that in the daytime we would each pursue a different path. Dave consulted with police and doctors that might have seen Angela as a patient. We couldn't imagine that Angela wouldn't attract notice. Her bright smile and chatter had always drawn attention.

I scoured the city, walking through parks, watching mothers and children, and especially grandmothers with their grand kids. From one of the few leads, the RCMP thought the woman who took her must've been an older woman. All the young women on the bus were accounted for soon after the accident.

Even Dr. Robinson felt that I was wasting my time wandering the city, but I couldn't stop. I had started to see 'my psych-doc' on a regular basis, twice a week, soon after we moved into our house. She was helping me grasp the idea, that in wanting to see my friend Jill, I was not being irresponsible and foolish. She said, "Our modern life has taught us to think that we control our lives, but not so. In every life there comes a day when we must accept that there are things we can't change."

I saw many little blonde girls, and my heart caught at every one, but it was never Angela. Only once, I got the feeling that Angela was near. I had gone down to the lake harbor where the ferry to the islands docks. The ferry was loading when I showed up, and there where dozens of children-- some in their parents' arms, others being dragged back into line but there were always a few getting loose and racing around.

I thought I heard Angela's voice. Desperate to see the kid I'd heard, I ran back and forth along the line but she wasn't there. I watched everybody that got on the ferry. I caught a glimpse of one little girl with bright blue eyes and a face that might have been the same shape as Angela's, but her hair, under a big floppy hat, was dark brown. She was with a dark- haired teenager.

Before I could fight my way through the crowd to get a closer look, they'd disappeared. I called out her name but there was too much noise. I got trapped behind a man the size of a mountain. It's unlikely that I could have been heard through the crush of people. Half of them were talking loudly, trying to make themselves heard to a friend two feet away.

That was a low point in my search. I was beginning to lose hope.

I never did tell how it ended--that crazy affair with Dalton. It was a kind of reckless behavior that I remember now with cringing regret. Like a lot of foolishness, it came to a bad end. Maybe it wasn't so bad-- the end, I mean. That's the only part of it I can remember and laugh.

Because of the long trip into the city, and how hard it was to get away at night, we often met at lunchtime. One morning I woke up and felt as if my skin was on fire--a fire that only seeing Denton could quench. That's how far gone I was.

I hadn't used my fake appointments with Dr. Robinson for a while, so got away from home without the usual inquisitor's hassle. My alternate clothes were stuffed in a large purse that I'd taken to carrying everywhere. The subway train had barely stopped when I pushed my way out, cell in hand, onto the street.

Denton answered at the first ring, and seemed surprised that I was downtown and hadn't made arrangements beforehand. However, his hesitation lasted only for a second. "I am at the law office but will make some excuse--- a long client lunch or something. Wait for me in the lobby downstairs." His voice, laced with sexual overtones stirred a pot of memories. I clutched the phone and had to lean on a wall to keep my legs under me. I wanted to talk, but he said he had to go and hung up. Was he with a woman? But no, I'd heard another man talking in the background.

I looked around the lobby but couldn't see a ladies room. 'I've got to find a place to change,' I thought. 'I'll go on up to his floor-- there's sure to be one there.'

Minutes later, I found the ladies room. I changed into my short lavender dress with a pale yellow sweater draped over my shoulders. In my high-heeled sandals I felt sophisticated and daring. I went to the mirror to check my makeup. It was alright but was this outfit a bit--? I didn't want to think 'sluttish'--Denton would love taking it off, but now I wasn't sure it was the right choice. There was an instant when I wondered if this was a foolish thing I was doing, but I had come this far, and this was no time to chicken out.

The door, its brass plate gleaming, gave me pause. It shouted, 'Business, serious business done here.' My hand hesitated before pushing down the brass handle. This action literally seemed detached from my brain. I walked in but left the door open; probably for the first time in its existence--- maybe I was leaving an escape hatch.

I saw that the receptionist had already left for lunch. Her desk was cleared and her chair pushed in, so tidy, so uptight; not Denton's style at all. Everything was so posh that I suddenly felt a premonition -- how would this intrusion seem to anyone's business sense; Denton's father's for instance.

Denton had always made the rules for our meetings, and now I was breaking a really huge one by appearing at his work place.

The reception room was beautifully furnished with a leather couch and three matching chairs. On a glass and steel coffee table, a crystal vase filled with red and white roses, sent some kind of message. I didn't have time to think what exactly. A gorgeous antique rug, not from any village souq, but from rug makers of exquisite taste-- covered most of the dark wooden floor.

My mind was skittering all over the place.

It struck me that Denton wasn't short on funds these days. At law school, he used to live in a rat hole of a place, and constantly complained how his father hardly gave him enough to live on.

I could hear voices from behind a door that might have graced Eden-- it was so beautifully carved in arabesques of vines and leaves. A fleeting thought, as I pictured the Denton I knew. He'd never come from anywhere near Eden!

At first the voices were muffled and I couldn't make out the words. Then the handle unlatched and the door opened a sliver, no further, as if the person inside had hesitated and turned back. That's when I realized it was Denton, talking with his father, and they were talking about me. My first impulse was to say something, but a second later a herd of wild horses couldn't have pulled me away from eavesdropping.

"Listen to me, Son. You have to stop seeing that woman. I'll not have it! Sooner or later someone is bound to tell Miriam. I thought you wanted this marriage. What in hell are you playing at? The arrangements are all made."

"Calm down, Dad. Remember your blood pressure," Denton drawled in that butter smooth voice that always curled my toes. "It's just a little last-minute bachelor fling. She's one terrific lay. Miriam isn't exactly a sex kitten, you know. Besides, even if Miriam does hear, she knows our family, and that I'd never bring a woman like Sarah into it." He chuckled before continuing. "She's a pretty trophy to sport around town, but the makings of a Jewish wife? She's not!"

With that last piece of wisdom, he opened the door.

I went so fast from, 'I can't believe my ears', to red-hot rage it's a wonder I didn't go up in flames. "You, you son of a bitch!" I shrieked. They had to have heard me at street level.

Denton was struck dumb, practically in mid step. His father ran into him and staggered back to catch his balance.

I remember that my hands fit perfectly around the vase with its fluted shape. I raised it over my head and hurled it in their direction. With a satisfying crash, it burst like a bomb against the doorframe. Broken glass, water and mangled flowers sprayed over the two men, and most of the reception area.

I don't know whether I was so angry with Denton for his remarks about me, or his disrespect toward his innocent fiancée, Miriam-- a woman whose existence was news to me!

All at once, my anger fled, and in its place was hard cold reality. I had looked and acted like the crazy woman I'd become. The nearly transparent dress was now clinging to my body from all the water splashed about when I lifted the vase. My hair hung in rat tails around my face. I not only looked like a hooker, I felt like one.

I swung around so quickly that a high heel on one of the sandals I'd bought to look beautiful for Denton, snapped off.

Trying to leave now with any dignity was beyond possible. I tore the sandals from my feet and flung them at Denton's head. He neatly ducked the first -- the other hit his father in the chest.

The Jewish curse-- or maybe an Anglo-Saxon blasphemy—I didn't hang around to ask-- that burst from his mouth, made me want to cackle like a lunatic. But, the final humiliation was Denton's ringing laugh that followed me, as I ran barefoot out the door.

As soon as I was sure I was out of their sight, I raced to the washroom and changed back into the flats, jeans and T shirt that I'd worn on the subway. I thanked my lucky stars that the bag hadn't been stolen while I was making a fool of myself.

By the time my hair was dried under the hand dryer, a backbreaking process, I had calmed down. As I looked into the mirror, I began to giggle. I played the ridiculous scene over in my mind-- me the crazy, with Denton and his father smuggly righteous about their family and its long traditions.

My one time lover's outraged face!--I wished I had a picture. But Denton had managed to look debonair, even dripping wet: one red rose hanging from his hair and another like a badly placed boutonnière: on the fly of his pants.

Afterward, I was of two minds. One part is glad when all the pleasurable things that are bad for you are taken away; another still longs for their return.

There would be no return for me and Denton.

Chapter 43

Sarah

Soon after the break up with Denton, Dave came from Ottawa bringing Grace and her nanny, Amy Chow. I took to my room and only heard Amy's voice from a distance. I'd never actually seen her, but I knew she was from Korea.

It was time to go back to Dr. Robinson and take her therapy seriously, but there was still a black hole that I was afraid to look into. Grace's every cry pierced my head like a needle. Playing sick was no fun and I made a miraculous recovery. God, I was hungry when they left. The night raids on the fridge hadn't replaced Mom's three generous offerings per day.

Then the call from Lila came. I didn't want go because I knew she would mount a full-scale attack to make me remember the lost time. But, I just couldn't think of a good excuse without looking meaner than I had been brought up to be.

That trick with Lila's wheelchair didn't fool me for one minute, but I wanted to see how far she would take it. If she was really sick, she'd continue using it, but if it was just a ploy, she'd never be able to carry it off.

Somewhere in the middle of standing there watching her helpless act, I realized I knew her. Not remembered her from years ago, but recently.

The month there helped heal me. Not only did I remember a lot from the missing years, but there wasn't a remnant of feeling for Denton left.

It's hard to remember all the emotions that tore through me when Dave stepped out of the SUV. I know there was fear and amazement that I could have forgotten how much I loved him. He looked tired and sad and older than I remembered.

His eyes fastened on mine, but I couldn't read the expression on his face. I felt nailed to the ground waiting for him to take the first step. He glanced back to where the nanny was busy with Grace, but it was a mere flick of his eyes before his gaze returned to me. He said, with a ghost of a smile, "Well Sarah?"

"Dave," I replied with a tremor I couldn't control and went into his arms. Although his body felt as solid and warm as ever, I detected a slight holding back. I dismissed it, thinking, 'He's just shy in front of Don and Lila. There is no way he could have heard about Denton.'

Throughout the dinner, Amy and Grace were at the table; Lila had insisted. Throughout the meal, he talked about the search for Angela and answered a deluge of questions from his parents.

While listening to Dave, I became aware of Amy's exotic beauty. I saw her as a woman, not that generic being: 'the nanny'. Her skin was satin smooth. Her eyes were larger than usual for an Asian woman. They lifted her from pretty to beautiful. Her hair, piled up in a knot, gave the impression that it might spring loose at any moment, and pour down her back in a gleaming black waterfall.

There was something about her, as if she concealed an inner secret. When she caught me looking at her, a ghost of a smile pulled at her full lips before she cast her eyes down.

I had thought that Dave and I would fall into each other's arms after we talked. I could apologize for my behavior and tell him how I now remember our life together.

We were hardly in the bedroom when he said, "I need a shower," and disappeared into the bathroom.

He was gone so long that I got cold, standing around naked, and put on my pajamas and crawled into bed. When he came back, he'd put on fresh boxers and a white T shirt; his usual sleeping garb.

After he got settled, I pretended to wake up and slid my hand across to caress his shoulder. Slowly he rolled back and turned onto his side facing me.

"Sarah, I'm not able to do this now. The stress these last months has killed my sex drive."

I knew he had more to say, but I was too shocked to wait, and jumped in, saying, "With anyone, or just with me?"

"Sarah, can we just leave it? I love you and always will, but until we find Angela . . ." He turned over, leaving a cold bare patch of white sheet between us.

I was opening my mouth to argue, but remembered my affair. Dave had taken one road and I had taken another. "Will you hold me at least," I whispered.

He stretched out an arm and I settled in beside him. It felt like coming home. We lay for a long time, talking about how we had met, and how we had parted those years ago, thinking it was goodbye.

I was travelling alone on the ferry to Vancouver Island. I saw a good looking young guy leaning over the rail, watching something in the water beside the ferry. I strolled over to see what was holding his attention.

"Come look," he gestured. When I came to his side and looked over, I caught sight of an Orca whale riding the bow wave. I grabbed Dave's arm, awestruck, and turned my face to his. I saw wonder there that I knew was mirrored in mine.

After that, we just naturally hung out together. We exchanged names within seconds, and learned that we were both bound for the beaches of Tofino. We spent a magical night on Long Beach lying amid huge grey driftwood logs-- stars overhead, waves breaking on the beach. It was as close to heaven as we would ever get in this world. We spent every moment together, horizontal if possible, before it was time to go. We'd fallen in love with the rainforest, mountains, sea and each other, before we took the ferry back to the mainland a week later. We parted-- he to go to medical school in Ottawa, and I to law school in Toronto.

Between our studies and long-distance love, we began to lose some of the closeness we'd felt on the island. Still we wrote letters and got together every few weeks. We were both busy, but so in love; I thought we would never want anyone else.

The next year, Dave met someone, and when he told me, I threw myself into a relationship with another Law student to wash away the pain of his rejection. It didn't last. I couldn't forget Dave, although I had to accept that I had lost him. I turned to my studies. Although I went out with other students, Denton being one of them, we were friends, and that was all.

Nearly three years later, one rainy morning while I was leaving my small apartment, I nearly fell headlong over a bearded figure sitting in the dark hallway.

'Damn bums! They're moving off the streets into respectable buildings now,' I thought as I scrambled after my books that had skittered down the hall.

"I was waiting for you," Dave's voice struck me dumb. I seemed to be standing on a precipice, my heart beating double time, unsure of which way to jump. My body made the decision for me, and I flung myself into his arms. The bushy black beard was scratchy against my face, but the sweet familiarity of his smell and the way our bodies fit together made me want him, as if we'd been together yesterday. In an instant, my class was forgotten.

Back in the apartment, he told me how he'd gone to Cuba as a doctor in training. I could feel it had done something to him. The guy I had loved had changed into a man who knew who he was, and what he wanted, and he said he wanted me; if I would have him back.

Chapter 44

Jenna

After the court hearing me and Jo tried to keep things in the apartment as quiet as we could. Any step on the stairs and we stopped whatever we were doing praying it wasn't Jo's father. It didn't take much to set Angela off. She had nightmares and wouldn't go to sleep without her bunny light on. Nearly every day she asked if the monster was coming back. At bedtime she hung on to me asking if a bad man was going to come for Jo. I worried that it was going to take a lot longer for her to get over her scare than we thought.

It was good they had the daycare. Jo said that Angela seemed happy there. She was playing good with the other kids. I was awful glad Jo was with her. Our biggest worry was that they might meet Arthur on the street and he would go for Jo and scare Angela half to death.

As the days went by and we didn't see or hear anything about him we began to be a little easier in our minds. At the end of that first month the landlord sent people to clean and get rid of everything in the downstairs apartment. Jo had no idea where her father was living and didn't want to know.

She said to me he's probably shacked up with some of those old hookers who hang around the corner bar. I'm awful sorry Mom's dead but she's better off than living with him she said.

I felt bad that such a young girl was so bitter but then thought of how I was at that time. But a few days after she said I'm not going to let him keep me down, Jenna. I'm going look after you and Angela and go to school and make something of myself.

Jo took to the job with the day care as if it was the best job in the world. She didn't have the training to be much else but a helper but she soon found ways to be a real part of the team.

Angela was always saying Jo did this Jo did that. I could believe it because she was so smart at drawing and the puppets she made here at home each one talked different. She never forgot what voice went with who.

The other day I heard one voice say, gitcher big feet offen me. Jo said the puppet was mad because Beau stepped on him.

Angela giggled and said He never.

I quit work. The money from Children's Aid for fostering Jo helped us get by. It was a relief not to have to spend my days dreading to go to work every night. It got so that I could hardly drag that vacuum from room to room let alone up them stairs. I could rest in the mornings and do a little housework and shopping whenever I had enough energy I worked on fixing the secondhand clothes Joe got at the market on Sundays. There was a woman there that sold them for us when I got enough done over.

I haven't got a long time to live but if only the good Lord gives me this summer I kept thinking.

It was about this time that I got my old rosary out. For a long time I made believe I didn't know where it was or care but now all I needed was some time to set things right for Jo and Angela.

We got some word of Jo's sisters. Tammy and Kathy was happy with their new family. The day Jo was allowed to visit them they barely took time to say hello. She told me about the toys and the new dresses.

She said I hardly knew them. They were clean all over and didn't fight but played nice and quiet. Can you believe miracles do happen.

I asked her if she wished she had been adopted. No way had she said. I look after myself. Someday I am going to medical school you know.

I believe her.

Gillian was another matter. She had run away from the group home and tried making money on the street but was caught. They tried another place where she seemed better but Jo didn't give it much hope. Gillian's a born streetwalker--she's been practicing since she was six years old. The best thing they could do is teach her to protect herself and let her go but I guess they can't do that. She was trying to sound mean but I knew she cried in the night.

Alex disappeared. Jo gave him even less chance than Gillian. She said they might find him in Vancouver or Ottawa living on the street or in jail.

I felt bad to hear her putting down her brother and sister because I knew it was her anger talking. The one thing it did for me-- it made me realize that if I couldn't get Angela back to her family this would be what waited her. My poor little one passed around, cared for by people who only did it for money. I had to tell Jo. She had to know what to do if I died in my sleep before we got everything done.

But then I thought I've been feeling better lately. The rest is doing me good. We might even make it to Christmas.

I even let myself have a daydream of how we would have a little tree and act like a real family.

Jo's birthday was in the middle of August. As soon as she told us Angela started to dance around singing have a party! Have a party! Of course we had to do it.

Jo ran out to get some balloons and a toy or two for Angela. Angela and I made the cake. The sight of her standing on a kitchen chair with egg yolk and flour all over the floor and table and a big smile on her face was worth all the extra work. We hung blue streamers all around the kitchen and the meatloaf came out good. We even had ice-cream with the cake.

Beau wore a bib around his neck and sat in the old high chair that Angela didn't need any more. We sang fool songs and played hide and seek. That night Angela didn't look in the closet before she got into bed.

Jo read her favorite story about the little kitten that was lost and then found. That story always put her off. When she couldn't keep her eyes open she drifted off with one hand hanging over the side of the bed to touch Beau curled up in his box.

Jo headed for the kitchen to wash dishes but I called her from the living room. Come sit down. The dishes will wait.

Jo sat on the edge of her chair looking at me. Those days she seemed to shrink into herself-- worried all the time that the next time anyones mouth opened it would be bad news. She hunched her shoulders as if she might be hit.

I was never any good at talking about love-- any kind of love but lying in bed the night before I'd practiced what I wanted to say. But when it came to saying the words out loud I stumbled around before I could get started.

You know I-- la-la- love you like a daughter Jo and I think I know how you feel about me but there are things you don't know. I did a terrible thing.

I don't care what you've done! Jo sat up straight ready
fight for me. Then she said it's about Angela isn't it.

It is. I took her from a bus I was on--that bus that crashed
near Kingston last Christmas." I said this so fast it took a
second for her to understand.

Jo clapped her hands over her mouth. I had no idea what
she was thinking. That picture in the paper the one about
the little girl that I said looked like Angela. Remember
you said she was younger than Angela and blonde and you
didn't see it. It really was her wasn't it? That's why you
won't let me wash her hair. What do you put in it?

I thought she would be upset but she jumped up and fell
on her knees in front of my chair. She wanted all the details.

It's the same dye I use on my hair. And I told her some
of the story of the bus crash and how we got away. Stealing
someone's child was the farthest thing from my mind until
then. It was like somebody else took over and told me what
to do. I thought that God was answering my prayers and
giving me back Julie but I don't believe that anymore. It was
like lifting a stone off my chest to tell someone.

Jo wasn't surprised. You do what you have to do was
her take on life. Her mother had sometimes had to steal
food but Jo always ate it. There was only one worry getting
caught.

The scared girl twisting her hands was gone for now at
least. In her place was bright eyed Jo the bad girl ready to
talk. She told me that she'd felt something wasn't right but
never dared ask questions. In her family asking questions
got you a clip up the side of the head her father's cure for
sticking your nose in his business.

Then her face changed again. What are we going to do?
They must be looking for her. Should she be going to the
daycare?

What's that word for when the bad things you do catch up with you payback fate or something. Whatever it is that's what I felt was coming down the road. Maybe that's what the cancer was.

We'll hope for the best for the rest of the summer I told her. If your father stays away we'll be all right. I was so scared when the police were here. I don't think I could stand that again. When you go back to school we'll decide then. I hate her growing up here. It's dirty the air's bad and she's getting older and will soon start to notice things.

You mean my father the criminal don't you? I don't blame you. She was quiet a time. I could almost see the wheels turning in her head. Oh no you're going to send her back. Please don't. We can look after her. Tears started down her face and she squeezed my hands so hard they hurt.

She doesn't belong here Jo. Your father made me see that. Let's leave it for now. I've been feeling better so let's get out and do some things. I was thinking as I talked. I've always wanted to take that ferry boat to the islands. What say we do that?"

I told her I decided to let Angela's hair grow out. We'll make sure she has a hat on until the blonde gets long enough to cut off the brown. Tell them at the daycare that she got into my hair dye and we are letting it grow out.

Jo smiled. I'll buy her a pair of those kid's sunglasses. They'll help against anyone looking for her. We could dress her as a boy but she wouldn't put up with that would she. I had to agree. I could just hear Angela telling everyone within half a mile that she was really a girl.

The next morning when they was gone I dug out the purse I taken from the bus. I found a small notebook with addresses and phone numbers.

I found what I wanted. The grandparent was my best bet but how was I going to do it? You can't just call up to someone and say I'm dying and I want to give you your kid back. But I can't think of anything else.

Jo's going to have a fit.

Chapter 45

Dave wheeled his new Honda into the driveway. He'd felt it was ridiculous to drive a big van in the city. The motor purred so softly that he was hardly aware of it. Now, on turning off the key, the silence of this suburb surprised him all over again. He'd loved the deep silence of the woods on their country property, but had given it up for Sarah's sake. Here, if you listened hard, you could hear the subdued murmur of the city, but the mature trees around the house, and the fact that a wide ravine ran down one side and across the back gave the illusion of forest. It had cost him a fortune, but he'd got a good price for the Ottawa property.

The effort of getting out of the car, going into the house, and acting normal with Sarah, suddenly felt impossible. Sarah had told him about her affair with Denton on the second night as they shared their new bed in this house. Touching Sarah seemed impossible to avoid; his treacherous body wanted her, although he was far from over desiring Amy. The next night he moved into another room.

That problem, of making the final break with Amy, whose help they still needed--he couldn't do it until he'd told Sarah, and yet he couldn't tell her before he made the break. Thinking about it made his head ache.

He was trying to be forgiving, but flickers across his mind of Sara with Denton, still made his blood boil. When he had met Denton a few years ago, they had disliked each other at first sight. They knew nothing about each other, and neither had any claim on Sarah then, but every word out of Denton's mouth had grated on him.

Secretly, he suspected that Denton had lured Sarah into an affair, knowing full well that she was his; Dave's wife.

A tap on the window jerked him back to the present. Sarah was bent over, smiling at him. She stepped back while he got out 0f the car, and with a hand on his shoulder, gave him a quick kiss on the cheek, pressing her body against his arm and shoulder in a way that he had loved ever since they had met.

"Where have you been?" he asked, then cursed himself as he watched her face shift, as if a shadow moved across it. 'Damn,' he thought, that didn't come out right. In spite of all their efforts, the affair haunted their most common exchange. It was as if they tiptoed across a glass bridge; each trying to prove that they trusted the other again.

"I went down to the waterfront to watch people getting on and off the ferry. I don't think I'll go again. It's useless. Today I could have sworn I heard Angela's voice, but by the time I connected the voice to a kid, she was quite a ways away -- plus the little girl had brown hair. I didn't get a look at her face because she was wearing a floppy hat and seemed bigger than I remember Angela being. Although I suppose she has grown."

"That's too bad, Sarah. I know you had high hopes. My practice is already full. Soon we will be able to afford a new television blitz. You know, it just occurred to me last night when I was flipping through the TV channels; that program, 'America's Most Wanted'? I thought it was only criminals they looked for, but I wonder if we could get

Angela's search on it. They like a dramatic story, and they might be interested in ours."

"I'm ready to try anything, even if it makes me cringe to think of our lives out there for everyone to see. But, if you think it might help, you go ahead and look into it," she said.

With a new surge of optimism quickening his step, Dave took Sarah's hand as they walked up to the big front door and into the house. Sarah went to the kitchen to prepare dinner and Dave trotted up to the room he was using to change, and wash away the smells, and cares of his work day.

Sarah hadn't said a word about the separate rooms, and he knew why. She'd found it as hard as he had to find herself snuggled close to him in the mornings, and not make love as they used to.

Dave went into the nursery to spend time with Grace, but she was sleeping. At eight months, she was becoming quite a little person, sitting up, handling toys and interested in her first books.

Watching her, he had one of those agonizing moments, as a thought flickered like a half-forgotten pain. 'We need Angela. She should be here learning to love her sister'. He decided to go ahead with the application to 'America's Most Wanted', in spite of Sarah's lack of hope that it might help in their search.

He felt a soft hand slide around his waist. "She sleeps-- your wife makes dinner-- come with me. I give you a nice back rub."

Dave knew more than a back rub was offered in that playful smile. He wanted to refuse, but an image of Sarah in Denton's bed blindsided his resistance. He scooped up Amy's dainty body and carried her up the stairs to her room.

Chapter 46

Autumn came again with rain and shut in days for all children around the city. Angela had enjoyed the daycare over the summer, and missed Jo during the days, now that Jo had gone back to school.

Jenna did her best to amuse her, even letting her watch cartoons on their old TV any time she asked. She tried to find amusements that didn't include getting up and down off the floor. She remembered a game from her own childhood. Tie a long string around a piece of paper and pull it by the cat. It can never resist trying to catch it.

Angela ran up and down pulling the string, with Beau pouncing on the paper, only to have it jerked away. This gave her exercise and fun, with a minimum of work on Jenna's part.

Every day Jenna's energy diminished. The time was fast approaching when she wouldn't be able to take care of Angela in the hours that Jo was at school, and she would need professional nursing soon. Jo did the cleaning and cooking when she came home, gave Angela her supper and prepared her for bed.

By the end of September, Angela's hair looked bizarre; half brown and half almost golden. One day, when Angela was in a co-operative mood, Jenna suggested a new game.

She sat her in the old high chair and put a towel around her neck. She made up a story as she trimmed the brown hair away.

She told Angela that she would look just like Cinderella, saying, "Remember she had gold hair? We'll get out the book and read the story again."

Angela loved stories, and besides, she was really taken with her new look. Jenna had half expected that in the middle of the cut, Angela would have one of her meltdowns. But when she'd finished, Angela looked so cute, Jenna nearly collapsed at the thought of giving her up.

Angela stared at the child in the mirror as if she'd never seen her own image before. "Mommy," she said, and large tears trembled on her long dark lashes.

Jenna was struck dumb. On the bus, she hadn't really looked at the mother. But she and Angela must really look alike for the kid to remember all these months.

While she was still searching for something to say, Beau pounced onto the hair littering the floor, scattering it in every direction. Angela screamed in delight as he rolled in it, scattering it about.

Chapter 47

Jenna

We must decide right now I told Jo after she said over and over how different Angela looked with her hair cut. I didn't have to explain what I was on about. It had been in both our minds for a while now.

I could take her to her grandmother's. The cops wouldn't catch me. I could just ring the doorbell and when someone answers leave her and run. Jo said.

Yes but the cops would be here in a flash if they did see you. That would be the end of you living here. And think of school. They would make you into some sort of criminal for helping me-- maybe even send you to one of those awful jail places for young people. No we can't chance that. I'll think of something. I just mentioned it tonight because the pain pills are losing their battle and I know I won't be able to carry on much longer.

A few days later the check for the foster care came through the letter slot. The next Saturday we decided to take Angela to the big shopping center near the address I'd found in the purse.

I took extra medicine before we left. I needed to dull the pain so I could make the trip. We took us a bus to the nearest subway station and Jo bullied a couple of boys out of their seats so we could sit together. Thank heaven the shopping centre had its own station and escalators to take us up to the main floor. It was big as a city block and for a second I felt weak and wanted to turn around and go home.

All the stuff the herds of people pushing by and the smells from the food court made my head whirl and my gut feel like I was going to vomit. My knees shook and my heart beat so loud I could hardly think. I lost my balance for a second but Jo was there to help. I dropped Angela's hand but Joel caught it and slid her other arm under my elbow to hold me steady.

It's just nerves. C'mon we can't chicken out now Jo whispered.

Her courage made me buck up. I turned to thank her but the words wouldn't come. I always thought that when people say someone's face is glowing that it was just foolish talk but now I saw it for myself. How had I ever had the luck to have this girls love? me who dont deserve it.

Jo hoisted Angela onto her hip although she was getting too big to be carried. Everything around her was so strange that she didn't complain. We wandered along looking for a good place to set up a meeting.

One day last summer we had decided to take the ferry boat out to the islands. That day I found out that Angela's mother was alive. I thought of this as we're walking down the mall because that day Jo was carrying Angela. I got a bit behind and caught in the crowd as they started up the gangplank. All of a sudden I saw Jo turn sideways and whisper something to Angela. They leaned over to look down where she was pointing. I was already tired and scolded them for holding up the line. Jo told me that she had seen the mother watching kids.

She wasn't waiting to get on the ferry. Jo was sure. Jo was afraid she hadn't turned Angela away soon enough but when no one stopped us she knew the floppy hat and the brown hair had fooled the woman.

We brought all the money me and Jo made over the summer with our secondhand clothes business to the mall. I wanted to buy Angela some new clothes. I know it was foolish but I didn't want them to think I hadn't taken good care of her. Bad as I was for stealing her. They would hate me anyway.

Along the way was a children's shop. I had never been in one. I only had Julie with me for six months and I made her clothes. I couldn't believe it. There was just so much I had to find a chair and sit down. Angela and Jo didn't seem a bit taken aback. They disappeared into the racks like it was just another game.

Soon they were back both grinning from ear to ear. Angela was wearing a little dress with a matching sweater in a bright blue and green print. This one Aunty Jenna she asked and hopped from foot to fast enough to make me dizzy.

The price was crazy high but I didn't have the heart to say no. There wouldn't be enough money for shoes but Jo said a new pair of socks would go a long way to smarten up the old sneakers.

Angela's face screwed up getting ready for a real storm when we tried to get her to change back into the clothes she had been wearing.

Oh let her wear it I said. If it gets dirty we can wash it.

Now that she'd got her way she walked quietly between us. We hadn't gone far when Jo saw a good spot. She pointed out a corner store where two wings of the mall met. The store she was talking about had two entrances, one across from a jewellry store and another into the main mall where we could quickly hide in the crowd there.

We'll ask the woman who comes-- she rolled her eyes at me-- to stand over there facing their window. We'll be inside here and send our package over when we're sure it's the right person and whoever comes is alone. Once she picks it up, we're gone. She pointed to the second door out of sight to a person across the corridor.

I had never been so glad to see my place--poor as it is as when we got home. Angela was quiet except for walking up and down swishing her pretty dress from side to side. She must've been tired because she went right to sleep with only one story.

In the living room we plotted like the criminals we were.

We'll warn them not to bring any police or other men, I said. The women will be so glad to see Angela she won't look for us. Heavens that cat! We'll have to send Beau-- there's no way around it.

I could hardly believe the words out of my mouth. Six months ago I'd have booted him out onto the street without a second thought.

The secondhand shop has a cat carrier. It's an old one really only a box with a screen door. I'll pick it up tomorrow Jo said and began to cry. She said I don't know how I can go on alone. I'll miss you so much.

I took her hand. I have a while yet but we have to get everything settled. I'm leaving what little I have to you. My old house. I never told you I owned a house did I? Well I do but I hated the memories in it so much I just shut it up and left it. It'll be yours to do what you like.

And you should be able to get some welfare help until you finish high school if I don't make it till then. You'll have your scholarship so you'll be all right. I know you're scared.

Let's write down what you will say when we call. Do you think you could do it? I get so out of breath.

When will we do it she asked? I knew she wasn't talking about making the plan.

Soon, it will have to be soon. I felt as if I might die right there and wanted nothing more than to go lie down. Still I felt wouldn't give back one hour that Angela was with us.

When I asked her if she felt the same as I did Jo giggled. Well, maybe when she had some of those wicked tantrums. I knew she was joking.

Chapter 48

Sarah

It was near mid October when everything changed. I woke early, as had Dave. I could hear him moving around in his room. This was new with us– this awaking alone. We used to squeeze out every drop of sleep, and then leap up to our day's activities. Or we'd wake early and lie awhile, still warm from sleepy lovemaking or just talking. We'd share our thoughts, as we never do now.

This particular morning, he left early and I was still lying in bed, thinking, remembering. There, at the farm Dave hadn't known about Denton and, we didn't want to worry the James' by their finding out that we weren't sleeping together.

It was one of Dr. Robinson's suggestions that one start their day centered. It wasn't real meditation; that took more concentration than I could hold on to, but a stream of thought ranging through my past to the present, did the same for me. I avoided the future, as it was still a black hole that nibbled away the days. Trying to plan led to despair, and made my search for Angela seem useless.

But that morning I couldn't help but smile at the thought of how Dr. Robinson asked me to call her 'Sylvia', and our relationship had changed. Because, I still wanted to keep a distance, I spoke to her as 'Dr. Sylvia' which seemed to feel right.

Every visit, I had to get by the shame I felt for the time I'd wasted, by not using the help she had offered. I'd thought I was so clever, not realizing that she had seen through me from the first. We tried hypnosis, but it turned out I wasn't a good candidate, and we learned nothing that might help in the search. Therapy helped in other ways. She led me to see the woman I'd been, and to find my true adult self.

Dave filled me in as to what had happened after the accident, of which I had no memory--not surprising when you consider that I had been unconscious.

I could call up of very vague memory of visiting Jill, and of the bus station in Toronto. I could remember what Angela was wearing and how difficult it was for me to keep her next to me. She had absolutely no fear of strangers, and if I didn't keep a tight hold on her she would run into a crowd, in the most maddening manner,. She had thrown one of her infamous tantrums, that garnered me quite a few 'bad mother' looks while we were waiting for the bus in Toronto.

Dr. Sylvia had begun hinting that I should be thinking about the future and consider having another child. I was shocked and angry. It smacked of running out and getting another cat, if yours died. I couldn't replace a lost kid! What girl or boy would want to grow up suspecting that if I hadn't lost Angela, he or she would never have been born?

I was getting over agonizing, and blaming myself for the accident. If we knew the future-- what a life that would be-- waiting for happiness or death.

I'd been trying to become a real mother to Grace. She was such a sweet little girl, but I found it was nearly impossible to take her out alone, especially in the car. Once I suffered a terrible anxiety attack halfway to my folks' place. All those cars cutting in and out, huge trucks shouldering into my lane-- I suddenly felt the vulnerability of being shut up in that little tin box that could be crushed like cardboard. I'd had to pull into a parking lot, and manage to stop hyperventilating. When the dizziness passed, I turned around and went back home.

I swung my legs off the bed, thinking of a nice hot shower, and spending the afternoon strolling by daycare centers. Also, I had learned the times when the kids might be out playing in school yards or taken to a park. When my cell phone rang, my hand hovered over it where it lay on the table. I had stopped expecting good news. By the third ring, I picked it up. Fear choked my voice to a tentative, "Hello".

"Hello, Sarah! Is that you? Have I caught you at a bad time?"

The voice couldn't be anyone but Lila's, and I felt the tension running out of my body, because she and Don weren't in a position to have information about Angela. If they had heard anything bad they would tell Dave first.

After the usual assurances from her, that she was well, I heard a noticeable rising excitement in Lila's voice. I steeled myself for anything; a rumor, dream, a vision or Don's latest blunders.

She lowered her voice as if the Fates were listening. If Don was in town as Lila said, then who was there to hear, the cats? I'm afraid I never took Lila very seriously. I did like her though, and was willing to listen.

"I know you think I'm a little crazy, but I had a dream last night that I just had to tell you."

"No Lila, I don't think you're crazy, not any more than the rest of us anyway. Tell me." I was prepared for the usual boring dream stuff. I picked up the amethyst necklace that

Dave had given me, and ran my fingers over the smooth cool stone, as if it were an amulet to ward off evil.

"I won't go into all the ups and downs of dream symbolism as per Jung. I always thought he was crazier the most of his patients. Anyway-- at the very end, I saw Angela walking on a busy street holding a woman's hand. I debated about telling you this part; the woman was a skeleton under her clothes, which I think means she is either dead or dying. Then, I turned my head and saw you walking toward them."

Darkness swirled through my head, and I half fell onto the bed before I grabbed the headboard with my free hand to steady myself. The scene in my imagination was as plain as if the dream were mine. I could imagine myself standing behind Lila and seeing what she saw.

Although I had no intention of fingering over Lila's dream, I couldn't resist hearing more. Oh God, that's death, that walking skeleton--coming for Angela. The thought drowned out Lila's next words.

"What, what did you say?" My hands shook so badly that I clung to my cell phone with both hands. 'Keep grounded, keep grounded' I heard Dr. Sylvia saying. Dreams aren't real life.

"I think it means you're going to find her soon." Lila's voice was upbeat, as if happiness could start now, and my take on what she had said had never occurred to her.

After a few seconds trying to get a grip on reality, I said, "I hope you're right. I've been going out everyday." I told the story of having thought I heard Angela's voice at the ferry dock. I was anxious to hang up so that I could think about this.

My logical lawyer side said it was all nonsense; an older woman's desire to seem important, but there was another side. I wanted to believe her. I couldn't afford a panic attack, with its paralyzing symptoms and inability to think straight. I was afraid to believe her, but she was right sometimes, and I couldn't dismiss the way her dream had leaped into my mind, as vivid as if it had been my own.

I was scared of my thoughts, that they might drive me back to the dark. I thought of all the people I might tell, but no one seemed right. Dr. Sylvia might have been the one, but she was out west at a conference. I couldn't confide in Amy. I didn't trust her, and I'm not bringing up the race card. It had nothing to do with that, or her competence as a nanny. I knew she wanted Dave. But I had no time to dwell on that now.

For a second, I was standing in the farm kitchen with the aroma of Christmas dinner filling the room. Lila, waving her mixing spoon, announcing that travelling by bus from Toronto to Ottawa was dangerous in winter because of snow effect storms off Lake Ontario.

'It doesn't take a witch to deduce that--anyone who lives in Ontario knows that', I told myself. Somehow that vivid picture calmed me, and I realized that I was panicking over nothing; nothing but a dream.

'Tomorrow, I'll go down to the dock again and work outward from there. I'll look for daycare centers, and walk through some of those back streets. I've never been able to feel good about that little girl and the dark-haired teenager.'

Chapter 49

The shrilling telephone on the desk beside her broke Mary's concentration. She left her computer with a sigh. The book of short stories that she was working on was a great distraction, if only she could find the time to finish one. It was so annoying that everyone, but herself, thought that when you got older, you had years of time to devote to everyone else. Sometimes she wished that she had lived when a medieval lady could become a hermit, and be walled up in a little room on the side of a mountain, safe from all intrusion.

A ringing phone was something she had never learned to ignore. She knew many people with an answering service never bothered to answer, but it was something she couldn't do. What if someone needed her? She'd feel terrible. Impatiently, she jerked the phone from its cradle, expecting a voice asking to send someone to clean her carpets.

The caller didn't begin with any, 'Are you the householder?' She'd always wanted to say, 'No, I'm the cat burglar.' But instead she said, "Hello."

For a second there was silence, but she heard breathing. Someone was there. She was about to put down the receiver when the caller spoke, louder than necessary. "Is Sarah James there?"

Mary was so shocked she struggled for breath to answer, but fearing that the person would hang up, she forced her tongue loose, and said, "Who is this? Is this about Angela?" She could hear her voice rising in spite of her efforts to sound calm.

"Never you mind. Where can I reach her? Sarah James, her, and nobody else. If you don't tell me, I'll hang up!"

It flashed through Mary's mind that it was the height of foolishness to push a disturbed person to do something drastic. "All right, please don't hang up. I'm her mother, and I'll give you her cell number."

Mary opened her mouth but couldn't remember the number, and was fumbling for her address book when it suddenly came to her. She stammered out the digits, repeating them to make sure they were right.

There was no 'Thank you'; just a click and the dial tone. She stood for a moment unable to break the connection, although she knew the person was gone. She thought, 'She's young. Surely no one would be cruel enough to make a crank call about Angela so many months after her abduction. She was so serious and determined-- it just had to be real, not some prankster.' With that reasoning, she felt a surge of energy and ran down the stairs and to the back door.

"Ralph, Ralph, come in here," she shouted.

"Just a minute, I've only a few more of these rosebushes to trim," he called back.

"Don't be such a stubborn . . . It was a call about Angela."

Roses forgotten, his tools dropped, he rushed into the house. He was barely in the door, when Mary flooded him with words. "Somebody phoned for Sarah, but she wouldn't give her name. It sounded a bit odd. Could it be about

Angela? You think I should call Sarah? She turned toward the phone hanging on the kitchen wall.

Ralph caught her arm, and was pulled two or three steps by her momentum before he got her stopped. "Mary, Mary calm down. Better not to tie up the phone right now; you said you gave her Sarah's number. Sarah will call us back if it's anything important. I hope to God is not a crank call. That would be more than she could take; just when she is making real progress with Dr. Robinson."

He was right; she nodded, and sat in one of the kitchen chairs waiting for . . . she didn't know what. She bent her head and began a prayer. Ralph stood with his empty hands hanging by his side.

Ten minutes later Sarah burst through the door. She was all but incoherent, laughing or crying, they couldn't tell which-- trying to tell a dozen things all at once.

Mary ran to her and led her to the couch. She eased Sarah down to sit beside her and put her arm around her. "Ralph, bring her glass of water. Here, Sarah," she said, passing her a box of tissues.

After mopping her face and drinking a few sips, Sarah got control, and took several deep breaths. "She wouldn't talk long, but I got her instructions. I'm to meet her at the mall, this afternoon. You know where that jewellery store is? People's Jewellers? I'm supposed to be looking in their window at two o'clock today. Can it really be true? Maybe it's a trick. She said, 'Don't bring any police or any man at all"

A moment of silence fell before the older couple started asking each other questions, not waiting for one to finish before asking a new one. Sarah had no answers, but she got up and hugged them.

"We can't dismiss this call," she said in a sort of wonder.

"I don't think it's a scam either. There was something in that voice--a sort of desperation," Mary said.

"Did she ask for money?" Ralph asked.

"No, no, she didn't. I'm going to go do it," Sarah said.

"Have you called Dave?" Ralph asked.

"She warned me not to tell anyone. She was fierce in insisting no men. It had to be her, the one who took Angela from the bus. The only thing--the one sighting the police had was of an older woman carrying her. This person sounded young--maybe a teenager. And no, Dad I'm not calling Dave. Can you imagine trying to keep him away, if he knew about this? I expect that's the very reason she's made this demand. If it's a scam we won't be any worse off than we are now. We'll play along--although what could anyone get from it except some sick satisfaction out of making us suffer. It's not like we're going to meet in some dark alley; it's a mall. Oh God, I hope I can do this!"

"I'm calling the police," Ralph declared as he started to leaver himself from his chair. Sarah nearly gave in to a terrible desire to laugh. It was the kind of action he threatened when he felt the women were getting out of his control.

"No! You can't!" Mary and Sarah screamed. Then, after a moment of silence, Mary said, "You heard the instructions; she'll run if she sees anyone who looks like police."

When he saw that he was out voted, he subsided. His face seemed to age, adding years in seconds. It was obvious he hadn't looked on the positive side. He couldn't seem to get past the idea that this was a man's responsibility. He gave one last try. Dave had a right to be there was his argument; ground they had covered before.

"Besides," Sarah said, "I don't want to tell Dave until it's over. He's had so many disappointments. So many times he's got his hopes up only to find it a false lead. If nothing comes of it, I'll tell him then. I have to get back now. I'll call you again. OK-- before I leave for the mall."

Mary reached for Ralph's hand. She was so proud of Sarah, the way she was handling this-- so strong and sure, it brought tears to her eyes. "If only she would let me go with her," Mary kept saying to Ralph after Sarah left, and they went over everything they could remember that she'd told them.

Ten minutes later the phone rang again.

"Oh! For God's Sake! You can't hear yourself think around here." Ralph exclaimed. He mumbled a couple of curses for good measure, as he picked up the receiver.

Sarah's abrupt greeting tightened his hand on the receiver. Amy was sick, suffering from one of her migraines. Would they keep Grace while she went to meet the woman at the mall?

Mary visualized the crowds and the long corridors, and Sarah going in there alone. She reached for the phone.

"Listen Sarah, I've just thought of something," Mary said. "Let's go together and take Grace. I don't like your going alone. What if they want you to meet them somewhere else, after they make this initial contact? A grandmother with a baby stroller would be the last person that they'd expect to be a spy."

Sarah didn't answer for moment. Then she said, "Be ready at one- thirty"

When Ralph saw the state of Sarah's nerves when she arrived, just before the time specified, he insisted he drive them, and promised he would stay in the car.

Mary said that it wasn't a bad idea; the parking there could be a nightmare.

Chapter 50

Jenna

Well it's over. They left for the mall a few minutes ago. I couldn't go. I was throwing-up all night and can hardly hold a pencil but I want to tell this.

I know it was a selfish thing to do taking Angela but I was not in my right mind. That sore from Julie's death was still raw that day.

Such a useless thing for a useless man to do--the way he let Julie die. Billy wasn't a violent drunk just careless. He left Julie in the truck when he went into a bar to have a drink. One led to two and he forgot she was with him. After a long while she got the seatbelt off and set out across the street to find him. She was struck and killed right in front of the bar.

I blame Billy's father. He always had Billy in bars with him when he was just a kid. By the time his father staggered home Billy had drained the dregs from a dozen glasses. No wonder hes a drunk. If I dared to say anything it was a fist in the face.

My story-- I've only told a small part. How I left Montreal and tried to start a new life. When I got to Toronto I couldn't afford a place to live that wasn't a slum. The abortion took most of my money. The jewellery I stole didn't bring anything like I expected mainly because I had to hock it to a thief. That bastard said he knew the stuff was stolen and he would call the police if I didn't sell it to him. He only gave me a few dollars. Id picked that stuff out and knew it was worth thousands.

The new cleaner job that I wanted to find always seemed just out of reach. So it was back to the bars dodging grabby hands for long hours and late at night going home to a room over a dry cleaners shop where the smell made me cough as if my gut was on fire.

I was lonely. Although I spoke bad English I understood it well enough. I missed the jokey happy French Canadian drunks. Here the men were angry and mean and got nastier is that a word if I didn't answer their dirty talk.

There was a wild fight one night. One of the men stuck out his foot and tripped me. I fell on the table in front of me. A leg snapped off it and I went down with all their drinks on the tray in my hand.

It was a mess of beer and broken glass. A man from that table jumped up with a roar and struck the one who tripped me. His friends jumped in and a full blown brawl broke out. I had to crawl out as best I could on my hands and knees.

I was standing crying and trying to pick the splinters of glass out of my hands when a big man put his jacket around my shoulders and led me out to the back alley.

To get out of that place I would've gone with the devil himself. My short skirt part of the uniform was torn up to the waist. I had been walked on and kicked. I was soaked in booze and smelled worse than a pig pen.

Sam he said its name was. He offered to take me home. That little bit of kindness for he noticed my shoes were gone and said he would carry me to his car. It made me bawl like a baby.

I hadn't even got a good look at him. His voice was deep and gruff but he didn't sound young or old. It was dark behind the building and all I knew that he was being nice to me when no one else had been for a long time. He picked me up and I put my arms around his neck. He smelled of oil and cigarette smoke and warm man.

His car was an old clunker but the engine worked. By now I stopped crying but was shaking and couldn't seem to stop. My hands were still bleeding and he tore pieces off his shirt and wrapped them. I was such a terrible mess I couldn't believe any man would help me.

He didn't say much-- no questions except where did I live. I was glad he likely didn't have any more money than me. I was afraid of what he would think of my room with a hot plate in the corner a couch to turn into a bed and the bathroom down the hall outside.

Sam put me over his shoulder like a sack of potatoes, to carry me up the narrow stairway. I didn't have my purse or key. He kicked the door in and set me on my feet. For the first time I saw his face. He might have been handsome except for a scar that ran from his eye to under his left ear. I guessed he'd been in a brawl or two in his life.

We stood looking at each other. Then I remembered having seen him in the bar before. I wondered if he'd done this because he knew me from sitting in a corner watching me wait tables. Then I was afraid. Maybe he did all this help to get me where he could rape me. I think he saw how scared I was because he turned away and fiddled with the door. The lock was broken.

Maybe you'll want to shove a chair under the knob tonight. I'll come back in the morning and fix it. I'll be off now. You need to clean up. With that -no hanging around hoping to get lucky he left.

It was good to be safe. Bad as the old shower was with its stains and tiny booth, it felt like a fancy hotel one as I washed the dirt and blood away. I needed a few Band-Aids, but there weren't any deep cuts. I made myself a cup of tea and wondered if I would see Sam again.

He did come and fix the door and offered to take me that night to get my things from the bar. I knew I would be fired and I was glad to have a big tough guy behind me when I went in.

One look at Sam and my boss didn't say a word except you're fired and passed my purse and jacket over. Sam never said anything just stood there looking like for two cents he would tear that guys head off.

Of course it wasn't long until I was living with Sam. He had a small house in one of those back streets. He didn't want me go to go back to bartending. The garage he worked at needed someone in the office to write up bills and do simple bookkeeping so I worked there.

Sam asked me to marry him a few months later when I was expecting Billy. I had a bad time when Billy was born. He was a big baby that never was easy and it didn't get any easier as he grew up.

In spite of that Sam and I were happy for the first years. Then he was hurt when a car fell off the hoist. He couldn't work after that. I still did the book keeping but took another job at night in another nightclub. It was the tips. I could make more in tips in one night than I could make in a week at other jobs I could get.

Somewhere along the way Sam started to drink. He hated looking after Billy and doing what he called womans work. He'd come home staggering and swearing. It got so I didn't dare ask where Billy was. Sometimes he would have been left in his bed and other times when he was older I'd find him wandering the streets.

When he was drunk Sam often said that he wished he was dead. And I got to say that sometimes I wished it to. He got his wish ten years ago crossing the train tracks one night and for all his faults I missed him.

Billy quit school when he was fifteen and worked on and off mostly off. Then one day he said his girlfriend was going to have his baby but he didn't want to marry her.

She was a Catholic and wouldn't have an abortion so I said I would take it. That's how I got my little Julie. She was like some little angel not solid and set like Angela. Maybe she wasn't meant for this world.

I can't do more now.

Jo took loosing Angela real bad. I had a bad turn that day we was to take her back. She told me that the mother looked good and didn't even have much of a scar. She laughed through her tears when she told me how they walked up and down looking to catch her. She hadn't run away but waited until she was sure--any woman might have stopped to look in that window.

She saw the grandmother and the little girl baby. She could see from the fear on their faces that the only thing that mattered to them was to have Angela back.

I can go easy now. I have done this one good thing and have God's blessing in Jo. Tomorrow I'm going into the home for poor people to die in.

Jo will graduate from high school and go to the university on her scholarship. I know she will miss me but she is young and has her life ahead and she will make it a good life not the mess I made of mine.

She is the one that asked me to make this story. I like to think I will live in these pages--the good and bad I did.

Chapter 51

Sarah

After writing about the telephone call from Lila, I never got back to this until today. We're going again to Lila and Don's for Christmas. Lila has made great strides in recovering from her stroke, so much so that she has taken in two more abandoned horses. I think brushing them and watching them eat is a form of meditation for her.

Amy has left us. She claimed her headaches became so bad she was forced to quit. I accepted her reason, and was glad she was gone.

We didn't hire another full- time nanny. I decided to put off going back to work, until the children are in daycare. If we ever have another nanny, you can imagine who will do the hiring.

Unintentionally, I followed one piece of Dr. Sylvia's advice. In the fallout of Angela's return, I forgot to take the pill. The doctor says it'll be a boy this time for sure.

As a kind of closure, I want to tell what sprang from the call that I got from the girl whose name I now know. Jo. I still get goose bumps when I remember tearing down to my parents' place to consult them, and how Mom and I nearly ripped Dad into pieces when he wanted to call the police.

The distance had never seemed so long, or the traffic so maddening.

I wanted so much to call Dave. I hadn't been able to reach him before I left home. Even with his busy practice, he was always pursuing the search for Angela through private agencies, and the latest police reports. There had been hundreds of leads, but none had led us one step nearer to the truth.

Afterward, he told me that he'd been living in a permanently depressed state, and what kept him going was the progress that I was making at getting well.

He'd had so much hope for 'America's Most Wanted'. Hundreds of people had called in, but it turned out each caller had seen some mother, or other caretaker, going to a supermarket with a little blonde girl, or the person calling was hoping to make trouble for a neighbor.

About fifteen minutes before the mall meeting time, Mom and I, with Dad driving, arrived at the mall. The parking lot was full to capacity. We drove around getting further and further from the entrance.

Finally Mom said, "To hell with this going around in circles. Just stop and we'll get out. See if you can find a spot where you can see the entrance, Ralph."

Dad stopped along a curb near the entrance, and I jumped out to pull out the stroller, leaving Mom to get Grace out of her car seat. I was so nervous when I wrenched that contraption out of the trunk, I couldn't remember how to get the thing open. Drivers, piling up behind, tooted their horns and yelled at us. We hadn't wanted to get here too early but now I was desperately afraid we would be too late.

At last, with Mom holding a squirming Grace, and me nearly in tears, I wrenched stroller open and minutes later we entered the mall. Inside, it was a chaos of people walking up and down, in and out of stores; a flow of passing colours.

Mom and I exchanged a glance-- the type soldiers might exchange just before battle. We were excited but terrified that something might go wrong. We walked up the corridor, passing by the jewellery store without stopping. We wanted to scout it out. We still had eight minutes left before the specified time. Neither of us had any idea if the person we were to meet, knew what we looked like.

"Perhaps someone has been spying on us for weeks," Mom suggested.

I said, "Unless this is a gang, that's unlikely, Mom." I knew Mom was determined to be here, because she thought if it turned out badly I might have another breakdown.

We circled back to the jewellery store. Mom suggested going into a toy store nearby. "It will look a normal thing, a grandmother taking a baby to buy toys. While you stand by the window," I can watch from there, she said.

I was busy trying to remember the instructions, and to watch the people behind me reflected in the window, until I realized it was hopeless. I wouldn't recognize my best friend. I concentrated on staring straight ahead, an almost unbearable task, as I wanted to look behind me so badly.

"Oh God, don't let me faint!' I prayed.

I was so paralyzed with fear that I didn't register the first hesitant, "Mummy," but I did feel a tug on my jacket. Carefully, I turned my head.

"Hi Mummy," a little voice from beside me said. "Where you been? I look everywhere for you! You been lost a long time!"

"Angela!" I cried and fell to my knees and hug her to my body. No words can explain the surge of thankfulness and love I felt at that moment.

"I found you, I found you." Angela repeated over and over. "Jo said I could. But Aunty Jenna couldn't come today, she's sick."

In spite of her solid body in my arms, this all seemed too easy. Surely there would be someone to demand something, or to give an explanation, if not an apology. Angela looked alright. I took in the cheap but pretty print dress. Her hair had been cut short, but it was clean.

Just for a second, I couldn't resist looking around for someone suspicious, but I had no idea what suspicious might look like. For a moment, my eyes fell on a tall dark teenager, who seemed vaguely familiar, but the girl turned away, and I forgot her.

I know now-- she was the girl on the ferry ramp. It was quite a long time later that I remembered. My memory still has gaps, and I may never remember everything, but I don't care much anymore. How many miracles are we allotted in this life?

Mom came up with Grace. I knew she wanted to grab Angela up, but she softly spoke her name, and waited for Angela to come to her.

"Hi, Nana." Angela greeted her grandmother as if she'd seen her yesterday. "Is this my sister? The one Mummy went to get? Pretty isn't she? Nana look --there's Beau. I bet you didn't know I had a cat." She ran over to the battered cat box, poked her fingers in, giggled and was back in a second, asking another question.

Then, at the same second, Mom and I had almost the same thought. 'What are we standing around here for?' We were in shock trying to take in what had actually happened; her just appearing out of the blue. She was taller and more articulate, but the same ball of energy. Could it be as simple as this?

Mom broke first. "Ralph! We've got to tell Ralph." She wheeled the stroller around, practically on one wheel, and headed for the door. I picked up the old cat carrier thinking it was some weird piece of luggage that Angela had become attached to. Until it gave a loud indignant, 'Meow.' I nearly dropped it--there actually was a cat inside.

I took a last quick look around the area but everything seemed normal. Then, I hurried after Mom, who was trying to maneuver the stroller and answer Angela's questions at the same time. Her job wasn't made easier by the tears I knew were blurring her sight.

Angela ran back to me. She looked up, her face framed with short bouncy curls. She grabbed my free hand, "You were lost but now you're found. Isn't that right, Mummy?"

At first, I couldn't call up the words to answer. Instead, I lifted her into my arms and laughed through my tears. "That's right, my love, I'm found and so are you."

I felt so much anger at what we had been put through; all the months of fear and uncertainty. My affair with Denton; mixed together with such relief and joy. Angela was back! I wanted to yell out loud, and do a handstand right between the sliding doors!

Dave was there to meet us at the door of our house. After Mom and I had gone into the mall, Ralph had called Dave on his cell phone to tell him what was going on. Dave told him that he wanted to come, but there had been a terrible car crash, and he was the doctor on call.

Ralph told Dave, "There isn't any point in coming here. Angela will come or not. Meet us at the house." He said he'd send a message, 'Yes' or 'No' as soon as we came out of the mall.

There is still more to tell in my story; a year of pain and suffering, but growth as well. I wrote earlier about Angela's return. I'll let you imagine the joy and relief our family felt. But something still stood between Dave and me. I suspected it had to do with Amy.

I'd already decided not to pursue my law career until the children were at least in school, and if I was going to be a full-time mother, I didn't need a nanny. But I couldn't understand Dave. He was being evasive, and always had to do something when I brought up the subject of letting Amy go. I hadn't yet built up the courage to confront him.

For a father who had agonized over the loss of Angela for almost a year, he didn't seem as happy at her return as I had expected him to be. I'd hoped for the old affectionate relationship we'd had. He still slept in the separate bedroom.

One night, I lay awake thinking until I knew I couldn't go to sleep. I got up to go down to the kitchen to make some herbal tea. A crack of light beneath Dave's door told me he wasn't sleeping either. I put my ear against the panel, and heard him walking up and down.

I stood there with my hands clenched into fists and thought, 'this is ridiculous.' Whatever he's hiding-- Oh God, don't let him be sick-- nothing can be as bad as what we've been through.'

Maybe three o'clock in the morning isn't the best time to confront your husband, but there was no time like the present.

I tapped gently. Angela was still a light sleeper, and I didn't want her involved, if this was something so serious that it might lead to shouting, and wake her up.

Dave must have been pacing near the door because he jerked it open so quickly, I staggered backwards. He opened his mouth but only a strangled sound escaped. He gestured for me to come in.

I don't know who he had expected, but I suspected it wasn't me. His hair was on end, as if he had been running his hands through it. Behind him, his bed was a tangled mess.

He stood looking at me as if the weight of the world was on his back. His hands hung straight by his sides. Seeing him looking so beaten down, all my anger melted away and I went to him to put my arms around him. He was still so muscular that my arms wouldn't go all the way around, but I squeezed all I could reach.

"Tell me," I said. "Whatever it is, you can tell me. I've been through the fire--I'm fireproof now."

"I've wanted to tell you, Sarah, so much. I just didn't know how. It's so unfair, but it started after I went to Toronto to see you, and you pretended to be throwing up all weekend. Don't blame Amy, or think it was to get back at you. It just happened, the night we came back. I was so tired and discouraged, thinking I would never get you and Angela back-- I turned to her."

I felt his hands slacken, but I still hung on to him with my face buried in his chest. It was what I'd suspected from the moment I had seen how beautiful Amy was, and had noticed there was a certain ease between them.

"What are you going to do?" I was so frightened that I could hardly breathe.

It seemed like an eternity before he wrapped one freed arm around my back, and tilted up my face with the other to kiss me.

"I've already done it," he said. "I told Amy, when she left, that I was going back to you, Sarah. Tonight, I was trying to work out how to tell you that I want to be with you again-- and no one else."

A crazy laugh broke from my throat. I fell onto his bed and rolled around, hands over my mouth, trying to stop. Dave looked at me as if I were having a nervous breakdown, or had gone totally insane.

"Oh, this is rich; this is-- us beating ourselves up!" Another screech of laughter spurted from my mouth. It hurt to laugh so hard, but I couldn't seem to stop.

Dave leaned over-- looking very much the concerned doctor and slapped my cheek. Not hard, but it shut the laughter off like turning off a tap. I burst into tears. He sat down beside me and held me until I was calm enough to talk.

I grabbed the sleeve of his bathrobe and wiped my face. "It's just too ironic or crazy. All those times I told Mom and Dad I was seeing Dr. Robinson, I was having the affair with Denton."

I nearly had another laughing fit; remembering him with the wet rose in his hair.

'It was such a senseless thing, done by someone else-- that me of five years ago,' I thought, trying to get control of myself.

I didn't know what to expect, but I didn't expect Dave to laugh. His laughter wasn't hysterical like mine. He threw himself back on the bed, and pulled me down on top of him.

"This feels good." He kissed me. "This feels right. Tonight we start over." And we did.

It was amazing how quickly Angela slipped back into our family, almost as if she had never been away. She accepted Grace with, no other word will do-- joy. She has nightmares sometimes, but they get fewer as time passes.

When I went to get the mail one day in early December, a flat parcel, about the size of a school scribbler was in our mail box. When I opened it, I saw a number of hand-written pages in rather cramped pencil writing. Lying on top was a note in another hand.

I am sending you Jenna's story. She died yesterday. I want to tell you why she took Angela, and that she was very sorry in the end. I too am sorry for the pain I know you suffered, but Jenna and Angela saved me from a life of misery after my father murdered my mother. She took me in and I lived with them, and helped her take care of Angela. We loved her very much. I hope you can forgive us.

Jo.

Printed in the United States
By Bookmasters